Judy Finnigan is an author, television presenter and columnist. In 2004, Judy's name became synonymous with discovering and sharing great fiction, through the Richard and Judy Book Club, where authors including Kate Mosse, Rosamund Lupton and Victoria Hislop were championed and brought to the attention of millions of readers. This is her first novel.

Eloise

Judy Finnigan

sphere

SPHERE

First published in Great Britain in 2012 by Sphere
Reprinted 2012

Copyright © Judy Finnigan 2012

The moral right of the author has been asserted.

*All characters and events in this publication, other than those
clearly in the public domain, are fictitious and any resemblance
to real persons, living or dead, is purely coincidental.*

A CIP catalogue record for this book
is available from the British Library.

Hardback ISBN 978-1-84744-551-3
Trade Paperback ISBN 978-1-84744-552-0

Printed and bound in Great Britain by
Clays Ltd, St Ives plc

Papers used by Sphere are from well-managed forests
and other responsible sources.

MIX
Paper from
responsible sources
FSC® C104740

Sphere
An imprint of
Little, Brown Book Group
100 Victoria Embankment
London EC4Y 0DY

An Hachette UK Company
www.hachette.co.uk

www.littlebrown.co.uk

For Richard,
with all my love and thanks for his patience,
support and unfailing enthusiasm when I
thought I'd never finish this book.
I love you.

Prologue

Yesterday I almost saw her. I was standing on the sun deck, looking out to sea, revelling in the unexpected warmth of the February sun. A butterfly trembled on a nearby buddleia and suddenly I smelled her perfume, fragrant, drifting, elusive. The same fragrance which infused the little pink silk pouch in my bedside drawer. I touched the beads round my neck; perhaps the scent lingered on them. They were hers, given to me by her mother, and I kept them in the pouch.

Then a distant shiver of motion. They had put an old rowing boat in their garden, its prow vertical against the sky, secured in an alcove to use as a summer seat. Glancing past it I saw a shimmer, a translucent shift beside the lavender. It was as if her clothes, always wispy, drifted on the breeze: a glimpse of red, a swirling skirt, a gorgeously coloured silk scarf. The way I had so often seen her dressed.

She wasn't there, of course. How could she be, when I had seen her lying in her coffin just two weeks ago, the day before she was buried, her casket surrounded by the scented candles she loved. She lay in Cornish ground, now.

There was no possibility of her ever coming back.

Chapter One

The sea mist plays strange tricks in Cornwall. By the time we got back to Talland Bay it was impossible to see more than a few yards ahead. The sea lay invisible on the smoky-grey horizon and the trees loomed and dripped over the steep and slippery steps down to our cottage. Inside, we switched on the lights and Chris fetched logs from the little slate-roofed store tucked around the side path. Once the fire was blazing I sat on the rug, staring into it, trying to find comfort in remembering all the bedtime games we'd played with the children when they were little. With them cuddled on my lap in their pyjamas, we wove stories about the pictures we saw in each fiery nest of coals: jewelled caves glowing fiercely red, scary black petrified forests, witches' cottages and princesses' castles all cast their shadowy spells, and we watched, enchanted.

But today, as Chris brought more logs for the basket, all I could see in the flames were dark tombs, embers of death, coffins consumed by fire.

Chris watched me. I could feel his growing impatience but I ignored him. He poured two glasses of red wine, handed one to me and, with a loud sigh, sat on the sofa behind me.

'Come on, Cathy. Stop doing this to yourself. If you're not careful you'll get seriously depressed again. If I'd known you were going to get this upset, I wouldn't have come down here so soon after Eloise's funeral, and I certainly wouldn't have let you go to their house.'

'Let me?' I asked, trying to keep my voice light.

'You know what I mean. I'm only thinking of you,' he said with studied patience.

'Yes, well, don't, Chris. I don't believe you anyway. If you were *really* worried you'd stop trying to tell me off. You could try asking me why I'm so upset instead of lecturing me.'

'Cathy, I *know* why you're upset. Eloise has died. But we'd been expecting it for years. We're all sad because yes, it's terrible, and she was so young; but there's nothing you – nothing *any* of us – can do. Let it go, honey. You know you're not strong enough for this.'

'There speaks my resident psychiatrist,' I said bitterly. 'Could you just stop practicing your profession on me?'

'Cathy, you're tired and overwrought—'

'You bet I am! Friend dies, I get upset – that really makes me a basket case, doesn't it? Well, go on, Doctor Freud. Because once a loony, always a loony in your eyes,' I raged, getting to my feet. 'I'm going to bed.'

He stood up and held me by the arms, looking at me intently.

'Cathy, don't. Tell me what's *really* making you so unhappy.'

'I'm frightened, Chris, that's why I'm unhappy – desperately unhappy. She's dead – Ellie's dead, and she was the same age as me. And I thought she would beat it.'

He shook me slightly. 'No, you didn't. None of us did. We've been playing a game of let's pretend for years so as not to upset her. But there's no reason to be frightened, honey. It's not an omen that you're going to die. These terrible things just . . . happen.'

Beneath my misery and anger I knew he was right, but just because he was calm and rational didn't mean everything was all right. It wasn't. I was scared, yes, but not just of dying.

There was something else. Something very wrong. Something that gnawed at my gut like a restless rat, only I didn't know what it was, couldn't put it into words, and if I said it was 'a feeling', it would simply confirm Chris's fears that my depression was back.

Eloise had been ill for five years, her cancer diagnosed six months after her twin daughters were born. What she had confidently assumed was a milk lump was an aggressive tumour. At first she had conventional treatment: surgery, chemotherapy. But the lump in her amputated left breast refused to be vanquished. It reappeared in the right one, and Eloise fled into a fairy tale, a story she wove in a defence against the doctors whose grave faces terrified her every time she kept her hospital appointments.

It didn't work. So she stopped going for check-ups. Instead, she read dozens of self-help books, which told her the disease was rooted in her own anger and that if she exorcised the past fury from her mind, she would recover. She went to faith healers, visited spas in Europe where the water and the treatments promised miracles. She created her own sanctuary of denial, believing she could cure herself with coffee enemas and green tea. And the rest of us – her husband, her mother, her closest friends – the rest of us, to our shame, let her believe it. Crippled by pity, afraid to puncture her fragile sense of hope, we kept silent about her increasingly irrational routines, her avoidance of scans, doctors, hospitals. We allowed ourselves to think that keeping her spirits up was more important than insisting on proper treatment.

And for five years she seemed invincible. Still beautiful, still vibrant and full of energy, she convinced herself – hell, she almost convinced us – that she would beat the cancer, that she would live.

Of course, she was wrong.

Chapter Two

I went up to bed, leaving Chris to lock up and make sure the fire was out, but before I slept I pulled out my bedside drawer and immediately her scent floated softly into the room. I opened the little silk purse, impregnated with the perfume Ellie had loved, and gently drew out the beaded bracelet her mother had given me to accompany the necklace I'd been wearing earlier. Without waiting for Chris who, I thought sourly, would have given me a lecture on being morbid, I drifted off to sleep with Eloise's enamelled runes clasped close in my hand.

I wish I hadn't. Because I slid into the mist-edged landscape that I knew only too well would haunt me, and it had held me in its thrall for too long already. Whenever I felt my mind blackening, my thoughts darkening, I knew I had to hold on tight to my sanity. And bad dreams, nightmares that were almost Gothic in their horror, were often the first sign that my depression was returning.

In my cloudy dream I stood on a seashore. I was very small and distant, looking out toward the ocean; the night was dark and starless but there was a weak moon and, as I watched, a shadowy form pushed a wheeled stretcher across the sand with slow stateliness. Beyond this figure, shrouded in a long hooded robe, lay a calm sea rimmed with silvered moonlight, and I saw that on the stretcher lay a coffin.

The coffin was open, lined with white silk, and the body inside was my father's. His gaunt, cancer-ravaged profile was suddenly bathed in a deathly pale glow as the cloud and mist cleared and then, to my left, fire erupted from countless chimneys I hadn't seen until now.

I knew, because I first had this dream twenty years ago when my father died, that these were charnel houses, dozens of them, littering the rocky cliffside. Back in the Middle Ages these places had been used as repositories for dead bodies and bones; but in my nightmare they blazed with burning horror, infernos promising a passage to hell.

I also knew, though, as my father's corpse made its inexorable progress towards the furnaces, that its eventual destination did not lie in those flames, but across the black stillness of the sea. My father was going somewhere else, pushed by the hooded boatman, the guardian of the underworld, who would ferry him across to the land of the dead.

I woke up, my heart racing, my head pounding. I remembered my dad's death, his cremation, how I would dream for months afterwards of his slow, stately passage over the sands; how I would sometimes dream that I went downstairs in my parents' house to find my father grotesquely hunched up in the fireplace, half alive, half dead. I would wake, shaking and shouting for my mother, until Chris put his arms around me, hugged and shushed me until I calmed down and I would sob on his shoulder as he gently soothed me.

Dear, strong Chris. Of course he was anxious about my reaction to Eloise's death. He had seen me hyperventilating with panic, crippled by near insanity. Damn it, I thought, I don't want this horror all over again. Chris was right; I had to avoid all the negative emotions that had plunged me into clinical depression in the past. We'd go back to London tomorrow, I decided, although we had planned to see Eloise's husband – widower, I suppose I would have to call him now – Ted, and their little girls. We'd gone to their house – Eloise's house – this afternoon because I'd felt strong enough to cope with what I knew would be an emotionally charged encounter, but they weren't there. Now I felt guilty for thinking I couldn't face them, but I knew had to get away from the Cornwall I loved, the Cornwall that sparkled with clear green mornings whatever the season, as it had today. There were butterflies on the cliff path as early as Boxing Day and the daffodils in our meadow came out in November, and stayed golden and full of hope no matter how harsh the winter. The sea gleamed blue in the sunlight, and on rainy days its sullen pewter gloom was thrillingly brightened by crashing white surf that made my heart sing and my head clear of everything except the brilliant beauty of this wondrous place.

Cornwall filled me with peace and happiness. It had been my refuge for over twenty years, my sanctuary, and we'd planned this break long before Ellie's death, looking forward to time on our own with the boys away at their universities and our daughter on her school's ski trip. But now here, where Eloise had died, I was obsessed with death and gloom again. Worst of all, somehow I could feel Eloise pulling at me, filling me with dark thoughts, fear and foreboding.

Chris slept quietly beside me and I wrapped my arms round his warm, solid body. I would apologise for my irritation when we woke, tell him that we would go home.

*

In the morning, Chris was sweetly accepting of my apology, clearly feeling that it marked an upturn in my spirits. So much so that after breakfast he asked me if I still wanted to go back to London, glancing wistfully out of the window at the brilliant blue sky. It was raining at home, so the weather report had said, my night terrors were almost gone and it was a beautiful day.

'We could go to the beach at Polkerris,' he said. 'It seems a shame to waste a day like this and drive back to pouring rain.'

It did. Anyway, I could do with some sun and sea air to chase away the last night-time horrors. I looked at Chris and nodded. He grinned and kissed the top of my head. Outside in the garden the glorious salty tang of the sea helped revive my spirits and I wondered if Talland Beach Café was open. The season didn't really start until Easter but sometimes the young couple who ran it would open up before that if the weather was exceptionally good and it was a weekend. We'd stroll down in the afternoon for a cup of tea, I thought. Meanwhile we'd have lunch at Polkerris or Fowey.

We reached Bodinnick in twenty minutes and waited for the ferry. There were only two other cars in the queue, but in summer the lane was often packed with families waiting to cross to Fowey. I never minded waiting because I could look at the striking house by the water's edge and daydream about Daphne du Maurier. Painted white, with window and door frames picked out in vivid indigo, this was Ferryside, Daphne's beloved first home in Cornwall. Eloise and I were both passionate about du Maurier. Every year we would go together to the literary festival held in Fowey in honour of Cornwall's greatest novelist. This year, I realised sadly, I would have to go on my own.

The crossing took five minutes. We drove off the boat, turned right past the car park and instead of taking the left hand turn to Fowey we carried on until the road sign indicated Polkerris beach and Menabilly.

Ah ... Menabilly. The Holy Grail of anyone who seeks to understand and emulate the extraordinary talent and vision of Daphne du Maurier. Those of us who have been enslaved by her stories set in Cornwall know how her obsession with Menabilly, the house in which she wrote her most marvellous novel of all, *Rebecca*, still enchants and draws us. Ellie and I would sometimes walk down the lane and try to catch a glimpse of the old farmhouse, but it's so secluded and remote that it's impossible to see through the impenetrable thicket of trees surrounding the property.

Reaching Polkerris we had a choice of eating at The Rashleigh Inn, a very pleasant pub with lovely views of the sea, or at Sam's on the Beach, a truly great little bistro with a good fishy menu.

Today we chose Sam's, a converted nineteenth century lifeboat house, utterly unpretentious, all wood and glass, right on the glorious beach which in February was mostly populated with dogs and young children enjoying a fabulous sunny Saturday with their mums and dads.

We ordered prawns and scallops and watched the little ones on the sands outside, marvelling at their simple happiness with bucket and spade.

We had to talk, of course, about Eloise and, more particularly, about Ted and the twins. We hadn't seen them since the funeral but I really didn't want to just yet, not after last night's nightmare. We would call later and perhaps visit them tomorrow.

'We ought to see Juliana as well,' I told Chris. 'She's in the most awful state about Eloise – I called her last week and she simply couldn't speak. She just wasn't prepared for it.'

'Are you kidding, Cathy? Of course she was prepared. Juliana knew her daughter was terminal for the last couple of years.'

'Yes, but Ellie was doing so well just before the end. I know Juliana thought she had rallied, and her doctors thought so too. They told Ted and Juliana that she had maybe as much as a year; certainly another six months.'

'That was all speculative.'

'Obviously, as things have turned out. But Chris, of course Juliana's very shocked, and I want to see her. I'll call her now.'

'Honey, could you please leave it for today? I really, really want a quiet evening with just *you*. We could have some tea at Talland Bay and then head home, light a fire, and watch TV. We can have a couple of glasses of wine, and just relax. I think we both need that, and it won't happen if you get obsessed with Eloise again, as you did yesterday.'

I felt mutinous, but only for a moment. Chris had been wonderful when I was ill and I owed him some uncomplicated pleasure. I smiled and squeezed his hand. Tomorrow I would deal with Juliana, Ted, and those poor, motherless little girls, Rose and Violet. Tonight I would just try to make my husband happy.

Chapter Three

On Sunday morning I called Juliana – and she sounded desperate.

'Cathy, I'm so very glad you called. Can I see you? I'm in a bit of a state here. I'm really sorry to bother you but – well, things aren't right.'

'Of course. I'll come straight away. Do you want anything?'

'Oh God, Cathy. I want my darling daughter, and I want her daughters too.'

'I know, I know,' I said, aching with sympathy for her. 'I'll come. I'll be at Roseland in an hour.'

*

I don't drive. Well, I do – I finally passed my test after six attempts and felt too embarrassed to be triumphant. But it was all such a strain that I never really enjoyed it and always had the feeling that I was two steps away from a fatal accident.

Because of that, I now leave it to Chris, who loves driving; one of the many areas of our life together which I cede to him because I have so little confidence in myself; part of the catastrophic breakdown in my mind from which I was supposedly recovering. When I was ill, I became agoraphobic. I was terrified of leaving the house, and I hated meeting new people. I was much better now, but I still had no faith in my ability to drive. I have a little VW Beetle convertible that we keep in Cornwall, but I only drove it once last year, after my breakdown. Within yards of leaving the cottage to do some shopping, I hit an enormous boulder on the left-hand side of the road. I wasn't hurt and the only damage was a blown tyre, but that, as far as I was concerned, was that. Total failure. Despite all of Chris's encouragement, I refused to take the wheel again, even though he took a sledgehammer to the offending rock and smashed it to bits.

So the little cream Beetle sat forlornly on our Cornish driveway like a neglected pet: utterly sweet and begging to be taken out for a walk – or rather a spin. And hardly ever rewarded but for an occasional impulsive trip to the pub, on days so sunny it was irresistible not to drive with the roof down; but every time Chris or one of the boys was firmly at the wheel.

So it was Chris who drove me to see Juliana, and when we arrived he said he'd take a walk around the grounds, sure that Ellie's mother would prefer to talk to me alone. The gardens were magnificent, National Trust owned and cared for, so it wasn't exactly a sacrifice. Actually, it was a total treat.

Roseland Hall is a grand old manor house, built in the mid-seventeenth century, overlooking the lower part of the beautiful River Fowey. It's open to the public and is no longer the private domain of the Trelawneys, the great, ancient Cornish family to which it originally belonged.

Eloise had often shown me round it. She especially loved inveigling the curator to let us in late at night, when its ghostly grandeur easily persuaded us that it was haunted, as was its reputation. It's a remarkable house, astonishingly almost as cosy as it's grand, lit with exquisite French crystal chandeliers, and with a magnificent Long Gallery hung with the finest tapestries and paintings.

For any family, it would be a tragedy to leave such a house behind. But sadly, Juliana, the last Lady Trelawney, no longer lived there.

For generations, Eloise had confided to me, the Trelawneys had had problems with fertility and gradually, but inexorably, the line dwindled. Sir Charles, Eloise's father, the last baronet, was the only child of his generation, as his father and grandfather had been of theirs. He had no brothers, no sisters, no cousins. When he married the beautiful Juliana, a well-bred Cornish girl from an old, landed family, he had high hopes of producing a son and heir. And, after five years of increasingly desperate attempts to conceive, Juliana at last fell pregnant. When Eloise was born, Charles tried hard to hide his disappointment, but Juliana knew she had failed him. She never got pregnant again, and they never talked about it. She was afraid to plumb the depths of his despair. Juliana, though, adored her little daughter, and increasingly resented her husband's indifference to their child. She also suspected that her inability to produce more children was not her fault, but his. Her own family had no problems with fecundity.

Still, there was nothing to be done about it. Charles was so gloomy about Trelawneys no longer living on the estate that his wife knew to press him on the matter would open deep, irreconcilable wounds, wounds that could destroy their marriage, so she kept her peace.

Charles became increasingly maudlin about the future of the big house. He had a great deal of money, but the estate was a constant drain on his resources. And for what? There was no dynasty here, no reason to invest in his ancient family's future because there would be no future Trelawneys. If Eloise married, she would take her husband's name. And he sensed Juliana's heart was not in it. Charles was right. She was not enthusiastic about being forever responsible for an enormous stately pile, with all the sacrifices, discipline and hard work it required, and she had absolutely no wish to burden Eloise with the responsibility of maintaining an anachronism that had outlived its usefulness. She vowed to herself that if her husband died before her, she would give the house to the National Trust.

And that's exactly what she had done. Ellie told me it was the best decision her mother ever made.

Chapter Four

I knocked at Juliana's door. Since Charles's death, she had lived in a very beautiful old farmhouse in the grounds of Roseland Hall. I always felt a bit intimidated by its utterly perfect, though slightly shabby, patrician décor. But, to be honest, that was only my own inverted snobbery kicking in. And Juliana did not deserve that. She was so warm, so utterly enveloping, that her aristocratic background, her upper-class vowels, her complete confidence in her own being and her place in one of the most ancient and romantic families of distinguished Cornish aristocracy made you want to be close to her, to be involved with the rich tapestry of her days.

She looked wonderful, even though losing Eloise was, I knew, the greatest tragedy of her life. Tall and slender, she wore ruffled blouses with high collars, long flowing skirts. Her hair was abundant, ice-queen silver, gathered behind her head and then left to flow like a curling wintry river over her shoulders. She was completely beautiful at seventy-five, a graceful Cornish nymph, a dryad who could sit by a sacred well and comb her long hair to charm and enchant, even now in her old age.

She asked if I wanted tea, and one of her remaining devoted servants brought it. We sat in her pretty sitting room, and she talked about Eloise.

'She seemed so much better, Cathy. The doctors said she was in remission.'

'But you must know they just meant a sort of reprieve. Seriously, Juliana, you knew she was terminal?'

'Of course, but she was full of energy, and enjoying her life so much.'

'OK, I know she was, but we have to accept in an illness like that, things can suddenly accelerate. God knows, Juliana, we've talked so much about her pain. That's why she was taking the drugs. However much we wanted to deny it, we knew what was coming for Eloise.'

She fixed me with a long stare.

'Cathy, don't you think it's strange that I wasn't there?'

'What do you mean? When she died?'

'We were so close. She always wanted to be with me when . . . it happened.'

'But . . . well, you couldn't have been. It happened so fast. There was no time . . . '

'Yes, there was.' She gave me an unfathomable look. 'Tell me, Cathy, when someone is terminally ill, do they die suddenly as if they'd had a heart attack? I don't believe so. I saw Eloise the day she died, in the morning. We had coffee with the little ones. She was happy, so relieved that the doctors had given her a reprieve. You knew Eloise. She was always so positive, convinced she would beat it. And then, three hours later, she was dead? It makes no sense to me.'

I wasn't sure what to say. I had my own concerns about Eloise's death – a barely conscious doubt and unease that I suspected had caused my awful nightmare the other night. But I felt that if I gave in to Juliana's anxieties, it would send me into a realm of total paranoia. What was she saying? That my dear friend did not die because of her terminal cancer? After all those years of gloomy prognosis? Of course she did. The alternative was utterly ridiculous.

I asked her what she thought could have happened to Eloise, if her death was not from natural causes. There had been no need for a post-mortem, of course. There was no need to confirm what we all knew: Ellie died from her cancer, which had metastasised throughout her body. Her lungs, liver, spine and brain had been riddled with the hideous disease.

Juliana shook her head in frustration. 'I don't know. It's just an instinct that I can't shake off. Oh, I'm aware that I sound like a deranged old woman, unable to accept my daughter's death. Ted told me as much a few days ago.'

'You've discussed it with him?' I was astonished.

She gave a deep sigh. 'I tried to, but he became really angry with me. He said he had enough on his plate without having to deal with an eccentric old biddy who couldn't cope with reality. He even suggested I was going senile.' Her face darkened. 'That hurt me a lot.'

'But you and Ted – you've never really got along, have you?' I asked.

'Did Eloise tell you that?'

I nodded.

She sighed unhappily. 'Eloise got a bit impatient with me. Told me I was imagining things.'

'What do you mean? Imagining what?'

'I always thought he was a bit hard. To be honest, I thought he was a gold-digger. I never really trusted him,' she said.

'And what did Ellie say to that?'

'She laughed at me. She said she was grateful that I was looking out for her, but I was being ridiculous. She told me that Ted was a really talented artist, and that his paintings were increasing in value all the time. She said collectors were hungry for his work, and they both thought he was going to make a fortune in his own right. She said that what I took for hardness was actually fierce ambition, and a lack of sentimentality.' Juliana shrugged. 'She may have been right. She obviously knew him much better than I did. But Cathy, I never warmed to him – and he knew it, though we kept up a front for Eloise's sake. I'm so scared that now there's no need for that pretence that I'll see much less of him and . . . and the twins . . .'

I tried to reassure her that she was simply and understandably hugely upset, that there was no need to worry, and I told her I would think about what she had said, and call her the next day. We were supposed to be returning to London tomorrow, but I had no real reason to go home. Chris had appointments on Tuesday, but I could stay. As I left, I thought about Ted and Eloise. We knew Ted quite well, and on the whole they had seemed happy. They'd had the occasional row, and would sometimes arrive at dinner parties, each of them silently simmering with resentment of the other.

But so did every married couple. Chris and I certainly did. And Ted made Ellie laugh. He could be very witty.

I found Chris outside, mesmerised by the beautiful garden. I told him what Juliana had said and he sighed. Chris was kind, but like most men he wanted solutions, not problems.

'Look,' he said. 'She's her mother and she wasn't there at the most emotionally significant moment of her daughter's life. What she's feeling is natural. Not to have been with Eloise when she died makes her feel incredibly guilty. She feels she should have prevented it – and that if she'd been a better mother it would never have happened. You *know* all that stuff, Cathy. Comes with the motherhood territory. If it had been Evie, you would have felt exactly the same.'

Evie was our sixteen-year-old daughter. A flash of pain tore through me as I imagined losing her.

Then I felt furious. How dare he shift a mother's grief into something that 'comes with the territory'? Yes, of course, for a child to die before her is beyond the worst realms of a mother's imagination. But Chris spoke so glibly, as if he were explaining something to me that I was too stupid to under-stand. As if he had a paternal overview which was quite naturally superior to a mother's instinct.

I did feel strongly, at that point, a sort of tribal alliance with Juliana. We were both mothers. We were both, in dif-ferent ways, deeply uneasy about Eloise's death. I decided then that, however irrational, I was on Juliana's side. Something was wrong. And whatever Chris said, I was staying put in Cornwall until I had fathomed out what was troubling me.

Chapter Five

Monday. I woke feeling worried and oppressed. I had to do something and I really didn't want to. Then I remembered. Ted. We hadn't called him yesterday.

'Will you phone him today?' I asked, drinking tea on our little sun-drenched patio.

'Right. And what am I supposed to say?'

God. Men.

'Jesus, Chris – you're supposed to be his friend. You've always said he's one of the straightest guys you know. Can't you just talk to him about losing his wife? Then maybe we can talk to him about Juliana's concerns. And we have to check on the girls. See how they are. They must be so bewildered and sad at losing their mummy.'

'All right. Shall I ask them to lunch?'

'Yes. If they can make it.'

As it happened they couldn't. They were staying at Ted's parents' house in Manchester. They wouldn't be back in Cornwall until tomorrow.

'Well, I guess that's it,' Chris said when he ended the call. 'I've got to go back to London tonight, so we won't see him.'

Not 'we' – but I could, I thought. I didn't have to go anywhere. I would stay here until I had sorted things out with Ted and Juliana. For Eloise. But I wouldn't tell Chris for a couple of hours, until I thought of a way to convince him that I had to, that I needed to do this.

The weather turned on Tuesday. As I had waved a slightly surly Chris goodbye on Monday evening the sky was clouding over. Now the rain was hurling down in the relentless sheets that Cornwall throws at those of us who fondly hope for sun. It mocks us, really. 'Call yourselves lovers of Kernow?' the wind howls. 'What do you know about what living here really means? The hardship and bleakness?' And yes, Cornwall can be far from a paradise. A beautiful haven for family holidays for a few months of the year; a relentlessly harsh and difficult place to make a living for most of it. And so dependent on the weather. Every winter, every spring, the locals' eyes focus anxiously on the coming summer season. Will the sun bless the beaches? Will the holidaymakers flock to Looe, Polperro, and Penzance?

On a day like today, with the rain lashing down, and the wind thrashing the plane trees, it makes even the most devoted lovers of this beautiful, mystical county question their sanity. What was I doing here in this godforsaken, isolated place, so far from the shops, so shrouded in mist, rain and loneliness?

It was a day for staying in. I lit the fire and turned on the lamps although it was still morning. My little VW sat outside on the drive, but I had no intention of driving anywhere, so it was fortunate that there was enough food in the fridge to tide me over for a few days. Milk, eggs, bacon, cheese. And bread, fruit and salad. I made a cup of Horlicks and sat in my favourite place – a little yellow sofa tucked into a corner window, which made me feel warm and secure. I watched the fire – we could see it from everywhere in the big, open downstairs space; from the living room, kitchen, dining table and the little snug, which is where I sat now.

I loved this place, this cottage with its simple warmth, its big windows, the honey colour of the wide oak floorboards, the white, grey and blue of the walls and woodwork, the roaring fire and red and gold rugs. Sometimes I thought I could curl up here with a book and never feel the need to leave.

The afternoon passed slowly. The rain turned to hail, thundering down on the roof and windows. I put my book aside and sat on the little yellow sofa, immersed in memories of the lovely days here in Cornwall when Chris and I would meet up with Ted and Eloise, all our children in tow. Little Rose and Violet, the gorgeously beautiful twins, and our own kids, Eve, Tom and Sam, much older than the little girls but still young enough to enjoy the beach and demand ice creams. We would go to Polzeath or Daymer Bay, on the north side of Cornwall, far removed from our gentle southern coves. This was surf-land, all crashing waves, tanned public school boys and waif-like girls whose parents hired houses in trendy Rock at vast expense every year. Personally, I despised it, but Ted and Eloise were more forgiving, and, to be honest, quite relished the social vibe there. I suppose it's exciting up in north Cornwall, but I much prefer the gentle, cradling south.

We had some wonderful times, our two families. Chris and our eldest Sam would hire wetsuits and attempt to look convincing with surfboards, though they couldn't compete with Ted, a brilliant surfer, revered as a bit of a legend by the eager kids who holidayed on the North Coast and thought everything to do with surf was über-cool, while Juliana,

Eloise and I sat on the beach with the younger ones, feeding the tiny twins frozen yoghurt, laughing as the damp sand seeped up into our underwear. Soggy bums are very much part of the picture if you have small children in Cornwall. Photos of us all, raincoats on, umbrellas up, are among my greatest treasures. Lovely days. Full of the joy that having little children brings, as if you can believe, for a few fleeting moments, that life goes on for ever, that you can glimpse an extraordinary vision of bliss that will somehow endure. From here to eternity.

I felt achingly sad for those days now. With Eloise's death, that was all over. All that joy, that exuberance as you watch your children hold out the promise of eternal life – all snuffed out in an instant as your best friend, just forty-five years old, dies and shows you the true reality of your silly, ephemeral hopes for happiness, and the emptiness of what lies ahead for all of us. Oblivion. Darkness. That extraordinary god like link with our children vanished in a moment, leaving them to their uncertain fate, alone and motherless.

And us, the mothers. What happens to us in the void? Do we stop caring, watching? Or do we suffer eternal grief as we see our children grow up without us, knowing that however well their lives turn out, they will never be the same? Never be as happy, as secure as they would have been if death had not cleaved us cruelly apart?

And that, I knew with absolute certainty, was how Eloise felt now. I shuddered. Something had shifted inside my head. I could feel myself hovering close to the dark pit of despair that had engulfed me during my breakdown. I must, must not let that happen to me again, I told myself.

The phone was ringing. I had fallen asleep. My head was muzzy, and I was tempted to let the call go unanswered, but as ever I envisaged disaster. What if Chris had had an accident? What if one of the children was ill or in trouble or down at the local police station accused of some teenage carnage? That's the way you think when you're a mother. So I staggered to the kitchen and picked up the receiver.

'Hi, Mama.' It was Eve. 'I was just wondering – when are you coming home? I've just got back – it was brilliant, the whole trip, by the way – and I've spoken to Dad at the clinic. But why are you still in Cornwall? Dad says it's because of Eloise, that you're sad. Please don't be sad, Mama. Come home and I'll give you a big hug.'

Ah, my Eve. My baby. Always.

And Eloise?

No babies for her now. Never, ever. Or was she still here, still watching, brooding, desperate to get home to her little girls? Unable to let them go, scared for their future, wanting above all else to hold them once more, to protect them? My new, dark instinct, enveloping me as I veered ever closer to my old battle with depression, told me yes. But what did that *mean*? Could it be that, if I was right, Eloise's death was unfinished business? Was Eloise not at peace? Did Juliana's anxiety about how her daughter died mean that she shared my growing feeling that something very bad had happened?

Or was the stress of my best friend's death, my grief, my fear that if she could die so young, then so could I, pulling me back into the horrible black world of mental illness from which I had so recently escaped?

I gulped, got a grip, and forced myself to smile as I murmured soothing words of love and reassurance to my Eve, asked her more about the ski trip, said I would see her by the weekend, and meantime to give Daddy a big kiss from me. It seemed to work. She put the phone down sounding happy and well loved. Which she was.

I fried some bacon and eggs, and sat down to watch television while I ate. As usual there was nothing I wanted to see. Thank God for Sky Plus. I found the planner and accessed *Steel Magnolias*. If you're steeped in family sentiment you might as well watch a weepie. Besides, it reminded me of Evie. Julia Roberts, Sally Field, Dolly Parton, Daryl Hannah, Shirley MacLaine and the magnificent Olympia Dukakis never failed to grip me in a tight embrace of femininity. Evie and I had watched this movie many times. In fact, we were totally hooked on girls-only nights. Together we'd sniffled through *Stepmom* and *Mama Mia* when Chris, Sam and Tom were out, eating scrambled eggs, loving the silly sentimentality of our mother/daughter bond.

At about nine o'clock, when Julia Roberts was just about to expire, headlights swept past the sitting-room windows. I didn't think they had anything to do with me. We have two sets of neighbours on our land, both with rights of way past our house. It would be Jim and Mary, or Terry and his adolescent children arriving home after a day of work, school and football practice. I never closed the blinds in our cottage, just as, like everyone else in our tiny hamlet, I never locked the doors. There was no need. Our neighbours were benevolent, and no one else ever came down our remote drive unless invited.

The ceaseless heavy rain had turned into a violent storm, which can be pleasurably thrilling if you've got company, but much more threatening when you're on your own.

The kitchen door opened without a knock and banged violently against the wall as it was thrown open. I leapt up in alarm. Ted! He stood just inside the door and leant back against the frame. His knees buckled and I thought he was going to faint. I ran to hold and steady him.

'Ted, my dear. Are you OK? Let me get you a drink. Where are the girls?'

'I dropped them off at Juliana's. They're staying the night.'

That surprised me. Not that Juliana had agreed to babysit the twins, because she absolutely adored them. But if her relationship with her son-in-law was as difficult as she'd said, I wondered at Ted's preparedness to take advantage of her kindness. Maybe it was just a matter of convenience for him or maybe he didn't dislike her as much as she thought he did. I just hoped he'd dropped them off before he'd started drinking, because he was definitely not sober.

'I hope you don't mind, Cathy, but I was desperate for someone to talk to. I know Chris had to go back to London, but I really needed to see *you*. I'm sorry.' He shook his head. 'It's probably the last thing you need at this time of night.'

'Don't be silly. It's not that late and I'm glad of your company. Cornwall in the middle of a storm can be pretty lonely.' As I spoke, thunder rocked the valley and the rain pounded on the roof. I waited for the lightning. In truth, I *was* glad not to be on my own right now.

'Ted, what can I get you to drink?'

'Don't suppose you've got any whisky?'

'You're in luck. Left over from Christmas.'

Lightning flashed and cracked as I poured the Scotch while he collapsed on the sofa.

He looked exhausted and I studied him carefully. He was

an attractive man, tall, with hair bleached blond by the Cornish sun. His eyes, blue as the sea, were tired and sad.

'How are they? The girls?' I asked.

'Remarkable, actually.'

'And you?'

He laughed, sweeping his hand through his hair.

'Well actually, since you ask, I'm pretty crap.'

'I thought so. I'm sorry.'

'D'you know what? I'd really like not to talk about this at the moment. I mean, just being here feels like a bit of normality.'

But the conversation was stilted. There were things neither of us wanted to say and I felt I had a duty to have a deep and serious talk with him about Eloise, but it was obvious he didn't want it. He craved a blazing fire, female company, a large Scotch and *News At Ten*. And that's what I gave him, watching him relax and sink into his chair.

'It's been so difficult, keeping up appearances for the children,' he said eventually. 'I can't talk, can't cry in front of them. I think I'm going mad, Cathy – the world's turned over and I don't know what to do next. To be honest, all I want is to get drunk.'

'Well, you're entitled to that.'

'I wish, but not here. I've got to drive back to Fowey. Home.' He grimaced.

'Haven't you been back yet?'

'No. Couldn't face it. Have to tomorrow, though. Just couldn't bear it tonight.'

'Then stay here, Ted. Have a few drinks, sleep it off, and go back to collect the girls in the morning. I'll come with you if you like. And go back with you all to Fowey. You'll need groceries to keep you going. I'll help you shop.'

'Cathy, you're an angel. But I can't impose my sad, pathetic self on you.'

'Don't be ridiculous. I've nothing else to do, and besides, I'm pretty knocked sideways myself. I spoke to Juliana yesterday. She's still in shock.'

His face changed. Now he didn't look sad, just angry.

'She blames me, you know. Christ knows why. Eloise had been living under a death sentence for years.'

'It's really tough on all of you. I'm desperately sorry. Just stay here tonight. Have another drink.'

He acquiesced. I wasn't trying to get him drunk, but his mood was hard to read, and I was anxious to calm him down.

I brought him another Scotch. He tossed it down. His face relaxed and he turned to look at me.

'You know, Cathy, of all Ellie's friends, you're the only one I can really trust. I really like you.'

'Well, that's good. I'm glad you feel like that,' I said, feeling slightly uncomfortable. 'And I really want to help; I can't tell you how much I want to make this better for all of you. If I possibly can.' It was obvious now that he'd drunk so much there could be no effective conversation, so I said, 'Look, Ted. I'm suddenly really tired and I just have to go to bed. If you go downstairs, you can sleep in any of the kids' rooms. The beds are all made up . . . '

'Cathy, please can we talk?' He was anxious, somehow petulant, wanting to prolong the moment.

'Tomorrow would be better – you look exhausted. Really, you need to sleep; and so do I. Things will make more sense in the morning.'

He clearly needed something from me – some level of emotional input – which I was not prepared to offer right now. OK, he was more than a bit drunk, tired and sad, but I sensed he wanted to confide in me and I wasn't sure I was ready to hear whatever it was. But confide what? I felt on edge. In some indefinable way the mood had changed and I sensed something slightly unstable in him, a hint of aggression.

Despite my reservations about Juliana's negative opinion of Ted, I had in fact suspected for some time that all was not well with him and Eloise. It was only a vague, niggling suspicion, and I hadn't said anything to Chris, but I felt there was a distance between them, a lack of the warmth and intimacy that they used to enjoy. I told myself it was the cancer; that she was in denial and he was desperate. I felt she needed to stop racing around the world in pursuit of alternative miracle cures; over the last three years she had visited Switzerland, Austria, Germany, and Italy to get the unorthodox but hands-on treatment she felt she had to have to survive. Of course she could afford it. But the more faith she placed in people Ted thought were charlatans, the more distant she became from him. She would bring them back to the house and expect him to entertain them. And they took advantage. Eloise was rich. She was to inherit a great deal of money when her mother died, and in the meantime she was the beneficiary of a substantial trust fund. Her 'healers' knew this and found her comfortable home in Fowey a very agreeable place to stay.

And of course they charged highly for their ministrations; massages, reflexology, swimming in certain 'holy' spots along the coast. There were evening sessions where they would chant and bang drums, then there was the nutritional advice, the insistence on organic fruit and vegetables juiced up several times a day.

To be honest, their lovely home became a madhouse and Chris and I stopped visiting. Instead we asked them round to our place when we were down in Cornwall, or arranged to meet on a beach, or at one of the local restaurants, like the Old Quay House in Fowey, where we could sit on the terrace, watch the boats go by and pretend to ourselves that our beautiful, blessed life in Cornwall was still intact.

I told Ted I was going to bed, as firmly as I could. By now he was nursing yet another Scotch and I could hardly take him down to Sam's room and tuck him in. He and Eloise had stayed with us many times, but still it felt awkward that he and I were here on our own. As I turned away, he followed me. His voice was slurred and urgent.

'Cathy. I know you left a message on the answerphone for Eloise the day she died. You were returning a call she'd left on yours. What did she say, Cath? Did she sound upset? Did she tell you something . . . something about us?'

'No. She did leave a message asking me to call her, but when I rang back she didn't pick up. Why? Do you think she had something to tell me?'

He stared at me. His eyes were unfocused, and a little wild.

'Did Eloise ever tell you that I really fancy you?' he asked.

I was beyond shocked. 'Of course not, Ted! Don't be ridiculous.'

'It's a pity she didn't. Because I do. And Cathy, I'm a grieving widower. I need some comfort.'

He leered at me, and lurched towards me, clumsily putting his arms around me, spilling whisky over my shirt as he did so. I pulled back sharply, nervous and a bit angry.

'I know you're very unhappy, and that's why you're acting like this. But it won't do, Ted, it really won't. Tomorrow you'll be embarrassed about this, but don't worry, I'll forget all about it. I understand what you're going through.'

I walked quickly to the door, ran upstairs and shot the bolt on our bedroom door. Yes, we never locked the outside doors, but our bedroom was different. We had to feel we could have some privacy from small, inquisitive eyes when the children were little. How I wished that Chris were here with me. He could have taken care of Ted, just as I could have taken care of Eloise or Juliana. Gender is so important at moments of high drama in domestic life. We kind of know what is expected of us when it comes to comforting sad people, but it helps if there are no possible misunderstandings about sexual roles. Ted, devastated as he was, could stay the night but our contact had to be strictly limited. He was not himself, and I didn't feel completely safe around him.

Lying sleepless in bed, for the first time I allowed myself to acknowledge that there had been times in the past when I'd felt he'd held me just a little too close saying hello or good-bye, had stroked my arm a little too intimately when I sat beside him at dinner. I had resolutely buried such thoughts, told myself I was imagining things, that Ellie loved him too much for him not to love her back just as passionately.

*

Eventually I went to sleep.

And then, something strange and tumultuous. I saw Eloise. She fled through a drowned landscape. Clouds and water drenched her, but she pursued the clear sunlight of her dream. Only then could she get back to her babies, I realised, to the still bright world of the living. Away from the vapour-filled twilight of the dead.

This was madness, but by some strange sense, I felt the panic in her head. I knew what she was feeling. What to do? How to find an ally? How to close that huge hole in her belly, the space where her babies had lain so safely? How to rescue them from the awful place in which they were now, threatened, motherless?

In my dream I found her at the war memorial on the cliff path to Polperro. I really did not want to be there, but her spirit had prised me out of my warm bed, and now I too was drenched, cold and frankly unhappy to be in a storm-tossed landscape, the surf below battering the rocks, the noise of the wind screaming in my ears.

It was a dream, of course. I knew that even at the time. Another of those ghostly supernatural hallucinations that happened when I was stressed, like the terrifying dream I'd had about my father.

But I was scared and angry. This was all so stupid, so utterly unnecessary.

'Eloise,' I said, to the formless shade before me, 'I'm asleep. I'd really like to get back to my bed. Why am I here? What do you want me to do?'

'I'll tell you soon,' the rippling shadow told me. 'Above all, you have to keep them safe.'

'Who? How? What do you mean?'

'Just watch my girls, Cathy. Keep them safe. Don't trust anything he says.'

Chapter Six

The rain, the cloud, the fierce February cold receded, and I fleetingly felt the caress of the duvet on my chilled limbs.

And then I woke up. And I wasn't in my soft, warm bed, but outside in the garden. It was raining hard, and I was in my Grumpy T-shirt from Disney World. I had no recollection of how I'd got here. I must have sleepwalked out of the house. The rain drummed down and the wind howled as it had in my dream. I felt terrified. The Cornish night was as black as ebony. No stars, no moon, just a dim light from the porch, and as I stumbled back towards the kitchen door, a low moan curdled my scared, shaken brain. It seemed to come from the willow tree. I was very tempted to ignore it, to slide back into my inviting bed, but as I hesitated it came again, and I saw, as I reluctantly stared into the darkness, a figure lying on the ground. At first I was so scared I thought it was Eloise, somehow transported from her place in the churchyard just above us at Saint Tallanus; but then I saw it was a man. Ted. Completely drunk and passed out on the lawn. He must have tried to leave, angry and embarrassed at his clumsy pass at me. His car was in the drive, and the porch light glinted on the bunch of keys clasped in his hand. I stared at him. Eloise's warning sounded in my head. *Don't trust him*. But that was just a dream. And Ted, wet, cold and drunk, needed my help despite his behaviour.

I tried to shake him awake, but he was totally oblivious. I thought of waking one of the neighbours, but it was, and I checked my watch, gone three in the morning. In the end, I'm ashamed to say, I left him. I covered him with the waterproof tarpaulin from the barbecue, rigged an old sun parasol over him to keep off the worst of the rain, and went back inside to the warmth of the kitchen. I left the door unlocked so he could get back in. Then I went upstairs, stripped off my soaking T-shirt, and towelled myself dry before climbing into my welcoming bed. What's more, I fell instantly and guiltlessly asleep.

I woke up late and flustered on Wednesday morning. It was after eleven. I got up and went into the bathroom. Brushing my teeth, I tried to remember exactly what had happened the night before. I must have been a bit tipsy myself. Everything seemed hazy. No wonder I'd had such a frightening dream about Eloise. While I was plying Ted with Scotch, I must have been pouring too much red wine for myself.

My heart lurched as I remembered. Ted! He had passed out under the willow tree and, unforgivably, I had left him outside in the cold rain of a February night. I felt sick. Clutching my dressing gown around me I pelted down the stairs. The living room was empty. I opened the kitchen door and walked out past the patio, up onto the lawn to the willow tree.

He wasn't there, which filled me with relief, but the barbecue cover and the tatty old sun umbrella were still reproachfully and squelchily in place, looking sad and unsavoury in the grey, forlorn morning light.

I rushed downstairs to the children's bedrooms, flung open their doors and found nothing. No beds had been disturbed, and the bathroom towels were pristine.

Back up to the living room, and I realised even his car had gone from the drive.

I was relieved – or was I? Obviously I had failed him last night. I mean, who wants a grieving guest to pass out drunkenly on the lawn on a cold February night? But somehow I did not want Ted in our house, certainly not when I was on my own. And I was glad, in a shamefaced way, that I didn't have to make him breakfast this morning, or go back with him to Eloise's lovely home in Fowey, as I'd offered, or even talk to him.

In the kitchen, I put the kettle on. There was a note on the worktop.

Cathy, it read.

Sorry to have been a complete lout and a bore. I was drunk and stupidly thought I'd drive home. I must have tripped on a tree root, and passed out, which was lucky, really. I could have killed myself driving in that state. Forgive me. I have a horrible feeling I made a complete idiot of myself last night. You were so lovely to me that I even thought there might be a point to life again. Will you let me make amends by having dinner with me and the girls in Fowey tonight? Don't really feel up to cooking (not that I ever could) but thought we could have a bite at the Old Quay House?

No, I thought. Definitely not. Not until Chris came back anyway.

I busied myself with a bit of house maintenance. I put some bedding in the wash, did some ironing. I was pretty fed up at not having the confidence to drive, to go somewhere totally disassociated with my dark thoughts about Eloise, but being fed up wasn't enough to get me behind the wheel.

I phoned Chris but he was busy with a patient, so I left a message saying I desperately needed to talk to him. Two minutes later the phone rang. It was Ted.

'Hi, Cathy. You OK?'

'Yeah, sure.' I tried to keep my voice neutral. 'How are you?'

'Well, I'd really like to talk to you. You're the first person I've wanted to – well – let off steam to since it all happened. There's so much you and Chris don't know.'

'I think it might be best if we waited for him to come back to talk about all that,' I said primly.

'Why? Cathy, look, I know I behaved badly last night. I'm really sorry and embarrassed because you and Chris have always been such good friends. But the thing is, I'm not myself at the moment, and I have to talk to someone. There's so much I don't understand. I mean, did Eloise ever tell you about Arthur?'

'Arthur? Who's Arthur? I don't know what you're talking about.'

He gave a bitter laugh. 'Well, no, perhaps you wouldn't. Juliana does, though. She certainly knows the lot.'

I was beginning to feel faint and sick. I really didn't like Ted's tone. And I hated the way he seemed to be drawing me into a conspiracy against Eloise.

Was I being hopelessly romantic about her? Had I put her on a pedestal because of her beauty, her ancient and aristocratic family associations? And then I realised my reluctance to engage in a conversation with Ted was a kind of fear of finding out more about Eloise than I wanted to know.

I told him I was feeling ill. Which was quite true because at that moment I really wanted to throw up. But, always sensitive to my body, I knew that my sickness had nothing to do with a normal visceral reaction, and everything to do with what was going on in my head.

'I can't see you tonight, Ted. I feel like shit and I've got loads of work to do. So, not tonight, but of course I want to meet up soon. And who is Arthur?'

Ted chuckled, but it was a dark and nasty sound.

'Arthur? Well, he's just a spanner in the works. That's what Arthur is. Not that I had the slightest idea about his existence until a few weeks ago. But, God, talk about betrayal. It's about as bad as it gets.'

I realised then that he was possibly still a bit drunk from the night before. He sounded slurred and stressed. But also incredibly vindictive and angry.

I told him I'd call him back later. I really needed to talk to Chris.

Late that afternoon Chris called. I told him about Ted's strange mood and how disturbing I found it. 'He made me feel . . . quite frightened really.'

'You're imagining things, Cath. Ted's bound to be under a lot of stress at the moment. That's probably what you picked up on.'

'No, Chris, I'm not imagining anything. He made me feel really uncomfortable. I think he . . . well, he tried to make a pass at me.'

There was a long pause. Then Chris spoke in the stony voice I'd come to dread, the one he used when he thought I wasn't doing enough to stop my darker thoughts and emotions taking me over.

'Right, that's it. You're coming home.'

I bristled. 'No, I'm not. Stop ordering me about.'

He sighed. 'Cathy, look. You've been very ill. So seriously depressed that at times I thought – well, you know what I thought. I wasn't sure that you were going to get better. But you have. You've been doing so well, and now here I am stuck in London and you're having some kind of meltdown on your own in Cornwall. This is not good. You must know that.'

'I'm not having a meltdown. I'm just ... well ... concerned about Ted.'

'It's not that I'm worried about. Look, I know the signs. The way you've started anguishing about Eloise. The way you can't let it go. I know when these things get a grip on you. You're getting obsessed with your dark thoughts again. It's the start of a downward spiral.'

'What are you talking about? I'm not obsessed. I'm not having dark thoughts,' I protested, although of course I knew I was. 'I'm just telling you what Ted was like with me last night. Are you suggesting I imagined it?'

'Cathy, you need to come home. You need to be with your family. You really shouldn't be alone. And I can't come down because I have patients all day for the next few days. But if you won't get the train, I'll drive down overnight and pick you up. You leave me no choice.'

'Jesus, Chris! Who do you think you are?'

'Your husband. Who loves you. Cathy, this situation is intolerable. And if you are determined to be so completely stubborn that you won't do what is obviously right for your mental health, then I have no choice but to act and get you home.'

'Oh, I see. And when I get back, are you going to have me sectioned?'

'Don't be ridiculous! Will you get the train or do I have to come down and get you?'

'Do you know what, Chris? You can get lost. I'm going nowhere. You can go wherever the hell you want.'

I banged the phone down. There was no mobile signal in Talland Bay, so it was still possible to be melodramatic on the landline. I was furious, though. And also despairing. If you've had a breakdown, as I'd had, does that give everyone carte blanche to question your sanity ever after? I knew what I had heard in Ted's voice, his angry attitude to Eloise. I wasn't imagining it. How *dare* Chris decide I was being delusional? Did this mean that every time I told him something he didn't want to hear he would assume I was mad again? How could any wife live with that?

Two summers ago, Evie had been ill. It had started with headaches so severe they made her weep. And then she started vomiting. We were staying in Cornwall, and the doctor referred her to Derriford Hospital. The consultant could find nothing wrong and Chris said it was probably just a stomach bug, but as the days went by and Eve's pale face stared reproachfully at me as she lay on the sofa, clearly in dreadful pain, I became convinced she was suffering from something much more terrifying. I decided she had brain cancer. And I insisted on a scan.

Chris felt I was over-reacting, but persuaded the consultant to indulge me. Evie had the brain scan. There was, said the doctor, absolutely nothing wrong with her. He showed us the X-ray. It meant little to me but Chris smiled with relief when he saw it. As he and the consultant looked at it, they laughed and joshed each other and I regarded them with disbelief. What were they laughing at? Our daughter had a brain tumour, and Chris was chuckling about the X-ray?

On the drive back to the cottage, I sat stunned, sick with horror. When we got back poor Evie, clutching her painful tummy, went to bed with a hot water bottle. Downstairs, I confronted Chris.

'I want to get Evie back to London straight away. I want a second opinion, another scan.'

Chris looked at me, concerned at my shaking voice. 'There's no need, Cathy. I saw the scan. She's absolutely fine, honey. It's just a tummy bug, and now she's taking antibiotics it'll clear up in no time.'

I started to tremble. 'Chris, she's got cancer. I *know* she has. I just know it.'

He sat down beside me on the sofa, and took my hand. 'Darling, I'm a doctor and I can assure you she hasn't.' He stroked my hair. 'I think I know what this is about. It's Eloise, isn't it?'

I rounded on him. 'Eloise is dying,' I hissed. 'If it can happen to her out of the blue, it can happen to anyone. I *won't* let it happen to Evie.'

Chris looked nonplussed. 'But, darling, nothing's going to happen to Evie. I promise you.'

'Yes, well, that's what everyone always says, isn't it? Look at the way everyone told Eloise she was going to be fine.' I started crying hysterically. 'She's dying, Chris. My Evie's dying!'

And that was how it started. The dreams began that night.

I remember the first one. In it, Evie was a little girl, around three years old. She looked sweet, happy, singing to her dolls. But as I watched she started shrinking, dwindling. I snatched her up and she became a newborn baby in my arms. And then, she was gone.

I was distraught, panicked, frantically rushing around the house looking for her, lifting cushions, opening drawers. My baby had gone, she had left me. And then, on the mantel-piece, I saw a matchbox. I picked it up and slid it open. Inside, tiny as a mouse, lay my child. She looked perfect, as if she was just sleeping, but I knew she was dead.

There were many other dreams after that night, night-mares of Gothic horror, in which I wandered through a green valley, and all around me severed heads rose up out of the ground, watching me gravely, almost pityingly, as their blood dripped onto the grass.

There were dreams where, everywhere I walked, I saw bodies of dead baby animals strewn along my path; calves, kittens, puppies, foals. They made me feel ineffably sad.

And the worst one of all. Eloise sat before me with the matchbox containing my dead daughter in her hands. She smiled at me, but without warmth. She looked gloating, gleeful.

'You see, Cathy, it's not just me. I'm not the only one dying before my time. Now you'll know what it's like, how I feel about leaving my daughters. Now YOU will know about unbearable grief, not just me.'

She looked so evil, staring at me, her beautiful face twisted with triumph. And then she began to cackle.

Night after night, I woke screaming or sobbing and Chris took me back to London, where I began treatment. For months my nights were filled with horror, my days drowned in a lethargic stupor. I was almost catatonic with fear and loss. I was diagnosed with severe clinical depression.

And Evie? It turned out she had a grumbling appendix. A few days after we got back to London, she was rushed to hospital for an emergency operation. At the time, I knew nothing about it. Chris was too frightened to tell me that our daughter had, in fact, been in danger, albeit for a condition much less terrifying than brain cancer.

And yet, afterwards, even when Eve had recovered and was manifestly well and cheerful, I still felt dread in my heart. I still dreamed she was dead in a tiny matchbox. I still dreamed Eloise was gloating over my grief.

Eventually, with medication and therapy, I got better. By winter I had returned to sanity, accepting that Evie was well, and that I had had a breakdown precipitated by my fear for Eloise. I had been living in terror and denial about my friend's impending, inevitable death, and when my daughter became ill, my anxious mind flipped into a kind of madness.

I was better, but I knew, from the way he watched me, looked at me, that forever after Chris would watch me for signs of instability. And although I prided myself on my recovery, my rationality, of course I also knew I was perpetually on the edge of an abyss. If you've been there, you don't ever forget it. You can't possibly ignore it. Once you've glimpsed the profound horror of the chasm which opens up beneath your feet, once you've felt the inexorable pull which draws you to the edge, once you've understood that down there lies not just madness but the total destruction of your life, your happiness, all hope of love and comfort ... then, and only then, can you understand the unspeakable magnitude of what lies beneath. And how utterly vile it is, how barren of everything but death. And even when you're feeling better, when pills and therapy have restored you to a fragile normality, you always know there are demons out there, life-sucking, soul-sucking vampires.

Never far away. And always ready to pounce.

It was ironic that I was married to a psychiatrist. Someone who knew me so well but couldn't treat me. I had to see one of his colleagues because of medical etiquette, which I found terribly embarrassing. *Hey*, I imagined him saying at dinner parties when he'd had a bit too much to drink, *did you know that Chris's wife is nuts?*

Chris told me I was wrong when I wept my fears to him. The man who was treating me was, he said, scrupulously observant of the rules of confidentiality. Chris would trust him with his life – or at least, I responded with bleak humour, with his wife.

Chris didn't like it when I was flippant. But then, I would tell myself, he was desperate to help me, wasn't he? And, like any man trying to cope with a suicidally depressed wife, he was desperate anyway. Because during my breakdown, I had left him in no doubt that if anything happened to Evie, I would kill myself.

The phone rang again. Convinced it was Chris, I let the answerphone take it. But the voice which came from the machine was soft, mellifluous and quite definitely female.

Juliana. I suddenly saw an answer to my problems and flew to the phone.

An hour and a half later, having called a taxi, I was sitting in Juliana's house, a cup of tea in one hand and a beautifully ironed handkerchief in the other, unable to stop crying. I could hear myself sobbing loudly and I was mortified by my self-absorption. Juliana had just lost a beloved daughter, her only child – all that had happened to me was that I had had a row with my husband.

Typically, Juliana, who had asked me to spend the night, was completely sympathetic and warm about my ridiculous emotional crisis. I told her something about my breakdown – all she'd known was that we had stopped coming down to Cornwall for a time and because Chris hadn't wanted to worry Eloise with the truth, he'd said it was because Tom was studying hard for his A-levels and that I was busy with writing commissions. Concerned with her own deadly illness, Eloise had accepted the excuses. I didn't tell Juliana to curry sympathy, but to explain how rocky my judgement was at present.

'Darling,' she said. 'Of course you're upset about everything. But I had no idea that you had been going through such a terrible time.'

'We tried to hide it from you, Juliana. God knows you had enough on your plate with Eloise.'

'Yes. That's true. I appreciate your kindness. But still, you've had a horrible time. I wish I'd known.'

'Do you know what, Juliana? I just wish I could go to sleep. Sometimes I think I could sleep for ever.'

'Eloise used to say exactly the same thing.'

'She was depressed?'

Of course she was. She was dying. How stupid of me.

'I'm so sorry, Juliana. She was so ill.'

'Well, there was that, of course. But she didn't mean that. She meant that her life, quite apart from the cancer, wasn't worth living.'

'But she was desperate to live,' I protested. 'She fought death with everything she had!'

'Oh, yes. But that was because of her children. She knew how much they needed her.'

'So what do you mean? Surely her life meant everything to her with her babies?'

'Yes. But there were other things.'

'Ted? Is that what you're talking about?'

She looked down. She was sad, tired. 'Darling, I really can't talk about this tonight. But I am so utterly delighted that you are going to stay with me. I think we both need company and we have a lot to talk about. Let's start tomorrow. In the meantime, I'm going to ask Annie to put you to bed.'

If that had come from Chris, I would have told him that nobody puts me to bed. But Juliana's suggestion felt as if it came from a mother. *My* mother, Not that mine was the most loving and kind maternal figure, never had been, and God, how we all long for that care, that absolute conviction that we are loved, wrapped round with affection. That we are still small, still passively able to accept the physical absorption into the soft loveliness of our mothers' bodies.

Annie, who was was over eighty and who had been Juliana's loyal lady's maid from their teenage years, tucked me into bed with a hot water bottle and a cup of hot chocolate. She had already unpacked my suitcase and hung up my clothes, few though they were. I felt like a fugitive from a Jane Austen novel. I was tired, upset and totally appreciative of the soft linen sheets and warm quilt on my new bed. I felt cared for, cocooned. I fell asleep, feeling, for the first time in years, that I was being mothered. It was utter bliss.

I dreamed again that night, but this time, Eloise's spirit came gently. As I slept, I felt she wound her essence around me. She was glad, clearly, that I was with Juliana. She was pleased that I was on her own familiar ground. She was sweet, in my dreams. Full of comfort.

'Cathy, you're with my mother now. That's good. I can really talk to you here. Please stay at the farmhouse and I can tell you about my children. There's so much I need to say to you. But I'm weak, trying to get the strength. It comes sometimes, then evaporates and I am nothing. Nothing. Just vapour on the breeze. Can you imagine how that feels? To be nothing, to be so powerless when so much is at stake?'

No. I could not even begin to imagine that desperation, and I had known huge despair when I was ill, had been so frightened for Evie, believing her to be in terrible danger. Was that what Eloise was trying to tell me about her little girls? That she was terrified they were facing great danger?

No, it was a dream, only a dream, I struggled to tell myself. Eloise is dead, quiet in her grave. I don't believe in ghosts. I'm just prone to horrible nightmares.

Chapter Seven

Eloise drifted softly through my dreams all night, but not enough to wake or alarm me. Annie woke me in the morning with a cup of tea. Juliana, she said, was waiting for me in the breakfast room; I would have plenty of time for a bath; there was no hurry.

Half an hour later, bathed and dressed but with no make-up on, I joined my hostess at breakfast. She smiled, lovely as always, but there was strain in her blue eyes.

After the usual morning pleasantries, she stirred her tea and asked quietly, tensely, 'Cathy, did anything strange happen to you last night?'

'No,' I said quickly – and regretted the lie immediately. 'Well, truthfully, I did have vivid dreams. About Eloise, actually, but they were calm, nothing really worrying.'

'Have you been having *troubling* dreams about her?'

'I suppose I have, but then I can be a bit . . . well, odd.'

Juliana gave a short laugh. 'I don't think so. Or if you are, so am I. But . . . I feel I must tell you. She left me a message.'

'What do you mean? Eloise left you – what? A letter?'

'No. She left me *Wuthering Heights*.'

I didn't understand. 'I'm lost. How do you mean? She left a book with you?'

'It was in the library. I know that for a fact because I was re-reading it last week. It's one of my favourite books and it was comfort reading for me when she was so ill, and especially after she . . . '

I swallowed. 'Sorry, Juliana. What are you saying? That Eloise left a book for you in the library?'

'No. It *wasn't* in the library. Not this morning. That's the thing. It was there yesterday. Eric, who's been with the Trelawney family longer even than Annie, leaves the newspapers out on the library desk each morning, and I saw the book there yesterday when I went to collect them. I keep asking him to bring the newspapers to me in the sitting room but he always forgets. Anyway, *Wuthering Heights* was on the desk exactly where I had left it. That was yesterday.

I remember it bothered me. I didn't want to look at it again, because I was so upset about Eloise.

'But this morning, when I woke, it was on my bedside table. And it was open at the page when Cathy Earnshaw's ghost haunts Heathcliff's new tenant when he sleeps at Wuthering Heights.'

I closed my eyes for a moment, feeling my world tremble.

'Juliana,' I said, trying to keep my voice even, 'I'm desperate to understand, but I can't. You've had a terrible experience. Are you absolutely sure you left the book in the library? Perhaps you took it up to your bedroom without remembering?'

I could hear Chris in my ear. *Of course she did. She's traumatised. She doesn't know what she's doing and you'd be mad to believe her.*

Maybe, I thought. But you think I'm mad anyway. So, what do we have here? Two mad women? Both convinced there is something terribly wrong about Eloise's death? Sisters in hysteria? Or maybe an extraordinary moment of combined female intuition?

I hardly dared to let the suspicion form in my mind. Eloise, her mother and me. Could we be joined in some kind of psychic triangle, and was there perhaps something real happening here, a message sent by dreams and misplaced books, a message from Eloise from beyond the grave? I shuddered.

Don't forget, don't forget, I whispered to myself. *Your mind is fragile; you imagine things. You thought Evie was going to die and she wasn't.*

'I know how this must sound,' Juliana said in a voice uncharacteristically tremulous. 'But I am absolutely certain that *Wuthering Heights* was not by my bed when I went to sleep last night. You know, it was one of her favourite books too. I first read it to her when she was ten, and she's always loved it.' Juliana looked sad, exhausted and utterly defeated. 'I'm sorry. Forgive me. I've had a bad night. I felt sure she was trying to contact me, tell me something vitally important. But she was just all ... I thought I could see her ... almost ... but then her face became so indistinct and her voice was lost – hollow, and too faint for me to hear.'

I had to tell her. 'Juliana, in my dreams she seems to be warning me about something. Something to do with her children. Do you know what she could possibly mean?'

Juliana stared at me for a moment, then suddenly shook her head sharply.

'No! Oh, Cathy, I'm such a self-indulgent fool. Having stupid supernatural thoughts about my daughter when she is dead from that horrible disease. Why am I even thinking like this? I was her mother, and I suppose that made me deny that she could possibly die so young – just as much as she denied it herself. But still. I had years to come to terms with it. I *knew* what was going to happen to my lovely daughter. I wept, I raged, I begged God to spare her. But He didn't and I can't bear it – forgive me.'

She stood up. She put a book before me and abruptly left the room. I picked it up. *Wuthering Heights*. There was a delicate tapestry bookmark within the pages and, suddenly feeling unbearably confined, I decided to take it into the garden and read it there.

Outside it was cold but sunny. There was a little gazebo beneath the rhododendrons, with cushioned seats and a wood-burning stove against one whitewashed wall. It wasn't lit but the room still felt cosy enough. I settled down with the book on my lap, but before I had time to open it, Juliana's old manservant Eric shuffled slowly in with matches, bellows and kindling, his frail body bent almost double. He was so ancient I thought his spindly legs would buckle under the weight of his burden. He was closely followed by Annie, bearing a tray of tea and a tartan rug tucked over one arm.

I leapt up, feeling horribly guilty at making them feel I needed looking after when I was so much younger and fitter. 'Annie, Eric, this is terribly kind of you, but I'm fine as I am. Perfectly warm enough, thanks.'

'Oh no, Miss,' said Annie.

Miss? I was forty-six next birthday. The spirit of Jane Austen was surely still alive within the confines of Roseland.

'The mistress asked us to look after you, and you'll catch your death out here without a fire. It is February, after all.'

Eric said nothing, but lit the fire, smiled gummily and creaked off. Annie fussed about with the tea and the blanket, tucking it solicitously around my legs, informed me that lunch was at one o'clock, and followed Eric out of the gazebo.

This is ridiculous, I thought; Juliana is living in the nineteenth century. Yet Eloise had been so modern, so down to earth. No servants for her – although, thinking about it, she could certainly have afforded them.

Money. Was that the elephant in the room between her and Ted? We had never discussed it. Eloise always seemed slightly embarrassed about her aristocratic background, although she loved her mother fiercely, and Ted had sometimes referred obliquely to his wife's wealth, teasing her about what they could do, the lifestyle they could enjoy, if only Eloise could persuade her mother to release more of her trust fund now, instead of waiting for Juliana's death. But his teasing was always light and playful, and Eloise had seemed to be nothing more than amused.

'Oh, Ted,' she'd laugh. 'Always wanting to be the gentleman landowner. Well, I find you much more sexy as you are. An impoverished artist. That's what Cornwall's all about. And we're hardly living in a garret, are we? We've got more than enough.'

And in truth they seemed happy then. Very physically wrapped up in each other. Sometimes when Ted looked at her, his eyes smouldering with desire, I felt quite jealous. Not that Chris and I weren't close. We were, but somehow Ted and Eloise seemed such a romantic couple, she so beautiful, he so glamorous with his dirty-blond surfer good looks. She from such a rich and distinguished background, he a talented artist whose paintings were attracting more and more interest, with an exhibition due in London later this year. Chris was a psychiatrist; a professor no less, doing a distinguished and important job. But somehow Chris's worthy profession lacked the edgy glamour of a Cornish painter . . .

I sank down into the comfy squashy armchair, old but beautifully upholstered with white linen cushions, poured a cup of tea and, looking at the glowing wood fire, felt impossibly pampered. Looked after. Like a child again, I thought to myself, not entirely happy with this regression into childhood, a mood that had enveloped me deliciously ever since I arrived at Juliana's. I loved feeling so protected, but I couldn't possibly accept it. This was all part of a dream, a fantasy into which Eloise's death, Juliana's grief and my own sense of dislocation and shock had sucked me.

I opened *Wuthering Heights*.

The pages parted easily and fell open at the part when Mr Lockwood, the unsuspecting new tenant of Thrushcross

Grange, an isolated mansion in North Yorkshire to which he has retired to escape 'the stir of society. A perfect misanthropist's heaven' pays a visit to his landlord, Mr Heathcliff, at the latter's gloomy and festering moorland pile, Wuthering Heights.

'A capital fellow,' enthuses Mr Lockwood, at first welcoming as a fellow recluse the satanic neighbour into whose lair he has just unknowingly strayed.

That night, because of driving snow and howling winds, Heathcliff is reluctantly forced to admit that his visiting tenant cannot possibly cross the moor to reach home. With extreme bad grace, he allows Mr Lockwood to stay the night, and in a distant, cold and lonely bedroom, the poor man attempts to get some rest.

The quietude he craves doesn't happen. He discovers the window ledge on which Catherine had inscribed her name, for this had been her bedroom as Catherine Earnshaw; 'Here and there varied to Catherine Heathcliff, and then again to Catherine Linton.'

Lockwood, filled with a maudlin curiosity, reads Catherine's diaries, lying mildewed on the window ledge. After falling eventually asleep, his dreams are vivid and tortured.

Then, his thoughts mangled by strange and vivid images, he wakes up. Or believes he does.

In Juliana's copy of *Wuthering Heights*, the following

paragraphs charting the rest of Mr Lockwood's hapless night were heavily underscored in black ink.

This time, I remembered I was lying in the oak closet, and I heard distinctly the gusty wind, and the driving of the snow; I heard, also, the fir bough repeat its teasing sound, and ascribed it to the right cause: but it annoyed me so much, that I resolved to silence it, if possible . . . 'I must stop it . . . ' I muttered, knocking my knuckles through the glass and stretching an arm out to seize the importunate branch; instead of which, my fingers closed on the fingers of a little, ice-cold hand! The intense horror of nightmare came over me: I tried to draw back my arm, but the hand clung to it, and a most melancholy voice sobbed, 'Let me in — let me in!' 'Who are you?' I asked, struggling, meanwhile, to disengage myself.

And here the narrative changed. For in the book, of course, the ghost replies 'Catherine Linton.'

But on the page of Juliana's *Wuthering Heights*, that name was heavily crossed out, and written in large black letters above the type was

ELOISE TRELAWNEY

Her maiden name.

And underlined in the same heavy black ink next on the page:

I'm come home, I'd lost my way on the moor!

Startled, I jumped up from the chair. What *was* this? A true message from Eloise, sent to her mother from beyond the grave? Or a result of Juliana's own grief, a deep, tortured but unconscious response to the absolute despair she felt that her only daughter had left her so abruptly, so completely bereft? Suppose Juliana, in a fit of furious denial, had altered the words in her copy of *Wuthering Heights*? What if she, in the middle of the night, sleepwalked from her bed downstairs to the library, took up the fountain pen which lay on a blotter on the cherrywood desk, and wrote her daughter's name so boldly in the book which had meant so much to both of them? And then took it back to bed with her, and woke up in the morning to find, with genuine shock, that she had received a supernatural message from her beloved dead child.

I didn't know. Agitated, mind churning, I left the book, the rug, the tea tray and the cosy stove, walked out of the gazebo and blindly followed a narrow path which wound away from the farmhouse.

As I pursued the lovely, ancient way, I gradually felt soothed. Cornwall was timeless. These grounds, this parkland of Roseland Hall, had remained unchanged for centuries. Eloise's ancestors had played as children underneath these trees, secure and loved. And, of course, the whole estate lay just at the foot of Bodmin Moor.

With that thought peace fled and I shivered. Those haunted words wailed through the wintery trees.

I'm come home. I'd lost my way on the moor!

Juliana was waiting for me when I got back to the farmhouse and we sat down in front of the fire in her sitting room. She was agitated.

'Did you read it, Cathy? *Wuthering Heights*? Did you see what she . . . ?'

Eric came slowly in with a decanter of sherry. He placed the silver tray it stood on on a little sideboard, and poured the sherry into two small, exquisite crystal glasses. We said nothing until he had left.

'Yes, I read it,' I said non-committally.

Juliana leaned forward eagerly.

'Well, what do you think? I just don't know what to make of it. What was she trying to tell me? I mean, she wrote that in the book, but what did it *mean*? Oh Cathy, please tell me I'm not going mad.'

Luckily, because I really didn't know what to say, before I could answer Annie came in and announced that luncheon was served. Juliana had perfect manners; if she felt irritated, she didn't show it. We moved into the dining room and sat down at the old oak table, beautifully laid, as always at Juliana's, with white linen, silver and crystal. Great vases of daffodils and forsythia stood on polished tables around the room. The atmosphere was gracious, tranquil and welcoming, but it did not calm Juliana's obvious nerves.

She said nothing until Annie had served the first course, pea and ham soup, and withdrawn.

'I can tell that you think I'm being fanciful and ridiculous.'

'No, no, I don't. Because I've had the most extraordinary thoughts and dreams about Eloise myself. But the thing is, we have to make sure we're being sensible about all this.'

Juliana gave me an incredulous smile.

'Sensible? Do you really think any of this, what I feel and *know* with every fibre of my body, could possibly be called *sensible*? Cathy, you know something is terribly wrong, I can tell. So please don't tell me to be sensible. There's very little sense to be found in any of this.'

I murmured my agreement. I was on her side, I really was, but at the same time I was becoming increasingly anxious to leave Roseland. The comfort and solace I had revelled in had given way to a febrile hysteria. Juliana, I thought, was even more fragile than I was. The mutual support and reassurance I had hoped for when I left Talland Bay was clearly not going to happen.

Again I heard Chris's voice when I'd rung to tell him that I was going to stay the night at Roseland.

'Darling, nothing good will come of your stay with Juliana. You're both too damaged – she by Eloise's death, you by your delicate mental state. I'm coming to get you, honey.'

I would go home now – gladly.

Annie and Eric served the main course – chicken and leek pie, so delicious it lulled me into a drowsy and contented stupor. By an unspoken agreement we no longer talked of Eloise; but it was an uneasy alliance, both of us keenly aware that we were skirting an issue of vital, urgent importance.

Instead, we discussed domestic things. I, with genuine curiosity, asked her if she always ate like this.

'What on earth do you mean?' she chuckled. 'Everyone has to eat.'

'No, I mean so formally. With the table beautifully laid and everything? It's absolutely lovely, of course, such a gorgeous room, such a delicious lunch. But these days everyone tends to eat much more casually, unless it's a special occasion of course.'

'And what makes you think this isn't a special occasion?' she smiled. 'Eloise's best friend has come to lunch. But, no, I'm teasing. I only eat in style at lunchtime. This is my main meal of the day, you see. Supper is just beans on toast or scrambled eggs on a tray in the sitting room while I watch the news.'

She smiled. 'Charles would be horrified. He was always such a stickler for doing things properly. I think that's why I feel I must have at least one formal meal each day. To appease his memory – and it's good to preserve some discipline in one's day-to-day life. Also it gives Annie and Eric something to do, a familiar routine. That's important at their time of life.'

She went on to talk about her worries about her elderly manservant, who was an astonishing ninety years old.

'I mean,' she said, 'it's not that I'm worried he won't be able to work. We have girls in from Fowey who do the real housework. No, the worry is looking after Eric in his great old age. I will be totally responsible for him, you know. He has no family, no home of his own. He will stay here, of course; I will never ask him to leave. But Annie is eighty-one, you know. Hale and hearty, thank God, but still ... And I, of course, am an incredibly youthful seventy-five. Goodness, I might as well turn this place into an old people's home!' She looked suddenly wistful. 'You know, I had always hoped I would hand the farmhouse over to Eloise in a few years' time. There's plenty of money, and she could have hired staff to keep the house cared for, not to mention us,' – and with that she gave a small snort – 'the decrepit pensioners' army.'

'But surely you could hire staff yourself to . . . to care for you all?'

'Oh yes, I suppose I could. And now of course I will have to. Employ staff to look after my staff. And me. Not a prospect to be looked forward to, but inevitable.'

She looked up at me, her eyes wet. 'Don't you see, Cathy? I am old. I have no future. *Eloise* was my future. And now, nothing.'

'But you *do* have a future. You are a grandmother. You have two beautiful granddaughters. That's your future.'

'I don't think so. Ted won't let that happen.'

Annie came in with dessert. Juliana straightened her back and thanked her elderly maid in a soft but controlled voice. But Annie was not fooled. She gave her mistress a sharp and worried look, then looked at me accusingly. I had obviously upset her beloved Juliana. She put the apple crumble before us and left the room with a troubled backward glance.

I felt awkward and brutal but I had to say it.

'Juliana,' I asked abruptly. 'Who is Arthur?'

Chapter Eight

She froze. Completely shocked. She looked stricken.

I asked again. 'Juliana, tell me, who is Arthur?'

'I don't know what you mean. Arthur? I've never heard of him.'

Her reaction surprised me. She sounded jumpy, her voice uncharacteristically sharp.

'Well, OK. But Ted mentioned him and he sounded pretty fraught when he did.'

'Ted mentioned him? What did he say?' she asked suspiciously.

'He said something about a huge betrayal.'

Juliana laughed awkwardly. 'What utter rubbish!' She sighed. 'Look, Ted's not always – reliable. He gets bees in his bonnet. And, to be honest, he was always ridiculously jealous about Eloise. He watched her like a hawk. Eloise came to see me so often in despair about his ludicrous suspicions that she was having an affair.'

'And she wasn't?'

'Of course she wasn't. Do you really think Eloise would do anything to harm her daughters? She'd never risk a break-up with Ted. She knew how vindictive he could be.'

'What do you mean? Did she think he might try to take the girls away from her?'

Juliana looked annoyed, as if she knew she'd said too much. She leaned forward fiercely.

'My daughter was, more than anything else, a devoted mother, you know that, Cathy. She adored her children and she put them first, before anything else. Everything else in her life came second.'

'Including Ted?' I asked, then immediately thought better of it. Juliana looked at me, almost pleadingly.

'If you knew, Cathy. If only you knew.'

'Knew what?'

But Juliana had said everything she was going to. Her expression was cold, steely, completely different from the warm woman I knew. I had gone too far. It was none of my business; I had no right to pry into her mind. I would never normally dream of being so pushy, so ill-mannered. It was as if my dreams of Eloise had changed me, taken me over.

I felt disorientated, shaken and on dangerous ground. Juliana was obviously not telling me everything. I hated that. People creeping around shiftily, professing to be utterly truthful, while withholding information they wanted to keep to themselves. I knew I was over-reacting, that I was being paranoid, but since my breakdown I had become increasingly aware of lies and evasion. Not normal for me; I had always been open and receptive, happy to welcome people into my life, to accept them with warmth and lack of judgement.

But no longer. Now I withdrew like a snail into its shell whenever I scented duplicity or evasion. I felt sorry for Juliana, but if she did not intend to be honest with me then I didn't want to risk my own vulnerable state by confiding in her.

So, out of self-protection I began to retreat from Juliana; I felt alienated from her, which was intensely distressing. I had always admired her; and over the last twenty-four hours I had become dangerously close to regarding her as a surrogate mother.

She wasn't, of course. She was Eloise's mother. Her daughter was, rightly, the only person she cared about, and her maternal loyalty was absolute.

I needed to disengage.

'Juliana,' I said, standing nervously, hesitantly. 'I don't want to let you down. I know how much you are grieving for Eloise, as am I, but I don't think we can help each other at the moment. I need to go home. To be honest, I need to be with Chris and my family. I thought I could help you, and you could help me, because there's no doubt we both feel there's something terribly wrong about how Eloise died. But I don't think I've got the strength now. I need to go home and get some rest.'

I felt agonised. Again, I was letting Juliana down. Just as, I thought bitterly, I had let Eloise down by not being honest with her about her fanciful attitude toward treating her cancer.

Yes, I thought. Here I go again, backing away at the first sign of trouble. I'm not a very admirable human being, but I desperately need to get away from this. To get away from ghosts, and dreams of disturbing clifftop encounters with my dead friend, whose spirit seemed so troubled, but whose body was now irrevocably consigned to the sacred ground of the graveyard at Talland Church.

I was fed up. Tired, lonely and desperate to retreat. I would call a taxi to take me back to our cottage. And I would call Chris. Lovely, loving, cross, disapproving Chris; my lifeline, my anchor, the love of my life.

Juliana took my hand, nodding her understanding. She sat

me down again, found Annie and asked her to call a cab. Twenty minutes later I was off, curled up on the back seat, my mobile phone clasped to my ear as I waited, weeping gently, for a signal, so I could talk to Chris.

I fell asleep in my bed at home in Talland. I couldn't reach Chris, even through the landline, and I quickly gave up. I was disabled by the familiar torpor of depression. There was no point talking to him anyway. What could he do? The world was lost; nothing could be changed. I was way, way back, deeply submerged in the old trough of despair, without hope, without anything except a deep desire to sleep, to escape.

And so, armed with Nytol and my Virgin Airlines eye mask, I sank down beneath my beloved, snuggly duvet and prepared to – what? Surrender to the horrible but irresistibly overwhelming impulse so familiar to anyone who is depressed? To end the torment? No, let's not be melodramatic. I wasn't suicidal, although I had been in the recent past. What I wanted was oblivion, if not for ever, at least for as many hours as I could force my brain to switch off.

My head turbulent, but with no perspective, no proportion, only a heady desire for self-annihilation, I sank into a deep sleep . . .

If I had wanted peace, lack of torment, a brief time-out from anxiety and dread, I was to be horribly disappointed.

Eloise came back with a vengeance during my longed-for rest, filled with fury and reproach.

She snatched me up from my bed, hurled me a long way from Talland. She put me in a strange rock formation on a most godforsaken wild stretch of moor. I couldn't believe that something happening to me in a dream could seem so real. I could feel the cold, smell the mud, see the stars. I was wearing my Gap pyjamas and the stones hurt my bare feet. Her outline glimmered angrily before me.

'What now, Eloise?' I asked her wearily.

'What now? What do you think? You've run away again, haven't you? Typical of you, isn't it? Just when I need you, all you can think of is yourself. I genuinely thought you would help me, but you've let me down. Cathy, you're useless.'

Cathy, you're useless. Those words which had haunted me for so long. Of course she was right. I was, as my mother used to say, neither use nor ornament.

I rallied slightly before Eloise's indignant shapelessness.

'Do you know what, Ellie? I may be no good to man or beast, but at least I'm alive. Yes, I'm a mess, but one day I'll get better. And you won't. You're dead, Ellie. You are buried in Talland Churchyard. Stop bothering me. Especially if you won't even tell me about Arthur. Ted told me about him, but you've never mentioned him, not once.'

Then there was such a wail, such a surge of heartbreak, that it blasted me off my feet.

'Don't,' she said. 'Don't ever . . .'

And she was gone. And I was locked deep into a troubled, thrashing sleep.

There was someone bending over me. My head was cloudy, throbbing painfully from my artificially induced sleep. I tried to open my eyes, succeeded only enough to see a blurred form hanging over my head. I shrieked. It was Eloise, surely, come to claim me, to bear me off to her ghostly lair on Bodmin Moor.

'Cathy, Cathy, it's all right. It's me, darling, just me.'

'Chris?' My mouth was full of cotton wool. 'Chris? Is that really you? Why – what – are you here for?'

'For you, of course. What else?'

'But you're in London.'

'Nope. Here, ready to take you home. I arrived a few hours ago and saw you were deeply asleep, so I kipped down in Sam's room to get a bit of down time before driving back. You OK to go now?'

I sat up. I felt groggy and my head swam.

'Sweetheart, I'll make you some tea. Just get your things together and we'll drive back. The traffic's really light.'

'Chris? Eloise. It's really bad, you know.'

'I do know. I talked to Juliana. That's how I knew you'd come back to Talland.'

'What did she tell you?' I was immediately defensive.

'Just that you were very upset.'

'Yes, I was upset. She was being so . . . odd about Eloise. She started lecturing me about what a marvellous mother Eloise was. I know that, but Juliana was just trying to avoid my questions. She pretended not to know who Arthur is, but Ted told me she definitely does.'

'Shush, Cathy. You get up; I'll get some tea. We can talk about all of this later.'

I knew he was humouring me. I very much wanted to argue my case, that everyone was conspiring against me, even Eloise, and she was dead, for Christ's sake. But I was exhausted, and pathetically glad that Chris had come for me.

We got into the car. It was warm, snug. I fell asleep again almost immediately, and didn't wake up until we reached our house in Chiswick four and a half hours later, in the early hours of the morning.

I was still sleeping, in our bed, when Chris left for work next morning. When I woke up, it was nearly midday. This didn't surprise me. The inability to get out of bed, to rejoin the land of the living, was a hallmark of my illness; and yet I had been so much better, more positive and energetic before we went to Cornwall, before Eloise's ghost had overwhelmed me. I shook myself. Ghost? What was I thinking? She was a dream, not a ghost. Just a nightmare, one of many that disturbed my troubled nights. But she felt so real, and what she said to me was so coherent. She was always trying to tell me something urgent. The dreams I'd had when I thought Evie might die were nothing like my night-time visions of Eloise. When I had my breakdown, I dreamed of a baby in a matchbox, tiny dead kittens, gruesome severed heads. None of it made any sense. But Eloise, as she appeared to me, seemed to be trying to have a rational conversation.

And yet, trying to be sane about it, what had actually happened? My friend had died of the cancer she had suffered for five years. It was not unexpected – just the opposite. And because my state of mind was still fragile – though I had hoped and believed I was better – I had allowed myself to be drawn into some Gothic fantasy, fuelled by Ted's surly anger and Juliana's obsession with *Wuthering Heights*. No. It was nonsense. This mad conviction that Eloise's spirit was unquiet, that her death needed to be avenged and I was her chosen weapon of retribution was utterly unhinged. I had read too much Daphne du Maurier in Cornwall. I had let myself become darkly obsessed by Manderley and the malevolent image of Rebecca, stalking her little cottage on the beach, desperate, even in death, to ruin her husband, Max de Winter. So who was to be Eloise's Mrs Danvers, I thought?

Who was the one who was determined to suppress the truth? Eloise was begging me to find out.

My head whirled. Was she a ghost? Or just a dream?

I closed my eyes in despair. I was going mad. Chris was right. I was very ill again.

Chapter Nine

It was June before I went back to Cornwall. Some of that time was a blur. Lots of hugs from my darling Evie and concerned faces from my sons, upset that their mum was once again drowned in a sad landscape they could not begin to imagine or share. Thank God.

Chris was wonderful. I had to have treatment again, and pills; but he never made me feel I was going mad, that I was a lost cause; an embarrassment as a wife or mother, which of course I believed I was.

Normal life gradually returned. My sleep was untroubled and I was, at last, completely better.

So, when Chris suggested we should go back to Talland in late June, I agreed in a spirit of defiance. I was going home to my lovely cottage, to my healing refuge in Cornwall. I was no longer afraid of ghosts. I would take Evie, who was tired after sitting her GCSEs, and Chris who was due a much-needed holiday, and we would have a wonderful break. It would be like the old days; lots of walks on wild empty beaches, Cornish pasties and cider consumed with gales of laughter on the steep fields leading down to Lantic Bay.

I couldn't wait. The boys had finished their university exams and had other fish to fry. I, meanwhile, needed to embrace my lovely county again, fresh and full of ravishing blossom and luscious green meadows, with my husband and beloved daughter in my arms; swaddled in bedclothes dried on the line and smelling of grass, lavender and honeysuckle.

On the first day back, Evie sat at the wide oak kitchen table, head in hand, staring out of the window at the clematis winding round the railing of our little patio.

'Mum,' she said dreamily. 'Can you fall in love when you're sixteen?'

'You can fall in love however young you are,' I said with a smile. 'Look at Shakespeare's Juliet. She was only thirteen when she met Romeo and was instantly besotted. Mind you, look where that got her.'

'Yeah, I know. But that's just drama. I mean, things can have a happy ending when you're just a teenager, can't they?'

I looked carefully at my sweet girl.

'Why? Have you met someone you really like?'

'God no, Mum. You mean like all those idiots at school like Josh and Harry? Do me a favour.'

I felt slightly disappointed at her dismissal of Harry. He was, in his gauche way, actually rather charming.

Eloise and I often talked about the kind of boy we'd like to see our daughters marry. We wanted so much for them — men who were successful but kind, ambitious yet sensitive, intelligent and funny. How strong the matchmaking instinct is. Ellie and I wanted the best for our girls — love, passion, happiness — the pot of gold at the end of the rainbow.

I sighed. Eloise would never see her twin girls married, never play with her grandchildren. I must be there for Rose and Violet, I told myself, I must try to make sure those motherless little girls grew up happy. Never mind that Ted and Juliana would look after them. I, too, would do my best. I was their godmother, after all. I would try to make sure that, somehow, Eloise's hopes for them did not die.

And then I remembered a conversation Eloise and I had. So many years ago, before she married Ted.

I had asked you if you were tired of being single, Eloise. I was long married by then, with three children who defined everything about me. You were only a few months younger, and you seemed sad. There were many days I sat beside you and watched your lovely face sink into a soft despair, especially when you watched my little ones squabbling, cuddling and wrestling their baby days away.

'Tired of being single?' you said with a weak smile. 'Devastated, more like. I long for what you have with Chris. That wonderful bridge of love and companionship. But I won't have that, I think. I lost it a long time ago, and it won't come back.'

I was shocked. What were you talking about?

'Tell me about it,' I said. 'I've never heard about this. Christ, Ellie, this sounds important. Tell me what's wrong.'

You smiled and shook your head.

'I can't. It's far too painful and only my . . .'

You suddenly sat upright and became your usual gay, sparkling self.

'Sorry, Cath. I'm an idiot. Can't help myself. Once a drama student, always a drama queen.'

Eloise and I had met when we studied drama at Bristol University. It had affected us both very strongly, but in completely different ways. She had loved the whole thespian culture; she was a classic exhibitionist, dressed in the New Romantic fashions and totally at home on the stage. She was a good little actress too, although it was clear this was always going to be for fun. Eloise, with her trust fund and stately home, was never going to need a serious career.

I, on the other hand, did. But I knew by the end of our first year that I was never going to make it as a professional actor. I so loved the poetry and the prose; was totally carried away on the waves of those gorgeous cadences, swellings and sighings of words; the sad sudden plunge from high romance into deepest tragedy; but I couldn't deliver the words at a level they needed. I never resented it. I was stoical. Acceptance was my lot. I just got on with it, got my mediocre degree, took a typing course and ended up at the BBC in London as a 'graduate secretary', working on the venerable science programme *Horizon*. Hoping, with all the other girls in those hallowed establishment offices, that I would somehow leap over the rest of us 'graduate' girls and get a job on the creative side. As a researcher. That's all I, and we, asked for.

And it might as well have been for the moon. You grew up fast in those little rabbit warrens at the BBC, full of testosterone and fear that a young girlie from the typing pool will make it onto the next rung, depriving an earnest Oxbridge graduate of his birthright; his admittance into the ranks of the fantastically pensioned and revered great and good of the BBC.

But I was never really that ambitious. I just wanted an interesting job. And then, in my early twenties, I met Chris, and that was it really, as far as my career was concerned. I fell in love with him straightaway and my entire focus changed. I knew that all I wanted out of life was to marry him and have a family. I know that's pretty old-fashioned, but I didn't care. Once we were married, children came along quickly, and it made sense for me to work from home. I left the BBC without a backward glance. I'd always wanted to write, so I settled for a low-key career in freelance journalism, mostly writing for women's magazines. I never made much money, but at least I felt I was contributing to the family income, especially when I was contracted to write a regular column on a weekly.

I was very, very happy.

Do you remember, Eloise, how I tried to pursue that conversation with you, to find out about your past secret love? But it never got me anywhere. And, in the end, what you said faded away. Normal life piled up its daily layers. Yesterday was soon obscured. A few years later you were telling about how you'd met Ted in St Ives. This sulky but sexy young artist with a huge chip on his shoulder. At once fascinated by you, and at the same time rudely and stridently dismissive of your privileged background.

I thought he sounded like a complete prat, and told you so. But you were already lost. He was great in bed, you told me, and I shrugged. He and a million other guys out there, I said.

No, you replied, not so. Not for you at any rate. For you there had been no one who moved you that way for many years. In fact, before Ted there had only been one; among all the boyfriends who had flocked to claim you, only one who had brought you to ecstasy and you wouldn't tell me who.

And now there was Ted. And you married him.

All this passed through my head as I watched my daughter's yearning face.

'OK, Eve, who is he?'

She blushed, giggled, sighed.

'Oh Mum, he's so gorgeous. I saw him on the beach this morning. He's new though. Not from round here. He's *so* fit.'

Oh God. My daughter had a serious crush.

'I tell you what,' I said, 'let's see if we can find him down at the café. I could do with a cup of tea and a toasted teacake.'

Eve giggled again. 'OK, but if we see him you won't mention that I like him, will you?'

'As if I would.'

'You told Harry I liked him. It was so embarrassing.'

'Sorry, sweetie. Lesson learned. Promise I won't do it again. Let's go down to the sea and see if we can spot this gorgeous boy.'

The café in our little cove is only a three-minute walk away. It was full of young families – the schools hadn't broken up yet – and a few teenagers free of GCSEs and A levels. Small children swarmed over the rocks while their parents called them back to eat ice creams and Evie and I sat at one of the wooden tables drinking tea and devouring toasted teacakes. Although she scanned the beach with anxious eyes, the glamorous one was nowhere to be seen.

'He's probably got really bored with all these mums and babies. Gone off somewhere much more interesting, like Newquay probably.'

Ah, yes. There was always that undertone; although our kids loved Talland Bay, Newquay, on the north coast, with its tempting surfer glamour and noisy nightlife was always the forbidden Holy Grail. And of course, it was our fault that they weren't there, having a great time with their peers, instead of being stuck in sedate south Cornwall, where there was no surf and the most exciting thing to do at night was to take some kindling down to the beach, light a campfire and drink lager listening to someone's iPod.

Just as I tried to think of a soothing counterweight, per-haps a reference to the barbeque and disco to be held that night at the Smuggler's Rest, a lively café just up the path from the beach, there was a shout from above us.

'E-e-e-vie!'

She jumped up from the table, whirled around and clapped her hands with pleasure as her father, with a huge grin, shepherded her middle brother past some squabbling children and joined us.

'Tom,' Evie screamed, and flung her arms around her sheepishly grinning nineteen-year old sibling. 'I thought you were off camping with your friends?'

'I was,' Tom said. 'But it was raining like anything in Scotland, so we decided to call it quits. And I wanted to see Mum — and you.'

My eyes filled and I looked at Chris. He gave me a sweet, crooked smile. I'd had no idea, when he went off to pick up groceries from the shop earlier, that he had arranged to meet Tom at Liskeard Station.

Eve was already telling her brother about the gorgeous boy she'd spotted on the beach and Tom was laughing. 'Come on, Sis. Not another one. I thought you were in love with Harry.'

'God Tom, you're just like Mum. I *so* don't fancy Harry. He looks like Justin Bieber. Or at least he thinks he does.'

'I would have thought the Bieber was right down your street, Beevs,' Tom laughed, using the boys' pet name for their sister.

'Yeah, like you'd know. You are just *so annoying*,' she shot back.

We started to walk back up to the cottage, Tom and Eve ahead of us. I was snuggled into Chris's side, enormously happy and grateful to him, beyond contentment. Two of my children, here with me on this beautiful summer's day in the most heavenly place on earth.

And then, walking towards us, came a boy. He cut in from the Talland Bay Hotel, which was just beside our house. Tom and Eve were ahead of us and didn't see him. But I couldn't help but stare.

He was beautiful. There was no other word to describe him. Mesmerising, a sort of sylph. Tall, slender, shaggy blond hair. A face that belonged to another world, a land of sprites and fairies. And yet sensuous, very much present and aware.

As he passed us, he gave a smile of such dazzling sweetness that we both stopped.

'My goodness,' breathed Chris. 'He's a remarkably good-looking young man, isn't he?'

I wanted to laugh. No, I thought, he's not a man at all. A boy, yes. But what kind of boy, human or elvish, I had no way of knowing. And yet I sensed something. I felt I knew him.

Chapter Ten

When we got back to the cottage, Eve and I started to cook dinner. Only spaghetti with a pesto sauce, cheese and fruit to follow. I'm a lazy cook. I can, actually, cook very well, as Chris and my kids will mournfully testify from time to time, remembering the homemade soufflés, steak and kidney pies, lasagne and treacle tarts that made their delicious way onto our table when they were younger. But I'd stopped enjoying cooking when the depression hit me and these days I was hard-pressed to open a can of soup. Depression is not just bad for the soul but the family stomach as well.

We ate around the old oak table and Evie once again started to talk about the gorgeous boy she had bumped into on the beach that morning

'I hope I see him again, Mum. My friends would kill to meet him.'

Tom rolled his eyes.

'Actually,' Chris said, 'I think we saw him earlier.'

Evie's eyes went wide.

'Dad, what are you talking about? Did you see him on the beach?'

'No,' I said. 'Dad and I saw him coming out of the hotel next door. At least, it may have been him. He was about your age, tall, blond and very good-looking.'

'How good-looking?' Tom muttered. 'Sort of Justin Bieber-soppy good-looking?'

'A lot better looking than you,' Eve fizzed back at him. 'Just because you're as ugly as sin, and he's gorgeous. You're just jealous, Camel-face.'

'Eve,' I said. 'Your brother is not ugly. In fact he's very handsome. Ask Maria.'

The mention of Tom's newly acquired university girl-friend, who had stayed with us at Christmas, made him blush, and Eve laugh.

'Oh yes, I'd forgotten about Maria. I mean, like, God knows what she sees in you. You really are the pits.'

Chris sighed. 'OK, Eve, that's it. I wanted to have a really happy family break here with us all. You know your mother's been ill and this was supposed to make her feel better. If you two can't stop squabbling, we'll go back to London tomorrow.'

Tom looked horrified and upset, Eve furious and defiant.

'Mum's *always* ill these days,' she burst out. 'I'm sick of it. Why does everything have to revolve around her? I've just met the boy I could fall in love with, but you lot are just putting me down.'

I was immediately flooded with guilt. It was true. I had been paralysed by depression at one of the most important points in Eve's young life. It had made me self-absorbed, removed from my most sacred and demanding duty; to be, above all, a mother to my children, focused on their every emotion. They needed me, and I had not been there.

I sat forward, motioning Chris to stay quiet. 'Darling, nobody's putting you down. Everyone loves you, including Tom,' I flicked my eyes at him, and to his credit, he took his sister's hand.

'Hey, come on, Beevs, I was only having fun.'

It was over as quickly as it had begun. Suddenly they were laughing and teasing each other, communicating in a language their father and I could not begin to understand but were deeply relieved to witness.

We went to bed, Tom and Evie to the rooms they'd had since they were little, Chris and I upstairs to our pretty beamed attic master-suite.

We hadn't made love since I'd left Cornwall in panic after my stay at Roseland Farm. I'd been too locked into the grey world inside my head to even think about sex; and Chris, God knows, was far too worried about me to make any kind of physical overture. But on this sweet summer night, together in our favourite place in the world, two of our beloved children tucked snugly into their beds downstairs, we turned to each other at last, in gratitude and relief. We were together again, each wrapped around the other, full of love and desire. There was so much time we needed to make up. I felt shy. Maybe it wouldn't be the same, both of us clumsy and self-conscious after our prolonged period of sexual separation.

But we slipped immediately into our old rhythms, and it was as strong and passionate as before. And in Chris's love and warmth, I felt renewed.

I drifted off to sleep, curled up in his arms. Totally relaxed, cherished and happy. All the anxiety and panic of my last stay here in Cornwall had evaporated. I was back in the room and the house of my dreams.

And then she came. She filled my head with her pain and fear, and although she let me stay in my own bed this time, her faded voice was urgent and demanding.

'Cathy, Cathy, why did you leave me? Where did you go? You must stay here for me. I needed you, I still do. Please don't go away again.'

I stumbled, slow to respond.

'Ellie, not again, not tonight. I've been ill; this is my first night back.'

'But Cathy, you must know how important this is. I was ill too, but I didn't get better. I'm buried now, dead and buried. I can't do anything for myself, but I need your help. You're all I've got.'

In my sleep, I turned and my leg caught Chris's. He mumbled and his hand shot out to catch mine. I held on to him hard. He was my lifeline in an insane dreamworld.

And as if she'd caught my thoughts, Eloise hit right back.

'Cathy, do you really think you're dreaming?'

'Of course I am. I'm in bed, asleep, what else could I be doing?'

'You aren't dreaming. This is real, important; a matter of life and death. I don't have much longer, Cath, it's been months since I died. The spirit fades. And if that happens, if I have to go before you know the truth, then everything I love, everything I care for will be lost. I have done a terrible thing. I am going to be punished for it, not just me, I don't count any more, but my lovely innocent children ... oh, I can't bear it any more!'

'Eloise, my love, you have never done a terrible thing.'

'I have. And I have to prevent what happens next, the consequences of that. And you have to help me do that. We are linked, you see. It is your destiny to help me.'

'And if I don't?'

'Then you, too, will suffer. Do you think your illness, your mental fragility, is just a random accident?'

'I don't know what you're saying. I have depression. It's pretty common these days. Stress and genetics are what it's down to.'

'No, Cathy. You must help me. You have to, or else your mental torture will be so unendurable that you will crash.'

'Crash?' I asked.

'You will go under. And you will take your family with you.'

'Are you threatening me?'

Her voice almost inaudible, she laughed. It was a horrible sound, sinister and pathetic at the same time.

'This is about the girls, about Rose and Violet. I know you love them. I trust you to keep them safe. There are things in my past that I have never told you about. It's all about to come out, and then . . .' Her voice in my dream broke. 'Then it will be too late. Don't trust him, Cath, don't trust him. Keep my babies safe.'

'No. I can't help you because you are sending me mad. Leave me alone, for God's sake, Ellie. Just leave me alone.'

I woke up in the morning, her words ringing in my head. They troubled me, of course they did. But now I thought I knew what this was all about. My own ridiculously doom-ridden thoughts about my friend's death had trapped me into a silly, supernatural fantasy. Time to distance myself, to grow up, to see Cornwall as it had always been to me; my place, my family's home. Bury the past and all that. Whatever this mad spirit was trying to tell me, it was time to cut loose.

I got up, pulled on a dressing gown, and went down to the kitchen. As I pottered about making tea, I felt more and more resentful. Actually, I was furious with Eloise. I had been incredibly upset by her death. I had mourned her for months. But, if I was not completely mad, her presence was preventing my recovery. Which thwarted everything I wanted at the moment. I was so angry with her, with her demands, the way she kept invading my sleep.

I decided I had had enough. I had my own family to think about. I was completely fed up with Eloise, her husband, her daughters and her mother. I stood before the kitchen window, staring at the mint and thyme in our little herb garden, and swore at her. Then I made a vow.

'OK, Ellie. I am now beginning the rest of my life. I miss you, but I am not responsible for you or your children.'

I was exhausted. I found a note that said Chris had taken the kids off to Lansallos Bay. I just wanted to go back to sleep, and for a while I did, until the knock at the kitchen door became insistent enough to force me downstairs.

It was Ted. Not just him but the little girls as well. Rose and Violet, the adorable twins, golden haired, gorgeously dressed in Oilily cotton frocks and little white socks.

I wanted to cry at the sight of them. Ellie's babies, still here when she was so very far away, so permanently removed from them; when they were so devastatingly no longer hers. And despite my furious vow to Eloise that morning, I knew I could never abandon them to the fate she hinted lay in wait.

'Ted. Hello.' How inadequate, I thought. Especially when I knew that he was the last person I wanted to see, although I was overwhelmingly happy to see the girls, wanted to drink them in, carry them upstairs to bed, tuck them in for a lovely safe sleep. Mother them, make up for the loss of Eloise.

'Cathy. The girls wanted to see you. They've been talking about you and Evie for days. James at the café told me you were here.'

The girls bounded towards me, flung their tiny arms around my neck. 'Auntie Cath. Where's Uncle Chris? And Evie? We want to see her. And is Tom here? And Sam?'

Overwhelmed by emotion, aware that the last time I'd seen these girls was with their mother, on Talland Beach, eating pasties bought at the little café, Eloise sounding certain that her latest treatment regime would work wonders, I swallowed my tears and held my arms open to them both.

'Well, my little darlings, how gorgeous to see you both. Let's go inside and I'll find you some sweeties. Eve and Tom are both here, it's just they've gone to Lansallos Bay with their dad. They'll be back soon. I know they can't wait to see you.'

The twins rushed into the sitting room, whooping around, picking up the little wooden figures of sailing boats and fishermen that lay around the window ledges, playing with them as if they were dolls. In fact they preferred them to the Barbies Eve had shown them, kept as childhood relics in her bedroom.

They hadn't been at the funeral. Juliana and Ted both agreed it would be too traumatic for five year olds. But I wondered. Where did they think their mummy had gone? And if they hadn't seen her grave, how could they accept she had gone to her final resting place? I suppose children can understand that their mummy's gone to heaven. But, surely, at some point, they need to find a place to sit and commune with her. And a grave can be comforting, a small grotto of peace, to contemplate your loss, and talk to the beloved person it commemorates. I decided to ask Ted if he would take the girls up to Talland Church soon; if he would explain to them that this was where their mummy now lay; that, yes, she was in heaven, but part of her rested here in Cornwall, somewhere they could always come and peacefully remember her.

But before I could screw my courage up to broach something so personal, the kitchen door opened and Eve, Tom and Chris poured into the room, laughing and wafting a sharp smell of ozone in with them.

Rose and Violet were beside themselves with joy to see Tom and Evie; especially Evie, because they saw in her the big girl they hoped they would become. My two took the little ones downstairs to play with Eve's old dolls and to watch cartoons. Which left Chris and me warily facing Ted.

Chris was his usual warm and sympathetic self. He'd dismissed what I'd told him about Ted making a pass at me as a fantasy conjured out of my confused mind, so he crossed the floor immediately and put his arms round Ted.

Ted's eyes grew wet. He leaned into Chris's body, allowed himself to be held in my husband's embrace. Because we hadn't been down in Cornwall since February, it was the first time they'd seen one another since Eloise's funeral

'I'm so sorry, Ted. Christ, it's so horrible she's gone. Are you OK?'

'Dunno really. Holding it together I guess. I could really do with someone to talk to. I mean there's no one really. My parents are good, but they don't really get it. How could they? And I've got no brothers or sisters. And, actually, precious few friends. Apart from you and Cathy, they were mostly her mates, not mine. I don't come from round here. And in the end, if you weren't born here, you're always an outsider.'

'What about Juliana? I know from Cath, who spoke to her on the phone only last week that she is still completely felled by grief. And she feels very isolated,. She needs you, Ted. You and the girls.'

Ted's face turned from sorrow to a mask of cold harshness.

'Juliana and I don't get on,' he said abruptly. 'And I don't want her poisoning the girls' minds against me, so I'd rather we both kept our distance.'

I had been sitting in our little snug, armed with books and newspapers, really glad to be well out of another emotional exchange with Ted. I was relieved that Chris was handling it, even wondering if I could sneak off downstairs to join the kids. But I knew I had to wade in after Ted's extraordinary comment.

I stood up. 'Ted, do you have the faintest idea what you're saying? Juliana is desperate, devastated. She needs to have her grandchildren near her. What on earth do you mean, that she'll poison their minds? She adores them, and has nothing but respect for you and your marriage to Eloise.'

Ted looked at me, and it really hurt to see it, with total contempt.

'I don't know how much my wife ever told you about our pathetic relationship. I suspect, knowing Eloise as I did, God help me, that she told you nothing that did not portray her in her usual fabulous halo of light. Suffice it to say that our marriage was a travesty.'

Chris and I stood in our pretty living room, shell-shocked. Then Chris, ever the pacifier, assumed a calm, doctor-like manner.

'Ted, please sit down. We all need a drink, and then we can talk about this without being melodramatic.'

He signalled to me and I moved slowly into the kitchen, anxious to help this horrible situation and at the same time desperate to run, to dash upstairs and wrap myself up in my duvet. To take a sleeping pill, dissolve into darkness, forget the whole bloody emotional rigmarole and wake up to a fresh clear day tomorrow.

Instead, I poured Ted a Scotch, and red wine for Chris and me.

It was Chris who started it.

'Right, Ted, would you like to tell us what's on your mind, what is making you so unhappy? Obviously you're in deep shock; your wife has died; you are alone; your children are motherless. Please believe I understand all that, and I also understand that you are feeling very deep anger, however irrational, towards Eloise herself. She couldn't help her illness or her death, which I know you realise, but you are harbouring a deep grudge against her. I've seen this so often, and, believe me Ted, it's completely natural. What you need to do now is to talk about it, all of it. Cath and I won't judge you, whatever you say.'

Chris stopped talking and there was a long, nasty pause. Ted looked at us both as if we were mad. Then he let rip.

'Jesus, Chris, your stupid fucking job! Do you know how you sound, so sodding pompous and sanctimonious? You're like a fucking Victorian parson, for Christ's sake. You don't have *any* idea about my marriage. It was nothing like it seemed on the surface. We were miserable, OK? Totally fucked, hated the bleeding sight of each other. To be honest, I couldn't wait for her to die.'

Chapter Eleven

It was eight o'clock that same night. Chris and I were sitting opposite each other at a small, candlelit table in the Talland Bay Hotel, a two-minute walk from our cottage. Our hamlet is remote and tiny, with only ten or so houses and cottages meandering down the steep lane to the cove, but all the land had once belonged to the manor of Porthallow, once known as Portlooe, which is listed in the Domesday Book.

We didn't have a shop or a pub in our village, and we loved our peace and tourist-free quiet, but we were lucky enough to have the beautiful old Manor House, which for a long time now has been run as a small, independent country house hotel. It's a Godsend to us, a place to eat and drink in the beautiful gardens with their gorgeous views of the sea, or, in winter, the oak-panelled dining room, logs blazing in the ancient inglenook fireplace. Our cottage is tucked around the back of the old Manor House, and it used to house the steward who managed the estate.

The evening was cool for June, and we chose to eat inside. Tom and Eve had walked across the cliff path to Polperro, aiming to get a pizza or steak and chips at the Crumplehorn Inn so, for a while, at last, Chris and I were alone. And we had so much to talk about that neither of us knew quite how to begin. Or at least I didn't. Chris, however, wanted to talk about Ted and Eloise. His analysis, I knew, would be spot-on. It was just that I thought there were things, feelings, irrational emotions playing out in this small family drama that needed a vast vista, a sweeping stage, to comprehend; we needed the Northern Lights here, the Aurora Borealis, to illuminate this sad, shadowy little Cornish tragedy.

'Ted's obviously in a really bad state,' said Chris. 'I want to help him but first he needs to admit he's got a problem.'

I swallowed my irritation.

'He just did. His wife has just died of cancer, and he told us he *wanted* her to die. I mean, he couldn't have been plainer, could he? Do you really think that's normal?'

'Of course it is, Cathy. Bereavement sends people into torments. He's so angry he doesn't know what he's thinking right now.'

Yeah, I thought cynically. Well I had a strong idea. He hates Eloise, and not just because she's died and left him with two little girls to bring up alone. There was something terribly wrong with Ted and Eloise, and it wasn't all down to her illness and the strain it had put on their marriage. I wished I could have just shrugged and consigned it to fate — other peoples' fates; their business, nothing to do with me.

But Eloise had made it my business too, and I knew with a weary spirit that I had been bound by her to find out the truth.

Oddly, I didn't hear from her that night. It seemed she had acknowledged I had had enough. That I needed some respite from her demands. That I actually just deserved some rest.

What a fool I was. That she, tormented soul, would ever think I needed a break. Really, I was nothing to her other than a means to an end. All that was left to her was a moral imperative; and that concerned her children, no one else. Not her mother, her husband, and certainly not me. She didn't care about anyone other than those to whom she had given birth. She certainly wasn't remotely worried about me, and the mental torment her 'visits' had caused me.

I no longer liked Eloise. Oh, I knew this was all about her

children, a mother's fierce and natural determination to put them first at all cost. But that cost now included me. And I had children too. They had already suffered because of Eloise's hold over me. They had seen me ill again. Of course there was a desperate craving, a real cry for help in her invasions of my dreams, I was sure of that. But I was just a medium, a cog in a complex supernatural equation aimed squarely at channelling my fragile mind. She was using me. I had no idea what this was all about, the big picture, as they used to say in Hollywood. But as much as I revered the memory of my dear dead friend, I had no wish to be involved in a ghostly mission for justice that might destroy my stability and the happiness of my own dear children.

So there you go. Your kids or mine, Ellie? No contest.

On Sunday, Chris and I went to church. The children stayed in bed, but, wordlessly, we knew we wanted to visit St Tallanus, our beautiful Celtic chapel. The church was the spiritual centre of our tiny hamlet. The very name Talland meant, in Cornish, the Holy Place on the Hill. It was built, as were all Celtic sites of worship, by running water, a tiny stream trickling down the slope beside the graveyard wall. The entire edifice had a powerful aura of mystery; it was said that the altar was built on a place where two ancient ley lines intersected. And it is true that to kneel and worship there was to experience a profound sense of awe and belonging. We had had our wedding blessed there ten years ago. We originally married in a Register Office, and neither of us had thought we were particularly religious, but the absolute calm we felt in Talland Church moved us to seek a blessing on our marriage four years after we moved into the cottage. This ancient place proffered a secure and holy roof, protecting the commitment we had made to each other, transforming it into a sacrament: we shall love each other, in sickness and in health, 'til death us do part.

We walked through the graveyard, past yearning, tragic headstones bearing witness to infants and young mothers who had succumbed to the carnage of death in childbirth. Past the more romantic and adventurous tributes to smugglers cut down by the Preventive Men as they brought their booty ashore on Talland Beach. And, inevitably, past the still-rounded mound that marked the passing of Eloise less than five months ago. Eloise had worshipped here, too, when they stayed over, and loved the peace and tranquillity, so it had been her choice to be buried here, with the endless sea before her and the gentle sound of the stream only feet away. It was too early yet for a gravestone to be erected – the earth had to settle first – but on my friend's still-fresh resting place lay a forest of flowers: tumbling towers of faded roses, garlands of pink clematis. I stared at it, seeing the sweetness of the flowers, thinking of the body of my dead friend in the casket below. Oh Eloise, why couldn't you rest in peace? Why, in this beautiful country churchyard, couldn't you give yourself up to eternal quiet, your tasks complete, your work done? And, after all your pain, sorrow and fear, sleep softly in this gentle bower, knowing that you had done your best, and your trials at last were over?

But there could be no repose for you, my Ellie. Not yet. Maybe not ever, unless I could fulfil your wishes. And I was not prepared to do that. You had frightened me too much, overplayed your hand.

I looked up. From Eloise's grave you could see a vast expanse of glittering sea, green hills swooping down to sand and rock, astonishing colours of blue, gold, purple and silver. It was a place of rest to be desired, to be devoutly wished. Paradise. But for the lonely spirit trapped below, Paradise was truly lost.

The service was calming. We took Communion, and when I settled back into the pew I felt a genuine sense of peace. If Eloise really was wandering about at night along the clifftop, scaring me to death with her dire predictions of doom, then I felt here, in this holy place, I might find the strength to resist her.

Afterwards the congregation, such as it was, gathered in the porch. We said goodbye to the vicar, a lovely woman with a marvellously confident pulpit voice, and various neighbours milled around exchanging gossip and invitations to Sunday drinks. An old lady I had not seen for nearly a year approached and eagerly embraced me.

'Winnie,' I said, happily returning her kiss. 'How are you? Have you got over that terrible flu?'

Winnie Wharton had been confined to bed for weeks with not just flu but a frightening lung infection at the time of Ellie's death. One of her neighbours had said darkly, at Ellie's funeral, that she might have to go into the hospital in Plymouth, and we all knew what that implied at her great age. She was well into her eighties and pneumonia was not a welcome diagnosis. But Winnie, always doughty and courageous, had clearly recovered from her illness.

'Oh goodness, yes,' she said. 'Fit as a fiddle I am now, though it took until May, and it's so grand to get back to church. First time I've been since January.'

'That's brilliant, Winnie. If you come next Sunday, maybe you and Wilf can come back to our house and have a sherry with us and a few friends?'

'Ooh, we'd love that. I must say it's been a bit quiet for us while I was poorly – hardly seen a soul in months. I'd like to have a bit of a knees-up again.'

I laughed. 'I'm not sure a few sherries on a Sunday lunchtime qualifies as a knees-up, but I'll do my best.'

'That will be lovely. Will Eloise be there?'

I was staggered. Surely she knew Eloise was dead and buried. Maybe I had misheard.

'Eloise? No, of course not.' Not exactly tactful, but I felt stunned.

'Oh, that's a pity. I'd like to talk to her again. Such a lovely young woman.'

I breathed again. Winnie, for weeks marooned in her sickbed, was clearly unaware that Eloise had died. And since Ellie had kept her illness secret from all but her closest family and friends, why should an elderly lady of the parish know that the lovely, glamorous, vivacious star of south Cornwall now lay buried just a few feet in front of her?

Winnie burbled happily on. 'I tried to speak to her this morning when I saw her outside church, but I don't think she heard me. And then I thought I'd see her at Communion, but she didn't come. She looked lovely in her red swishy skirt.'

I stared at Winnie. 'You . . . you must be mistaken. Eloise isn't here. Hasn't been for months.'

I couldn't bear to say the words: *Eloise is dead*.

'Well, I don't know about that.' Winnie was beginning to bristle, in the way old people do when they think their memory is being questioned. 'All I know is that Eloise was here this morning when I arrived at church. She was standing right there.' And Winnie pointed to Ellie's unmarked grave.

'She had someone with her as well. A young boy, about sixteen or so. Lovely-looking young man he was. They were both looking at those gorgeous flowers on that poor soul's grave. Don't know whose it is, but someone's been taking good care of it.'

I was dumbfounded. I stared at the grave, saw nothing but heaped earth and tumbled blossoms. I really didn't have the heart to remonstrate with Winnie, but before I could say anything, she let out a cry.

'There he is. That's the lad. He's on his own now, but before she was with him. And the way she looked at him, you'd have thought the sun shone out of his eyes.'

And wandering slowly among the graves, reading head-stones avidly as he meandered from tomb to tomb, was the young man Chris and I had seen coming out of the Talland Bay Hotel. Evie's beautiful boy, pale and unearthly, haunting the sacred ground where so many Cornish lay dead.

I whipped around, trying to spot Eloise among the small congregation in the churchyard. But of course she wasn't there.

I grabbed Chris's hand and set off to talk to the boy. Chris wasn't happy. He'd been in deep conversation with the vicar, about a psychotherapy self-help group they were trying to set up in the parish. But, with his usual patience and stiff upper lip, Chris allowed himself to be dragged away.

'What are you doing?' he hissed as I pulled him down the slope toward the place where I had seen the boy.

'We need to talk to him, Chris. I just know he is really important in all this; he's a clue to why I keep dreaming about Eloise.'

'Talk to who? And what on earth do you mean, a clue to your dreams? Are you still imagining all that rubbish about Eloise? You're not making any sense. And not for the first time,' he added.

I froze. Stopped and turned to him. 'Look, Chris. I've just about had enough of this. You keep implying I'm mad. I know I've been disturbed, depressed, but actually I am perfectly well at the moment. Something is going on here about Eloise. You heard what Ted said yesterday. Did that sound normal to you?'

'Absolutely normal behaviour after a bereavement. Cathy, look. I can't stand much more of this. Can't you get it into your head that there was nothing strange or unexpected about Eloise's death? Last time we came down here you started obsessing about it. You were fine back home in London, back to your old self, but now it's all starting again. I can see the signs. Look at the way you were staring at her grave just then. As if you'd never seen it before. For God's sake, she's *dead*. It's all over.'

He looked stricken, genuinely upset.

'I just don't know what to do about you any more, Cath. God knows I've tried. And I don't think you understand what you're doing to *me*. I couldn't have been more supportive or understanding. I've put everything on hold for you. My work, my research. I was supposed to publish my book on schizophrenia this autumn, but there's no way I'll finish it now. And that won't go down well with the Faculty.'

I interrupted him. 'Are you saying you can't work because of me? Because you know that's ridiculous. I've never stopped you doing your research, or writing your bloody book.'

Suddenly Chris looked furious. 'God, Cath, you don't understand anything, do you? You're so obsessed with yourself you can't think about anyone else. How do you think I can work when I'm worried sick about you all the time? You're so damned selfish, acting as if all that matters are your warped emotions. And I mean that. They are warped and twisted. Eloise died from *cancer*, for Christ's sake, no big mystery there, but you just can't let it go, can you? Jesus, I spend all my professional life dealing with mental patients. How do you think it feels to come home to one as well? You're my wife, not another sad case at the hospital. Don't you think I need some care and affection when I come home? Instead of which all I get is your stress and ridiculous delusions. I can't stand this much longer.'

He stared at me, his face contorted with anger and misery, and then wheeled round and stalked back to the church. Everyone was looking at us. They obviously knew we'd had a row. I was stunned at Chris's outburst, at the hostility and venom he had hurled at me. He had never spoken to me like that before, but I knew he was telling me the truth. He had had enough of me.

I walked away, downhill past the church. I no longer looked for Evie's gorgeous boy, or for Eloise herself. I suddenly knew I was on my own. Chris was at the end of his tether. He had tried to help with my depression, and then with my fixation about Eloise's death. But he could no longer go along with an obsession he regarded as stupid and misguided. He thought I was being self-indulgent, attention-seeking. Was I? No. My dreams felt real enough to me.

I felt dreadful. Everything around me was dead, over. Without Chris, how could I ever ride over this nightmare, this horrible thing that visited me almost nightly?

I walked up the hill, past the hotel, down our drive, past the fence wreathed with clematis, and down the steps to our cottage. The children were still in bed. I made a cup of tea and carried it out onto the terrace. I was suddenly seized with an impulse to visit our wildflower meadow and orchard, which we had reclaimed at eye-watering expense when we bought the house. The bills were frightening, but we never regretted it. The paddock was huge, around three acres, but had been completely overgrown with Japanese Knotweed, impenetrably neck-high, and impossible to hack through to get down to the very pretty pond which sat at the bottom of the valley. The landscape gardeners who at last transformed our paddock into a kind of wonderland also enlarged the pond, so that it now has a little wooden pier, and a skiff on which you can lazily boat among the water lilies and reeds.

I walked down there and sat at the little picnic table by the pond. It was perfect; an idyll so beautiful and profound that I thought I could die there, peacefully, and be completely absorbed into this lovely land. And have my ashes scattered around the pretty willow trees that lean around our little stretch of water. Although I wasn't sure if I wanted to be buried or cremated. The only thing I knew was that whatever was left of my body had to lie in the garden of my beloved Cornwall.

The bottom line now was that I was on my own. Chris had had more than enough of my ghostly suspicions. It was clear to me that beneath the anger and harsh words he desperately wanted us to be as we had been before. Which was close, happy and completely wrapped up in each other.

I had been blessed in my marriage. Why in God's name would I want to destroy such a good strong bond, because I felt compelled to look into the death, the perfectly legal, expected death of a friend who had been suffering from terminal cancer?

The answer crept into my mind with the sinister slither of a snake. It was the voice of my doctor, calm, soothing, slightly patronizing. 'Because, of course, Cathy, you are not well,' it whispered. 'You're on anti-depressants. A lot of the time you are miles away from reality, locked into a paranoid world. Somehow your mind has hijacked Eloise's death, her perfectly natural though tragically sad death, and turned it into a dark Gothic fantasy. Linked somehow in your brain with motherhood, and your own guilt about how you have neglected your children because of your mental incapacity. This is all a pathetic fairy tale, and you've invented it to divert attention from your own madness. There; now acknowledge it. And be done with it.'

And then I looked up.

And I saw her.

Strongly present, in her red skirt and long silk scarf. At first she was up on the horizon, silhouetted against the outline of the church. But then, in an instant, she was down, this wraith, standing by the jetty on our pond, her ethereal beauty streaming gorgeously toward me, bathing me in her irresistible light, her tragic need for love and redemption. The sight of her almost stopped my heart with awe and terror.

Would she speak to me? Would she tell me what had gone on between her and her husband?

'Eloise,' I said, my voice trembling. 'I can see you properly now. Will you talk to me, please? Just let me know, gently I beg you, because your visitations terrify me, what it is you need and want me to do?'

'I'm sorry I frighten you, Cathy.' Oh, to hear that voice again, as soft as ever, but infused with an urgency and determination I had rarely heard during her lifetime. 'I'm afraid I have no choice. Where I am you are given appalling . . . ' She hesitated. 'Insights. You can see the consequences of your past actions. And, because you are no longer alive, there is nothing you can do about it. Unless you can reach a friend, someone like you, who cares enough to help. The bottom line is that I need you to sort out a terrible mess I made, one which I died too soon to sort out myself.'

'I don't understand what you mean. God, Ellie, I never understand you in my dreams either. Can't you stop talking in riddles?'

What was I doing, trying to hold a conversation with a ghost? My mind reeled in disbelief. If Chris had found me now, he would have proof positive that I was losing my mind.

'I can't tell you everything, because I don't have the strength. I only know that you, and you alone, can help me.

I've seen it, Cathy. I've seen what will happen if he isn't stopped. It's up to you.'

'This is madness. I'm not hearing you. You're just an illusion. I can't bear it much longer. I thought you were fading, too weak to carry on meeting me. How come you've suddenly rallied enough to be here, in our paddock, talking sense – or nonsense. I just don't know any more. Ellie, am I just imagining that you're here? Am I having another breakdown? For God's sake don't mess about with my mind.'

She didn't flinch.

'I *am* real to you, Cath. That is, this is me, what's left of me. It's true I'm very weak, but I have been given a lifeline. Short lived, but I've found enough adrenalin in it to sustain me for a while longer. But you need to know everything. Only you can help.'

'Then tell me. What should I do? No more hints, Eloise, no more dramatic threats. What do you want me to do?'

I thought even as I said this that it was rubbish. My communication with Eloise had been so fragmented, so essentially meaningless, that I thought she could do nothing but hand out dire predictions of death and dread.

But then she surprised me.

'You don't know it, but you have already seen Arthur. He is the thread of life still left to me. You must go back to Roseland and talk to my mother. She knows almost everything.'

'*Almost* everything? Christ, *you* know all there is to know. Why all this secrecy? You're here, right now. Just tell me everything — tell me what this is all about. Stop playing games, for God's sake. This isn't a *fairy tale*. Or is it? Or worse still, are you some terrible figment of my warped imagination? Is all this just another symptom? Another indication that I'm going mad?'

Eloise had now drifted far away. Of course she had, God rot her; I'd become too close, asked too many questions. Or, I thought, I'd let my frail mind get too close to her. Maybe the few wisps of self-protection left inside my choppy brain had pulled me back, distanced me from her insistent ego?

And then I remembered what she had said about Arthur. I had seen him. Yes, I thought. The beautiful boy in the graveyard. The same boy I'd seen with Chris in the lane. The one who seemed familiar. I knew that. I was just terribly unhappy at the prospect of finding out more.

Eloise had gone. I looked up at the church, its strong reassuring outline on the crest of the hill. My lovely Talland. How could this life-enhancing little hamlet, this place of spiritual serenity, play a part in a drama, which was poisoning my mind?

And then the sky darkened. Purple thunderheads rolled in from the sea, waves crashed and boiled on the beach. She was back. I couldn't see her, but her voice was insistent in my head. 'You see, Cathy, I shouldn't be here. At least not yet. I was terminally ill but my passing was . . . premature. And it shouldn't have happened; it was a sin that I died when I did; I was trying to make amends for the mess I left behind, but I didn't get the time. I made terrible mistakes but God, I paid for them. Now I need someone – *you* – to put it all right. My mother will help you. Please Cathy, please.' The waves hurled furiously over the rocks, the wind screamed over the war memorial up on the cliff, the air was beaten up with crashing tension. The sky was indigo and black, swollen with huge clouds pregnant with doom.

I fainted. I was still lying on the grass, beside the picnic table, when Eve and Tom careered down the orchard slope and found me comatose beside our little spring. Eve immediately rushed up through the paddock shouting 'Dad! DAD! Mum's collapsed. Come back here.'

Tom, however, just cradled me in his arms and kissed my forehead. I was already coming round and deeply grateful for his uncomplicated affection. Chris pulled me to my feet. He looked upset, but I wondered if he was still angry with me. I murmured that I'd fainted, no idea why, and he roughly said that I was far too emotionally upset and that I needed to go to bed.

'And I'm going to give you a tranquilliser. You must calm down.'

I protested. I really didn't want that stuff in my system any more. I was still taking Prozac and surely that was enough.

He gently walked me up to the house and said I had to rest.

'Trust me, Cathy. I'm only doing what's right for you.'

And Eloise's voice echoed, soft and distant in my head.

'Don't trust anything he says.'

Chapter Twelve

I had taken the sleeping pill that Chris insisted I needed and I woke late next morning. As I gradually surfaced, I became aware of deep male voices in the kitchen below. For a while, I surfed on the cadence of those low, strong waves, finding them reassuring without understanding anything they said. I snoozed, groggy from the tablet, until I suddenly heard Chris's voice.

'Look, she's very vulnerable right now. Not thinking straight. I just want her to rest, but that's difficult while she's got this bee in her bonnet about Eloise.'

'Chris, I'm sorry I blurted all that about our marriage the other day. I know it upset Cathy.'

I stiffened. Ted was downstairs talking to Chris about me.

'The fact is I've been under the most horrible strain for so long now. Eloise and I were very unhappy, but it was all masked by her cancer. Of course I had to do my best to help her, but to be honest, if she hadn't been ill, we would have been divorced by now.'

'Could you tell me why?' Chris asked gently. There was a long pause.

'Look, Chris. There's a lot I'd like to tell you about Ellie and me. But now's not the time. Especially when Cathy has so clearly taken against me.'

Chris sighed. 'I think she needs to sleep for a day or two. She's still quite fragile, and she keeps jumping at all sorts of daft ideas.'

'About me, do you mean?'

'No more than anyone else, Ted. Look, I'll talk to you later. Perhaps meet for lunch at Sam's? The kids will do their own thing.'

'And Cathy?'

'Don't worry. I'll give her something to make her sleep.'

I couldn't believe what I was hearing. Chris was manu-facturing some kind of plot to keep me comatose so he could go and talk to Ted. Meaning that he thought I was so unstable that I had to be kept out of the picture. I heard him coming up the stairs and decided to pretend I was still asleep. When he came into the room he paused, then sat down gently on the bed. He touched my shoulder. 'Cathy?' he asked gently. 'Are you awake, darling?'

I groaned, turning into my pillow. Chris's voice was conciliatory. He acted as if his furious outburst after church yesterday had never happened. 'Sweetheart, I have to go out. Tom and Evie are fine, they're down at the beach. I'll be back soon, but now just take this, will you, darling? Sit up.' I struggled up, pretending to be only semi-awake. Chris opened my hand and put two tablets on my palm. He brought a glass of water to my lips, and said 'It's OK, sweetie. You just need to sleep. You'll feel so much better when you wake up.'

I brought my hand up to my mouth, accepted the water he gave me. Then I put my hand down and let go of the pills, shoving them underneath my pillow. Chris beamed. 'There you are, honey. Sleep tight. I'll see you soon and make supper for us all. Or we could just get fish and chips from the stall at Wayland Farm.'

He leaned over and kissed me on the cheek. I feigned semi-oblivion and turned over. He quietly bustled about the bedroom, picking up things he thought he needed, then gently closed the door behind him. A minute later, I heard the kitchen door close decisively as he and Ted left, and then the sound of two cars revving up and departing down our drive.

I sat up, stunned. This was like the plot of a Victorian drama. My husband had tried to drug me so he could talk privately to the man I was increasingly sure was contributing to my friend's fears for her children. I felt completely betrayed. Until today if there had been anyone in my cloudy orbit of depression, anyone at all I could have trusted absolutely to defend me, have faith in me, it was Chris. Now he'd changed sides. He was having secret conversations with Ted. The man of whom Eloise had told me not to trust a word.

I dressed, fumbling with my clothes. I felt sick with shock and sadness. If I couldn't rely on Chris to be my unquestioned ally, who was left? My children of course, but I couldn't possibly burden them with my concerns – which were strange, even to me. And really, if they had to choose between their mother's weird imaginings, and their father's resolute common sense, which one of us would they believe? They had seen me almost catatonic with depression, sleeping for days, unable to take part in their precious lives. But their dad was always there, always dependable. He was their rock when their mum was sealed away, locked inside a chamber as impenetrable as a dungeon in a fairy tale, cursed by a malevolent witch.

So no, I could not turn to them. Or to Chris.

Which left? Only one person.

I was in my little car, my cream Beetle, keys in the ignition, heart in my mouth. I set off down the drive, turned right up the lane. I was heading for Roseland, rushing to Juliana, hoping that her warmth, her motherly arms, would hold me and keep me from my encroaching crash into a dark, lonely abyss.

I can barely remember the journey. It was like one of those horrible dreams when you find yourself in charge of a car, but unable properly to reach either the clutch or brakes. Somehow I travelled along country lanes and scary dual carriageways. I was scarcely conscious, and have no idea how I managed to find my way to Juliana's farmhouse. I can't even remember crossing to Fowey on the Bodinnick ferry.

But, miraculously, I got there, and slewed the car to a halt outside the farmhouse's front door. Which was open; not unusual in this blissfully quiet part of England. No threat, you see. Everything perfect, safe, snug as a bug in a rug. I breathed a sigh of relief, surged out of the Beetle and rushed through the inviting open door.

Two people stood in the slate-flagged hall, a fire burning even though it was a warm day. One of them was the boy. The dazzlingly beautiful adolescent I had seen on my way back up from the beach, and again in the churchyard.

The other was Juliana. She stepped forward, surprised but obviously delighted by my arrival. She hugged and kissed me and then waved towards the boy.

'Cathy, I want you to meet Arthur. My great-grandson.'

Chapter Thirteen

Chris came in a taxi. He'd phoned, and told me to wait at the door. He didn't see, didn't *want* to see, Juliana or Arthur. He bundled me into my Beetle, took the driving seat, said he didn't want to hear even a word until later, and got us home in time to eat fish and chips with Eve and Tom. We were all quiet, Chris and I burdened with more knowledge than we wanted. The children, too, were muted, obviously sensing something they weren't part of. After supper, they went next door to play pool with our neighbour's children.

Chris and I faced each other across the kitchen table.

'Do you want to talk first, or shall I?'

That was Chris, supremely rational as always. I looked at him. I was so floored by what I had learned at Roseland Farm that I didn't know how to begin. I shook my head.

'You start,' I said. 'And by the way, I know you tried to drug me so I'd be out of the way when you went off to have your talk with Ted.'

Chris flushed and had the grace to look ashamed.

'Yes, I'm sorry, Cath. I just knew I had to talk to him straight, man to man. And that couldn't happen if you were there. And besides, you really did need to rest.'

'No, I didn't. Don't pretend you tried to give me sleeping pills because it was for my own good. If you wanted to speak to Ted alone, why on earth didn't you just tell me?'

He looked down and muttered, 'I thought you'd refuse to let me. You're so obsessed with Eloise, I thought you'd insist on being there.'

'Jesus, Chris. That's a pathetic excuse. You drugged me because I was an inconvenient barrier to something you needed to say to Ted. I can't forgive that. If you ever try to do that again, I'll divorce you. I really will. I can't believe that you, of all people, my husband for God's sake, would exploit your medical knowledge to gag your wife so she wouldn't interfere in a fucking conversation with a mutual friend.'

Chris was obviously embarrassed, but defiant.

'Look, Cathy, the conversation I had with Ted today was important. And I couldn't have had it if you'd been there.'

'Oh, right. Fine. Then next time just get me sectioned if I'm interfering in your precious life. Or maybe you can silence me for good. After all, you've got access to all the right drugs. You could slip me an overdose, and no one would ever know. "Just Chris's mad wife, on the old pills again, taken too many. It's been on the cards for ages, ever since her breakdown".'

Once again, Chris was furious with me.

'Grow up, will you? You aren't well. You *do* need medication, and you're far more vulnerable than you want to believe. I'm looking after you, for Christ's sake. You're my wife, and my absolute responsibility. You did need to rest this afternoon and I'm sorry that I used that opportunity to talk to Ted when I thought you were asleep. It seemed like a useful thing to do. He said things ... well, he said things about him and Eloise that he would never have talked about if you'd been there. Because you and Ellie were so close.'

'What did he say?' Eagerness to know won over my anger.

Chris leaned back into his chair, took a mouthful of wine from his glass, and said:

'Cathy, he's not a nice man. Not the man I thought he was. At all.'

I looked at him. I know this, I thought. This is what it's all about; this is why Eloise is so desperate to reach me.

Don't trust a word he says. Her words rang in my head.

Surely she meant Ted?

But Chris had drugged me. So which one of them was treacherous?

Chris looked down at the table.

'First of all, Cath, I think he married Eloise for her money.'

'What? That's ridiculous,' I said, despite knowing that it was something Juliana had believed when he and Eloise first got together. 'Of course he didn't.'

'Why do you find it so hard to believe?' Chris asked. 'Think about it, Cath. A dirt poor artist marries a Cornish heiress and we all think it's a love match?'

'But we did think it was a love match, didn't we? You remember the way he looked at her? And she was very beautiful. Why wouldn't he love her?'

'He said their marriage was dreadful. He implied she was unfaithful.'

'Eloise? No! She wasn't like that and, anyway, I would have known.'

'Would you, Cathy? I don't think she told you everything.'

That was certainly true. I stood up.

'Let's go for a walk. Just down to the beach. I need to clear my head.'

We walked slowly down the lane, between the little white-washed cottages and the ancient stone walls with their wild flowers bursting from every crack and crevice. We'd once seen a dormouse here, tiny and bold as it perched on a rock, the sweetest sight I'd ever seen. And at night there were badgers and foxes scurrying furtively around the hedgerows, burrowing and searching for food. During the day though, the most constant presence was the sea, glimpsed blue and golden over every gate, every stile, its waves murmuring softly, beckoning you down to the cove.

'Did Ted tell you anything about Arthur?' I asked.

Chris shook his head. 'No. Who's Arthur?'

'Eloise's grandson,' I replied.

Chris stopped. He turned to look at me, his face mildly amused, full of disbelief.

'You're being ridiculous. Her grandson? For God's sake, she was only in her forties when she died. What on earth are you talking about?'

We sat down at one of the picnic benches at the café on the beach. The café was closed, the beach deserted. I reached forward and took Chris's hands over the table.

'Listen to me, Chris. This is important, really important.

Eloise has been trying to tell me this story for so long but it was Juliana who actually fleshed it out for me today. It's a long story, but what she told me is that Eloise had a baby when she was only thirteen.'

'What?' Chris interrupted. 'That's absurd. Surely we'd have known about something as . . . as huge as that.'

'Please be quiet, Chris, and hear me out. Hardly anyone else knew. It was all kept very hush–hush, for obvious reasons. Let me tell you now . . . '

From the time Eloise was small, a lonely only child, she was educated at a private school in Truro, quite a way west from her home. She was a weekly boarder, coming back to Roseland Hall every Friday afternoon. At that point, her parents still lived in the huge family mansion; but they had no male heir. There was money, but not enough to maintain the immaculate house and parkland indefinitely and Charles refused to countenance opening the estate to the public.

'Ridiculous idea,' he snorted whenever Juliana suggested that could be the way forward. 'We're not exhibits in a zoo. I don't want the hoi polloi and their muddy boots all over the Long Gallery, or trampling through my shrubberies. My father would have had a fit.'

Charles was as snobbish as Juliana was pragmatic. She knew he would never agree, but she did tell him that the most practical option was to hand over the big house and estate to the National Trust. They would still have a considerable fortune, enough to ensure they and Eloise and any children she might have would never have to worry about money. They could live in the pretty old farmhouse in the grounds, which was more than adequate to house their small family in plenty of style, and they would no longer have to endure the suffocating responsibilities of running an enormous stately home that ate money.

But Charles hated the idea of giving up the house that was his heritage. He would have hung onto Roseland indefinitely, however much money it haemorrhaged, feeling that it was the emblem of his dignity, his worth as a man. In fact, he was less worried about money than the fact that he had no son to inherit the estate. He felt ashamed about that, obsessed with the fear that his Cornish peers regarded him as inadequate and emasculated.

It was while Juliana was trying to cope with her husband's emotional crisis that her loving maternal eye became diverted from her only child. But Eloise, encouraged by her mother since she was young to keep a diary, recorded the events of the traumatic summer she turned thirteen. And then, years later after her father died, she allowed her mother to read it. And when she married Ted, she left the diary with her mother, making Juliana promise to keep it secret, and above all to ensure that her new husband would never find it.

Now, after Arthur's miraculous appearance in her life, Juliana had at last decided to share Eloise's record of that momentous summer with me. And because she knew so much of what her daughter had gone through at such a vulnerable age, her knowledge, combined with Eloise's abandoned, love-ridden rambling notes, took me straight back into a world in which I had never known my friend; my dear, lovely girl whose life was now so cloudy, so lost to me.

In her neat, childish hand, Eloise wrote of how lonely she felt. She was shy at her boarding school and found it difficult to fit in with the other girls, burying herself in the roles she won so easily in the dramatic society. Back home every weekend, she was mostly on her own. Isolated, footsteps echoing round the vast empty rooms of the mansion which had once been so vibrant, so full of glamorous social gatherings, dances, musical evenings, dinner parties resplendent with the finest silver and most precious porcelain, she withdrew. She spent her weekends in her bedroom, reluctantly joining her parents for meals during which her father was silent, his eyes dull, eating little but drinking glass after glass of wine. And after dinner, when he went alone to his study, Eloise would watch from the stairs as the butler, Eric, brought him a decanter of whisky. Charles would not emerge from his lair, no matter how long she stayed up.

Twice, unable to sleep, she got out of bed and walked down to the study, standing nervously for long minutes before she hesitantly opened the door. Both times, she saw her father stretched out on the sofa beside the dying fire, unconscious and snoring, the whisky decanter empty on the walnut table by his side.

The long summer holidays started on the eve of her thirteenth birthday. Both her parents were far too engrossed in their marital problems to pay much attention to their lonely little daughter. And so, as she wrote so wistfully in her diary, she whiled away her days wandering around the lovely parkland, daydreaming and occasionally settling into the little gazebo to read her favourite books, *Jane Eyre* and *Wuthering Heights*.

And she fell more and more into the company of the estate manager's son, Jack.

Like Eloise, Jack was an only child, just a couple of years older than she. Although he went to the village school, and often had friends round to play football in his parents' large garden, he was a wistful boy, dreamy, with huge blue eyes and a thatch of golden hair. A Cornish child, brought up on the beach, who could surf and swim like a fish. Eloise had always been in awe of Jack. He could do anything; he made campfires with kindling and cooked sausages for his friends as dusk fell. He knew his way around the strange and mysterious places on Bodmin Moor, telling hair-raising stories to his mates about the ghosts and boggarts that haunted the misty wild stretches around Jamaica Inn. He claimed he had seen apparitions, grey and terrifying, howling in terrible pain among the ancient stone circles that dotted the moor, souls tormented by unresolved passions, by desperate injustices they could not put right.

No wonder Eloise fell in love with him, this beautiful Cornish boy, blond as the hay and brown as a nut, with his fearless tales of those murdered innocents now doomed to roam the blasted heaths of Bodmin until they found release.

All that summer, she wrote, she couldn't take her eyes off him. Shy and tongue-tied when she was among his friends, she longed to be alone with him. When she was, she told him about her favourite books. He hadn't read them, but watched her with grave attention as she talked about Jane Eyre and her mysterious intimations of the madwoman in the attic, the final flight from her beloved Mr Rochester, and the supernatural voice she heard across the wilderness of the Yorkshire Moors, summoning her back to her blinded lover's side.

And she told him about Cathy and Heathcliff, their dark, doomed love affair at Wuthering Heights, and how their passion outlived Cathy's death.

And he watched her, lying next to her in the fragrant grass, his head propped up on his hands.

Eloise's thirteenth birthday fell on the thirteenth of July. Her mother, distracted as usual by her husband's moods, asked Ellie how she wanted to celebrate.

'Do you want a party, dear? We could ask some of your school friends. And have some lovely party games, perhaps with a magician or something?'

Eloise shuddered. She had hardly any friends, certainly didn't want them to come home and watch her father drink. And party games? How horrible was that? It all seemed deeply unattractive. So she demurred. Said she really didn't want a fuss. Would be happy just to celebrate at home with her parents, a birthday cake and maybe a ride on her beloved pony, Daisy.

Juliana was relieved. Charles had been particularly difficult lately. He was drunk every night and when he sobered up refused to discuss what was to happen to Roseland. The servants had sensed there was a crisis, so the atmosphere at Roseland was febrile and unpleasant, and it was all Juliana could do to smooth things over, to continue to behave as the gracious lady of the Manor, even though she woke every morning with her heart in her mouth, her stomach crippled with cramps of anxiety.

*

On Ellie's birthday, there was a celebratory tea. Sandwiches, scones and a beautiful cake, made and elaborately iced by Annie. All the servants were there, plus the gardeners, the gamekeeper, and the Estate Manager and his wife, John and Angela Merchant. Their son Jack was there, too, the only other person in the birthday girl's age group.

Everyone sang 'Happy Birthday To You' with gusto, and afterwards, when the grown-ups began drinking wine, Jack beckoned Eloise onto the Palladian terrace, and then, his finger to his mouth, across the lawns and around the side to the stable yard.

Juliana had showed me Ellie's account of what happened next.

'Ellie, do you want to come on a birthday ride with me?'

'Where to?' she squeaked with excitement.

'Up onto Bodmin. I've got so many places to show you. Places so scary you wouldn't believe. Honestly, Ellie, it really *is* full of ghosts. But don't worry. I know how to handle them. I'll look after you.'

Ellie and Jack rode out on their ponies; Jack on a restive creature called Red, Eloise on her own docile pet, Daisy.

Bodmin Moor, on a dank and foggy day, is not just forbidding and austere. Sometimes, when the mist wreathes round the gorse, and you can see only yards ahead, you feel a shivering of fear as you realise you don't know where you are, that it would be so horribly easy to veer off the road, find yourself on a footpath that led nowhere. And all around you, the ghostly breaths of the ancient stone gods of this inhospitable country.

Jack was strong and confident on his pony. Although Eloise followed him with trepidation in the fog, she trusted him completely. She felt totally connected with him, knew he would keep her safe, protect her from any harm.

They reached Jamaica Inn, which had been standing in lonely isolation on the moor for over two centuries.

'Now this,' Jack told her quietly as they tethered their ponies to the hitching rail outside the inn, 'this is a properly haunted place. Not just after dark, either.' He pointed to a little meadow behind the building, visible in a sudden break in the mist. 'See that meadow?'

Eloise nodded, too excited to speak.

'There's something not right about it,' Jack said. 'People don't like walking across it. I know a woman who used to be a cleaner here who used to walk to work across the meadow, but she soon stopped, I can tell you.'

Eloise turned to him. 'Wh – why?' she asked breathlessly. 'What happened?'

Jack shook his head slightly. 'Nothing has actually ever happened – not to anyone. It's the feeling they get when they cross it, going either way. A really strong sense that they're being followed; and not by something that means them any good. I remember being here one day last summer, and I saw some hikers cutting through on their way back from Roughtor. As soon as they climbed over that stile you can see on the far side, and starting walking to where we are now, they started looking over their shoulders – all of them. They began to speed up and when they were close enough for me to see their faces, they were obviously seriously spooked. They couldn't get out of that field fast enough.'

Eloise stared at the innocent meadow. 'What do you think it is, Jack? What's in there?'

He shrugged. 'Search me. I have no idea. Do you want to try crossing it now, with me?'

Eloise shook her head violently. 'No! Not at all!' She shuddered and turned to look at the inn. 'What about that – is it haunted too?'

Jack laughed. 'Oh yes, Ellie. It is sooooo spooky . . . the oldest part of Jamaica Inn is the eastern side.' He pointed to the right hand side of the building. 'All the weird stuff happens in there.'

Eloise gaped at the east wing. 'What weird stuff?'

'Too much to tell you in one go. The restaurant's supposed to be haunted by a man in a green cloak. I know someone who saw him leaving the restaurant and walking very, very fast to reception. When he asked one of the staff who it was, they went white and said he couldn't possibly have seen anyone coming from the restaurant, because the door to it was locked. He checked, and it was!'

'More! I want to know everything!'

Jack laughed. 'We'd be here all day . . . ok, one more. One of my mates, his dad's a plumber. He was called out to fix a leaking water tank in the east loft. He was up there all alone and suddenly felt absolutely petrified. He didn't see anything, nothing at all, but he was convinced there was something terrible hiding up there and he was back down the ladder before you could say knife. Never went back. For all he knows, the tank's still leaking.'

Eloise shivered. 'I don't want to stay here any longer. Please can we go, Jack?'

He grinned. 'Have I scared you, Ellie? Sorry, birthday girl. OK, let's ride over to the foot of Roughtor. That's the most haunted part of the whole damn moor.'

As they rode towards Roughtor, one of Cornwall's highest points, Jack told Eloise the terrible tale of Charlotte Dymond. Charlotte was a flirtatious maid who worked at a local farm. On Easter Sunday 1844, she was murdered at the foot of Roughtor. Her throat was cut, not once, but twice.

'Dad's got a book about it,' Jack explained. 'It was a massive drama at the time. In all the London papers and everything.'

He told Eloise that Charlotte's body had lain undiscovered for nine whole days before someone stumbled on it. 'You can imagine what a state it was in after all that time – flies and maggots and everything.'

Eloise gagged.

'Want me to go on?'

She nodded. 'Yes. I'm all right, honestly.'

Suspicion had fallen at once on Charlotte's suitor, an illiterate farm worker, lame in one leg and barely in his twenties. Charlotte was said to have refused him.

The upshot was that the man was tried at Bodmin Assizes, convicted, and, four months after the murder, hanged – in public. The crowds, Jack said, were enormous.

'But here's the thing, Ellie – turns out the poor guy was innocent all along. I can't remember the details but soon after they strung him up the case against him started to fall apart. Too late for the poor bloke by then, of course. He was six feet under in the prison yard. He never should have been executed.

'Now Charlotte Dymond is said to haunt the moors around Roughtor. They say her spirit can't ever rest because her killer was never brought to justice and an innocent man died, kind of because of her . . . '

'I'm not surprised,' said Eloise indignantly. 'It wasn't her fault, but I think if I were her her ghost I would feel the same! I can't stand injustice. Who's seen her?'

Jack said the most reliable sighting had come from The Cornwall Rifle Volunteers, who in the early 1900s had been on night exercises near Roughtor and had seen Charlotte walking on the very spot where her body had been found, and where a memorial stone now stood. They'd been so terrified they had abandoned the patrol and fled home. A few years earlier men from the nearby Stannon clayworks had reported multiple sightings.

Interestingly, women never saw Charlotte Dymond's ghost. Only men.

Of course there was nothing to see when the pair of them reached Roughtor, only swirling mist and the stone memorial to poor Charlotte, erected after public subscription the year after she was butchered at the lonely spot.

Eloise tried to hide her disappointment. She really had been half expecting to be met by a weeping apparition of the murdered girl.

'Come on,' said Jack. 'I know a place you can't fail to be seriously scared by. It's much, much older than anything I've shown you so far. And it is so spooky, Eloise. I'm going to show you the Stone Quoit of Trevethyan.'

At last they reached Jack's intended destination. The stone chamber loomed above them. From Jack's description, she had imagined it to be like the witch's cottage in an old fairy tale, but the reality was vast, terrifying. This astonishing monument, so tall and uncompromising, so elemental in its ageless defiance of time, inspired horror in Eloise's soul.

'What's it for, Jack?' she whispered.

He looked proud to know. 'It's a burial chamber. They laid down the bones of Kings and Princes here. Do you know how old it is, Ellie?'

She shook her head.

'Five and a half thousand years. There were people here, people like us, all that time ago. And they built this. Come inside.'

She didn't want to. All those dead bones, all those centuries of haunted memories. She shook her head.

He laughed, took her hand. 'Are you frightened?'

She acknowledged it, looked at him and said she wanted to go back home.

Jack looked grave. 'Ellie, I promise you there is nothing to be scared of. I've been up here so much, even at night, and I've never seen a ghost. Although,' he paused, unable completely to let go of his supernatural hold over her, 'I have seen lights. Dim, purple and green. And I've heard things.'

'What kind of things?' Eloise asked shakily.

'Oh, just sounds. Like voices, but very far away. I couldn't hear what they were saying.'

Eloise shivered. 'No, Jack. I want to go home, right now.'

And Jack laughed softly, touched her cheek, and led the way back to their ponies.

Later that night, writing her diary in bed, Eloise could think of nothing but Jack, his charm, his knowledge, his confidence. She remembered his ghost stories, wrapped her arms round herself, enjoying the frightening thrill they gave her. And she realised that the thrill she felt wasn't just to do with his whispers about strange happenings on the moor. She knew it was also about his touch on her cheek, his casual assumption that he was in charge, that he would take her where he wished but where she also wanted to go.

She slept that night, and dreamed that he was next to her; that his arms were round her, his breath hot against her neck. She dreamt his body rocked against hers. And something happened; something so exquisite she could not understand what it was. Only that the tumult she felt left her breathless. And for ever Jack's.

He was a boy.

Her boy.

Next morning, Juliana was curious about her ride with Jack.

'Where did you go, dear? It was nearly dark when you got home.'

'Oh, we rode up to Jamaica Inn. A bit boring really but Jack knows loads of ghost stories about the moor, so that was interesting.'

'Yes, he's a nice boy. Very clever I think. It's a pity he goes to the village school.'

'Why? I'd love to go to the village school.'

Juliana sighed. 'Look, darling. We've been through this before. Truro School will give you an excellent academic education. You're very bright, and you're doing so well. Daddy and I want you to go to university.'

'Why? You didn't.'

'Yes, but things are changing. It may be important for you to make your own money, to have a career.'

'Is that what all the arguments are about, Mummy? Is that why Dad gets drunk every night? Is the money running out? Will we have to leave Roseland?'

'Hush, darling. We'll never leave here. All I'm saying is that in a modern world girls will need to be independent. And you've got the brains to do well.'

Eloise couldn't imagine leaving Roseland. It had drawn a magic circle round her and within its grounds she felt protected. But was her mother telling the truth? Perhaps they would have to go. Would she have to leave this warm and happy place, these beautiful gardens, her darling gazebo where she read and dreamed about Jane Eyre and Catherine Earnshaw?

And would she have to leave Jack? Never see him again? Her adolescent heart almost stopped in her breast.

'No,' she thought. 'Never. I will *never* leave Jack. I will always be his and he will be mine.'

Three days after her birthday, Eloise had not seen Jack again. She wondered why he hadn't sought her out. She was desperate to catch even a glimpse of his lithe brown body, to see his light blue eyes, to listen to his stories about the ghosts of Bodmin Moor. But more than anything, she knew what she wanted was his touch. His hand on her cheek, his arm round her shoulder. And more.

She felt confused. She could not have put a name to what she wanted from Jack. She was just sure she was in love with him, and that she would do anything to make him love her back.

Came the day, a week after Eloise's birthday, that Jack found her in the gazebo, reading as usual. He crept up behind her and put an arm around her neck. She jumped and he laughed. 'Look, Ellie, I've brought you a present.'

It was silly, a tourist shop piskie sitting on a rock, but her heart melted and her body throbbed. To think he had thought about her, had cared enough about her to give her something, a small tribute which showed he liked her.

She smiled and thanked him. There was an awkward

pause, and he asked, in a rush, if she would go for a picnic with him that night, after dark.

'On Bodmin Moor?' Eloise asked nervously.

'No,' he replied.

Just somewhere here, at Roseland, in the grounds. He would bring sandwiches and something to drink. And he had loads of spooky stories to tell her about the moor, but they would be quite safe down here. There were no ghosts, he told her gravely, at Roseland Hall. All the old spooks here were so posh they wouldn't be seen dead outside their swanky tombs.

He made her laugh. He always made her laugh.

They met later that night, after Eloise had endured supper with her silent parents. Her mother had at first tried to make conversation, but her father was sunk deep in his customary wordless angry stupor. He went to his study as soon as he could get away. Juliana tried to talk to her daughter in the drawing room, but she was obviously upset. After a while she kissed Eloise and said she hoped she wouldn't mind if she went to bed. She felt very tired, she said. Perhaps Ellie would like to watch television in the small TV room? And then Annie would bring her a hot drink at bedtime.

Eloise eagerly aquiesced. Once settled in the tiny, cosy room with the television on, Annie having fussed over her and brought her homemade lemonade, she waited impatiently. At nine-thirty, the house was silent. Of course the servants would still be up, waiting for a late summons from their masters, but Ellie was convinced her mother was asleep, and her father in a drunken stupor. She got up and went in search of Annie.

At the top of the stairs leading down to the servants' hall she called out: 'Annie. I'm going to bed now. Night night.'

There was an immediate flurry from downstairs.

'Don't you "night night" me, young lady. I'll be seeing you to bed. Now go upstairs and I'll be up in a minute.'

She smiled to herself. Annie was so comfortingly predictable. Ellie went up the stairs.

Her room was pleasantly cool, the windows open and the scent of roses from the garden below making her feel slightly intoxicated. Tonight she was going to meet Jack. Her head whirled. She lay on her bed, humming as she wrote her journal, until Annie bustled in with a tray of hot chocolate.

'Aren't you going to get undressed, young lady?' she asked as Eloise lay fully clothed across the counterpane.

'Yes, of course, Annie. In a minute. I'm just not sleepy right now.'

'Well, drink this and don't stay up reading too late. You're not doing your eyesight any favours, all the books you read.'

She left, muttering. Eloise lay quietly on her bed until her watch told her it was ten-thirty. Jack had said they should meet at the gazebo then. She got up, opened the door, listened to the complete quiet and edged down the stairs.

The back door was locked, but she knew the key was kept in a small cupboard in the corridor. She unlocked the door, walked out into the summer night, then locked it behind her and tucked the key inside her pocket.

It was a beautiful night, soft and warm. The smell of stocks, roses and lavender bathed her as she walked towards the gazebo. She felt light, dreamy. She did not quite understand what she was about to do, but she knew, without a doubt, that it was meant to be.

There were faint lights in the gazebo windows. She followed them and found the way easily. The wide doors were open, and she walked inside; the scene that greeted her made her feel she had come home. Her Jack sat on a sleeping bag in front of the stove. He had lit it even though the night was warm, and he'd put cushions on the floor. There were candles all around the little octagonal whitewashed room, and he had laid out a picnic supper on a rug before the gentle flames.

He grinned at her.

'Hey, Ellie. Do you like it?'

She thought it was the most wonderful thing she had ever seen. She sank down on the rug next to him. She felt shy, tongue-tied.

He showed her his picnic. Somehow he had managed to

scrounge cold ham and beef from home, cheese and bread. And cider. A huge plastic container of it, plus glasses filched from his mother's kitchen cupboard.

Eloise was enchanted. She had never done anything as naughty, as secret as this in her life. And here she was with this beautiful boy, this extraordinary angel whom she loved, and knew absolutely she would always love, whatever happened to them in the long future ahead. He was hers; she existed only in this moment, their young limbs reflected in the firelight, the golden glow on their yearning faces as true and perfect as a painting in an Italian church.

They ate the ham, some cheese and bread. But most of all they drank the cider, because they needed the courage to build a bridge across the childish history which bound them together but divided them in this new territory, this strange and sensual world of adolescence. They talked softly. Jack told her how his parents were desperate for another child, and how it had introduced tension into their family life. Eloise told Jack about her father's despair at not having a son to carry on the Trelawney name, and how unhappy her mother was.

They both agreed that, when they had families, they would never let these material concerns destroy their love. And then they looked at each other shyly, having mentioned the word that now swirled giddily around the room.

And Eloise felt herself melt. She was tipsy, for sure. But she was also in the grip of a sensation she had never known before. As they lay next to each other on Jack's sleeping bag, sipping cider, their tongues thickening as they drank and talked about their most secret dreams, she became impatient. She wanted something from him. Her head was muddled, but her body knew exactly what she was doing.

She told her mother later that Jack didn't take advantage of her. Although they were both more than a little drunk, she wanted him as much as he did her. They were cocooned in an urgent dream, unable to stop, blind to the consequences. In that little summerhouse, lit by flickering fire and candles, they lay together. Wrapped around each other. And it was the most perfect experience of Eloise's life.

In fact, it was the moment which laid the foundation for her future.

And for her untimely death.

Chapter Fourteen

Chris watched me as I finished off my tale.

'Did Juliana tell you any more?'

'Oh yes.' I said. 'But Chris, it's such a sad story.'

'Tell me,' he said.

I frowned. 'Why? I mean do you seriously want to know or is this yet another psychological assessment? If you don't believe me, I suggest you talk to Juliana. I know you think she's half deranged with grief, but, you know, I think even you would find it difficult to deny the existence of Arthur. You've seen him, for God's sake. You know who he is.'

'Well, I guess I know who he's claiming to be. Which is convenient, considering there's a fortune to be inherited.'

'But Juliana accepts him absolutely as her great-grandchild.'

'Well, of course she does. She's just lost her only daughter, her son-in-law hates her guts and won't let her play a significant part in her grandchildrens' lives. So, in her grief, isn't she bound to embrace the grandchild who does turn to her? Arthur seeks her out at this very vulnerable time. If his story is convincing enough, of course, she's going to see it as a lifeline to Eloise, and a complete answer to Ted who is making her life even more difficult than it's bound to be. Cathy, you do see, from an outsider's point of view, that this is all very dodgy?'

'OK, I understand I'm not going to be able to convince you about Arthur. But Eloise did have a baby when she was thirteen. Juliana showed me the birth certificate. And for crying out loud, Arthur is only sixteen. How do you think he would find out about his birthright?'

'Well,' said Chris. 'How about from his grandfather?'

His grandfather? That meant Jack, Eloise's childhood sweetheart.

'Do you want me to tell you the rest or would you rather argue?'

Chris softened. 'Yes,' he said. 'I do want to hear.'

*

The rest of the summer, Eloise wrote, passed in a dream. She felt she was floating above the fields and beaches around her home. She was desperately in love, looking for Jack's face in every tree, every blade of grass, every person she spied in the distance, sure it must be him. When it wasn't, she was wracked with despair. One day, she sat in the stable with her beloved pony. 'Daisy. I'm in real trouble. I love him and I am going to be so unhappy when I have to go back to school.'

Daisy swished her tail. She was comfortingly unmoved.

Jack did seek her out after a few days. He came round to the back door and asked for her. She rushed to see him, terrified that she would see indifference in his face, but his eyes told her his own torment was as great as hers.

They walked over to the gazebo, but this time sat down on the grass outside.

They tried to make small talk about the piglets in the new pen, their ponies and, inevitably, their parents.

'When I leave school, I'd like to be an actress, I think.'

Jack talked about his love of the land, how he longed for his own farm or smallholding.

And then he said: 'Ellie, my parents are talking about moving to Australia.'

She was stunned. 'When?'

'Early next year. They want their own farm, and they'll

only be able to afford a smallholding here – but they can get something really worthwhile in Australia.'

'And you'll go with them?'

'I'll have to.'

'But, Jack . . .'

He looked at her very gravely. 'Ellie, I think you're beautiful and I would love to be with you for ever. But let's face it, your folks won't approve of me being your boyfriend – my parents are your mum and dad's tenants.'

'I think you want to go,' said Eloise. 'You're just telling me that you won't stay here with me, even if I ask you to.'

Jack looked away, then turned fiercely toward her.

'Eloise Trelawney, you have no idea what it's like to be someone like me. To gradually become aware that my home is not really mine at all, but dependent on someone else's whim. There's no security, Ellie, none at all. Your father could turf us out whenever he wants. My dad's a skilled land agent, but he has no land. When we go to Australia, we'll get our own farm. And then I won't be a tenant's son any more. I'll have my own birthright, my own farm if I want it.' He paused. 'And maybe then I'd have something to offer you.'

Eloise went back to her bedroom. She felt ill and sad. Jack was going to move across to the other side of the world, and here was nothing she could do to stop him. She had nothing to give, nothing to offer except her love. And he was only fifteen, and his parents had opened up a new existence for him. And she, too, would have gone to Australia, given half the chance. A whole new world. Who wouldn't give anything for that?

Ellie had been feeling bad for a few days now. She was deeply upset about Jack and his decision, not just to leave her to emigrate with his parents, but, although he did not put this into words, his obvious desire to distance himself from her, and from the night they had shared.

The hurt she felt was beyond expression. And, as the summer wore on, Eloise began to fade; she lost her bloom, her loveliness. She would not leave her room; she felt faint if required to join company in the drawing room. She was often nauseous, and spent much time in her prettily tiled bathroom refusing to talk to her mother or Annie when they begged her to tell them what the matter was.

The matter was simple. Eloise was pregnant. But neither she nor her mother realised it for months. Only Annie suspected what was going on. And only Annie had the beginnings of a solution when everything came to a head.

It was early September when Juliana came to Eloise's room in a flurry of impatience.

'Ellie, come on, darling. You go back to school tomorrow.

You haven't even tried on your new uniform. And you haven't read the books on your reading list.'

'Mum, I feel so ill. Please leave me alone. I don't want to go back to school anyway. I hate it there. I'm not well. Can't I just stay here until I get better?' She felt so sick, so tired and heavy.

Juliana sat on her daughter's bed.

'Ellie, darling, I know you've been unhappy this summer. I'm sorry that your father's worries have affected you. But, you know, I'm sure everything's going to be all right, and I do believe you would be much happier back at school, with all your friends.'

Eloise sat up.

'Mum,' she shouted. 'How many times do I have to tell you I have no friends there? I don't want to go back. I want to stay here with—'

She stopped, burst into a storm of tears, turned her head into her pillow and told her mother to leave her alone.

Chris said, 'So, what happened? What did they do when they realised she was pregnant?'

'Juliana confided in Annie, who'd had time to think about what could be done. She had friends in Plymouth, who could look after a young girl in trouble. But actually, Charles knew nothing. Not then.'

'How did they keep it from him?'

'It was easy. He was totally obsessed with the future of the estate. As long as Eloise was out of the house, he assumed she was at school.'

'Whereas?'

'Juliana had taken her out of her boarding school in Truro, and sent her to live with Annie's friends in Plymouth. Juliana drove up to visit her at least twice a week.'

'And what about Juliana? Was she furious that Ellie had got herself pregnant by the land agent's son?'

'Oddly, no. Juliana was a bit of a free spirit, always slightly bohemian. As long as she could keep it secret from her husband she thought she could handle it and protect Eloise from any consequences.'

'Jesus!' said Chris. 'But what about the baby?'

'Well, yes. That was the fly in the ointment. Young though she was, Eloise absolutely refused to have an abortion. And Juliana, anxious to keep her daughter happy, tried to persuade her to give the child up for adoption.

'Eloise was very torn. She couldn't see a future for her and her baby – she knew her father would be probably be unforgiving – but she insisted he should know about her child, and that she should throw herself on his mercy. She hoped, in spite of herself, he would forgive her, and accept his grandchild.'

'And did he?'

'Of course not. As soon as he found out that Ellie was pregnant, he disowned her. Said she would only be welcome back at Roseland once the child was settled and adopted far from home.'

'So what did Juliana do?'

'She talked to Jack's parents. And they said that they would like to adopt the baby, and take it with them to Australia. Jack's mother had been told she had secondary infertility. Inexplicable, but it happens. She was considering adoption anyway, and taking on her only son's child as her own seemed like a gift from heaven.'

'And that was OK with Jack?'

'Jack was just a child, Chris. He was completely at sea, guilty that he'd made love to Eloise on such an impulse, terrified about the consequences. His mother assured him that the baby would be hers, not his. It would be formally adopted and he would have no responsibility for it. It would be his brother or sister, not his offspring.'

'How did Eloise feel about all that?'

'She didn't know. She went through the pregnancy in Annie's friend's home in Plymouth. She was desperately unhappy. She wanted to keep the baby but she was thirteen, for God's sake. And she knew her father was disgusted with her. He never came to see her in Plymouth, not once.'

It was late. Chris and I had started walking back up the hill toward our cottage. We were both weary and glad to stop talking about Eloise, when our kids leapt out at us from the front lawn, where they were playing an argumentative game of football.

'Mum,' shouted Evie. 'Guess what? Sam's coming down tomorrow. He says he'll be at Liskeard late tomorrow afternoon. He'll call and tell you when the train arrives.'

That was good news. The way I felt at the moment, the happier I was to be surrounded by my family. They had become a thick warm buffer, surrounding me with a quilted blanket which protected me from the crushing cold of Eloise's nightly visits.

Later that night, Chris and I fell exhausted into bed. We held each other tightly until we dozed off.

I dreamed a bulky object was pushing down into my stomach. It was firm and hard and gripped me so strongly that I couldn't breathe. I tossed furiously against the invasive pressure. I moaned so much that Chris woke up.

'Honey, what's wrong?' he mumbled, heavy with sleep.

But I was barely aware of him. I only knew that I was going under again, totally subservient to Eloise's domination of my dreams. And of course I knew from Ellie's diary what she had been through. I'd read her account of her baby's birth. She wrote it when it was all over, and she, heartbroken and bereft, was back home at Roseland.

I'll never be happy again. The last time I laughed was last summer, when I was so in love with Jack. Now he's gone to the other side of the world, and my darling little girl has gone with him. I've lost them both and I think I'm going mad. I'm back home now, in bed. I never want to get up again. I just lie here and cry. My body aches and bleeds. My heart aches and bleeds. I've lost the boy I love, the only boy I'll ever love, and to lose my baby too breaks my heart. When I got home my father told me I would never see either of them again. He told me to forget them both; to thank God I'd been given a second chance to have a 'normal' life. Normal! My life's ruined. He talked about the future, but without Jack and Isabella how can I have a future? My mother was gentler. She said when I'm older I can decide for myself if I want to see them again. I suppose that means when I've left school, when I'm eighteen. But that's more than four years away. My baby won't know me. And Jack will be twenty by then and he'll have found someone else. I can't bear to think of him in love with another girl. It's April now and I've got to go back to school in September. They've told the other girls I've had glandular fever, which apparently is a good enough reason to miss a year of school and that means I'll be a year behind so I won't be able to leave until I'm nineteen.

Nineteen! That's not for another five years. I'll die before then, die of a broken heart, I know I will. Some of the girls sent me get-well cards, which was nice of them. But I don't see how I can ever go back and pretend to be normal. I won't ever be normal again. I'm not the same girl any more. Not the Eloise I was. I was just a child last summer. Now I'm a woman. I've been in love, had sex, had a baby. And I've lost everything, for ever. My father's really ashamed of me. I'm ashamed of myself too. I did something wrong and now I've ruined my life.

I thought I'd never want to write about what happened at the hospital, but if I don't I'm frightened I might forget, and I never want to forget my baby. My waters broke at the home Annie found for me in Plymouth with her friends. It was so weird. I just stood up and then whoosh I was soaking wet. It was all over the floor and they took me to hospital. My mother had paid for a private room and that was good, because I never stopped crying the whole time I was there. They phoned Mummy and she came immediately and stayed with me all the way through. She was wonderful. I was so scared, especially when the contractions started. They were a bit slow at first, so they gave me something to make them come more quickly. I don't remember much of the labour; it was a nightmare. I've never felt pain like it before. Absolute spasms of agony. They gave me gas and air but it didn't help much. I thought it would never end and all I could think of was my mother. I held onto her like mad and it was only her love and reassurance that got me through.

But when it was over, when they put Isabella into my arms, for just a moment I felt wonderful. I felt such love for her, like nothing I'd ever felt before. And Mummy told me she loved me, and that my daughter was gorgeous and beautiful. But we both knew we couldn't keep her. And Mummy sobbed nearly as much as me.

They came for her the next day, the baby's new parents. I couldn't bear it! I cried and cried and begged Mummy to let me keep Isabella. She had tears in her eyes, but she shook her head and took the baby from my arms. Somehow I managed to stop crying and got out of bed.

'If my baby has to go, then I must be the one to give her to her new parents,' I said.

The nurse who had come to tell us that Jack's parents were here gave me a hug and said that she would get a wheelchair to take me to the room where Isabella's new parents were waiting.

As she pushed me along the corridor, I held Isabella in my arms and told her over and over and over again how much I loved her, how much I didn't want to give her away. And I told her that her new parents would love her, because I knew and liked them and was sure they would. And that her real daddy would be there to watch over her . . .

Jack's mother's eyes were full of tears as she took Isabella from me, and his father told me how very happy and grateful to me they were. They wanted me to know that the baby was already as precious to them as Jack, who hadn't come with them. I couldn't feel anything; I just felt so empty.

I went home the next morning. My dad was stern and distant. My milk had started to come in, and that night as I sat in the bath it streamed down from my breasts into the bathwater. I cried and shook so much that Annie heard me and came in. She realised what was happening, and later, in my bedroom, she bound my breasts tight with a bandage. She said it would stop the milk. She was wonderful. I truly think that without her and Mummy, I would have died of grief.

I'd read the diary earlier at Juliana's, and that night I dreamed vividly that I was Eloise, having her baby in that lonely little hospital room. I felt her pains, her labour; her joy as Isabella was born, her despair as she realised she could not keep her.

How can you deal with a loss like that? What do you feel like, your insides raw, your breasts aching for the small new life that has emerged from your body; your own; totally yours, flesh of your flesh? And yet this child has to be given to someone else. This is torture, surely. This is beyond endurance.

I woke with tears rolling down my cheeks.

Poor, poor Eloise.

Chapter Fifteen

When I got up, I couldn't shake off a feeling of foreboding.
I had to get out of the house, so I went to Polperro to pick
up bread, milk and newspapers. Now I was on my way back.
Walking along the familiar cliff path usually cleared my head,
but today I just couldn't get a grip on Juliana's revelations.

Why was Arthur here, in Cornwall? Juliana had written to
Jack in Australia after Eloise died, but Arthur had never even
met my friend. Obviously he now knew Juliana was his
great-grandmother, and that his grandmother was her dead
daughter. But, even so, why had he come halfway across the

world to see the grave of a woman he had never known? And at sixteen, why had his parents let him travel so far alone? Had Eloise left him some money? Had her solicitor suggested she wanted him to come to Cornwall to meet Juliana? Amidst all the revelations of Eloise's teenage pregnancy, I'd been too shocked to ask some of the more obvious questions. And then there was Eloise, or her ghost, still begging me night after night to do – what? Protect her children. But which children? Her twins, of course. But what about the baby girl she had when she was thirteen, who now had a teenage son of her own? Was Arthur included in those whom Ellie was so desperate to keep safe? And safe from what – or whom?

And I was so tired and isolated. I couldn't stop the horrible anxiety in my head, and I knew Chris was getting increasingly fed up with me. And I relied on him, his solid good sense, so much. I accepted that my mind could be fragile, and I needed his strength, his support. And I loved him. But close as we'd been physically last night, I knew he was pulling away from me, exasperated, but also worried that my mental health was deteriorating again. And that gave him power over me, I realised. That was why he had felt justified in trying to drug me while he went out to meet Ted. A wave of fury swept over me as I remembered his betrayal – because that is what it was.

Polperro was busy. It's such a pretty village, as enchanting as a film set, leading down to a gloriously beautiful working harbour. Clustered together are gorgeously picturesque white cottages, close-set, some of them built on stilts over the river that runs through the centre. Many of them are decorated with seashells, painstakingly gathered, and winking at you as you walk by. As a holiday destination, it's idyllic, but its deeply shadowed position in the valley has a dark side. From late October to the end of February Polperro sees virtually no sun. My own edge of darkness echoed its winter gloom as I walked up the village's enticing main street. Bright and lovely now, dark and forbidding for nearly half the year.

I shuddered. I was being silly. Polperro is enchanting, and I love it.

I bought some newspapers, and chocolate for the kids, and headed home. On the way back along the cliff path the heavens opened, and I cursed because I hadn't brought a coat. Hurrying as fast as I could to get home, I saw a man ahead of me, his head bent against the driving rain. I knew immediately it was Ted. He'd reached the War Memorial, where he stopped. He hadn't seen me yet, and I stopped too, glancing around me to see where I could hide. There was nowhere, of course. On one side the narrow path was bordered by a sheer rock face. On the other just a vertiginous drop down to the sea. I sighed. I didn't want to talk to Ted, but it looked as if I had no choice. Either that or wait here getting soaked until he chose to move on.

Reluctantly I walked on down the path. As I neared the Memorial I realised Ted was talking to himself. His blond hair was flattened by the rain, which streamed down his face. At first I thought he was crying, but then I saw that he was actually shouting, raging into the storm, like some mad King Lear. He looked crazy. I realised that if I didn't know him I'd be very frightened. Madmen on a lonely cliff path are not a welcome sight. And there was no other soul to be seen.

Ted had revealed a side of himself to Chris and me that I had never suspected. The language he'd used about Eloise was vile, riddled with suppressed violence. And as I watched him now, I suddenly saw a potentially violent man, full of aggression and hate.

He'd seen me. He stopped his ranting and stared at me with such hatred that I flinched.

'Hello, Ted,' I said as calmly as I could. 'This weather's foul, isn't it?'

He laughed. 'Do you really think I give a fuck about the weather? Suits my mood, anyway. I was looking for you. James at the café said you'd come up here.'

'Why? What's the matter?'

'Didn't your shrink of a husband tell you? That our marriage was a lie?'

'Yes, he did. But it's over now. Come on, Ted. Think about the girls. Stop brooding and try to move on. They need you.'

'Do you think so?' he sneered. 'Pity Eloise didn't agree with you.'

'What are you talking about? Of course she did.'

'Oh, right. So that's why she left me a bloody pittance in her will. The rest is all in trust for the girls. All I get is the house – and that's only until the twins are twenty-one. After that it reverts to them. Oh, and she's kindly left me a house-keeping allowance – a basic living wage to look after them. I get no capital at all. I'm no better off now than before . . . ' He broke off. 'But then you bloody knew that already, Cath. You and Eloise were always in cahoots.'

I was shocked and indignant.

'Ellie never ever discussed her will with me! Of course she didn't. I had no idea.'

'Oh, sure. Don't go all innocent on me. You two were as thick as thieves.'

'Look, Ted, you've gone far enough. You're being offensive. I thought you were grieving, but it's not grief you're suffering from. It's anger and resentment. And it's very ugly. I'm going home.'

I marched off down the path, trembling with anger. But he came after me and roughly grabbed my arm. I turned to face him and felt a sudden shock of fear. He leaned his face close to mine. He looked as if he wanted to kill me and I flinched as he spat out: 'Did you know what bloody Arthur got? Her bastard's bastard? Did she tell you? He got a bloody fortune. *My* bloody fortune. She left it all to him and the girls.'

He was pushing me now, closer and closer to the edge of the cliff. My foot slipped on the muddy stones. This part of the path was prone to erosion. At least twice a year it was closed off to the public while the council worked to shore it up. It flashed into my mind that someone had fallen off around here the previous year, tumbling down the precipitous rocky slope. He'd been lucky. A ledge broke his fall, but he had to be rescued by helicopter. Now the path was littered with signs warning walkers not to get too close to the cliff edge.

As Ted shoved me, I glanced down to my right. Just inches from where I stood the path crumbled, breaking away down a steep and slippery slope. Far below was the sea, grey and heaving in the heavy rain. The motion of the waves turned my stomach. I felt sick and dizzy. What was Ted doing? Was his rage so great that he would push me off the cliff? And then claim I'd had a tragic accident? Would that be his revenge against Eloise for not leaving him her money, and against me for being, as he put it, in 'cahoots' with her?

My head whirling with vertigo, I pushed back at him and he seemed to come to his senses. He pulled me back to safety and let me go, shouting obscenities as I ran down to the beach, then up the steep lane to our cottage. I was shivering when I got home, soaked to the skin. But I was also trembling with shock, horrified by Ted's rage. For the first time I was genuinely physically frightened of him. His hatred of Eloise was so intense, and now she was dead he seemed to have transferred it to me.

I needed Chris, his protection, but he'd left a note on the kitchen table saying he'd taken Tom and Evie to Liskeard station to pick up Sam.

I ran upstairs and into the bathroom. From the window I could see all the way down our long drive to the wooden gate which led into the lane. For a long time I just stood there, staring out at the driving rain, tense with the fear that Ted would follow me back to the house. What would I do if he did? I was alone. Our neighbour's car was not in his drive, and the weather meant the lane was completely deserted. I hadn't seen a soul as I ran back home. Ted had turned into a violent madman and I was completely vulnerable.

Eventually, I relaxed. There was no sign of Ted, and surely Chris would be back soon from Liskeard? I stripped off my dripping clothes and ran a hot bath.

Afterwards, I lay on our bed wrapped in a huge towel. I

must have dozed off, because suddenly I jerked up, aware of voices downstairs. I was frightened it was Ted but then Evie's giggle mercifully soothed the loud thudding of my heart. The bedroom door opened and Chris poked his head round.

'Hello,' he said, smiling. 'You having a nap?'

I tried to gather my thoughts. I so wanted him to hold me, cuddle me, tell me he would protect me. I told him what Ted had said on the cliff path, his rage and how scared I'd been. And that I was mystified why Eloise had left him so little in her will.

Chris sighed. 'I can hazard a guess. You know I told you Ted's not a nice man? Well, he boasted that he'd had a lot of affairs.'

'What? You told me he thinks Ellie was unfaithful but you never mentioned *he* was seeing other women.'

'I would have told you eventually. But honestly, Cathy, I thought that would make things even more difficult between us. Your obsession with Eloise has become the most dominant thing in your life. It's all you ever talk about, and it's ruining our marriage. I dread every day when we have to discuss it. So what if Ted had other women? It's all in the past now. Eloise is dead and you're the only one who can't deal with it. I can't stand to see you like this. You just won't accept how fragile you are, and I'm sick of it.'

'For God's sake, Chris. Ted's right about one thing. You *are* like some Victorian parson, just like he said when you were lecturing about bereavement the other day. You're so bloody patronising. Of course I'm not fragile, not now, and I don't need protecting from awkward facts. First you abuse your medical position to try and drug me and now you tell me I'm ruining our marriage. It's the other way round. For the umpteenth time, I'm not imagining things, I'm not mad, I'm not depressed and I'm not a little hothouse flower too delicate to stand on my own two feet. Oh, and by the way, I don't think you hear me the first time – Ted just tried to push me off the cliff.'

'Don't be so bloody melodramatic, Cath. Of course he didn't. He may not be the nice guy I thought he was, but he's not a would-be murderer!'

'How would you know? You weren't there.' I sounded childish and hated myself for getting worked up.

Chris opened his mouth, then thought better of it, and stormed out of the bedroom and down the stairs. I remembered that the children were here, and I desperately hoped they hadn't heard us arguing. I took a deep breath, pulled on a pair of jeans and a sweatshirt, and went downstairs to greet my eldest, Sam.

Chapter Sixteen

I hadn't seen Sam since Christmas. He'd spent the Easter holidays in the US with a fellow student whose parents lived in New York and I'd missed him a lot.

Tall and handsome, he was the spitting image of Chris, and, like his dad, he wanted to be a psychiatrist. He was at medical school in Edinburgh, doing well and enjoying student life. But his resemblance to Chris was superficial. In character, he was more like me. Of all of them, he had inherited my vulnerability and I worried about him; I dreaded that he might have inherited my tendency to depression. But I'd never seen any definite sign of it; it was more an instinct that made me watch him like a hawk. And right now he was smiling, his face suffused with the pleasure of being with his family again. He flung his arms around me.

'Mum. It's great to see you again. You look terrific.'

I returned his hug. 'So do you, darling. How's Uni?'

'It's good. I'm really enjoying it. Hard work, though.'

'Oh, well,' said Chris heartily. 'No pain no gain, eh?'

Sam had his back to his dad. He rolled his eyes at me. Chris and Sam were at that stage of a father and son's relationship where they constantly locked horns. They loved each other, but each found the other unbearably irritating at times.

I had no such problems with Sam. He was always wonderfully affectionate towards me, and I must admit that the way he sometimes sided with me in family arguments gave me secret pleasure, just as I knew it annoyed Chris.

We went next door to the Talland Bay Hotel for dinner. A big family celebration, the first time we had all been together since Christmas. I was stupidly happy. Everyone I loved, all together, my complete circle of devotion. For the first time since Eloise's death had haunted me in Cornwall, since I'd started dreaming about her, I felt confident that I had some back-up. That my family was whole and healthy.

But, like Eloise, my priorities were my children. That was just a fact of life.

Eve was talking about the gorgeous boy she'd seen on the beach. Like any sixteen-year-old, she could prattle on for ever about fripperies which meant nothing to anyone older. It felt strange that I could now put a name to him. She was talking about Arthur, my friend Eloise's grandson, although of course she had no idea who he was. Tom was sniggering and sniping, but Sam listened to her with complete attention.

'So, Evie, you think this guy is the love of your life?'

'No, Sam. Don't be such an idiot. I was just trying to tell you about this gorgeous-looking guy who's washed up here in Talland. He looks really cool.'

'OK, Sis. I believe you. Can I meet him?'

'No. I have no idea where he's staying.'

Chris and I looked at each other and I decided to be frank.

'Evie, your dad and I know where he is. He was here at the hotel for a while but now he's staying at Juliana's.'

'What? Why? What's he got to do with her?'

'Well, it turns out they're related.'

'How?' asked Evie, full of annoyance and frustration.

I bottled out. I couldn't tell her about Eloise, her baby, and that Arthur was her grandchild. 'Oh, it's just some distant relation from Australia. We'll meet him soon. Juliana's invited us round for lunch.'

Evie was thrilled. 'When, Mum? I need to think about what I'm going to wear.'

'I'm not sure yet, sweetie. I'll fix it with Juliana tomorrow.'

Chris gave me a withering glance. There was not going to be much harmony between us tonight.

Much later, Chris and I went to bed in icy silence. The kids were snug, happy and tucked up, but he and I were miles apart. I hated it. I wanted and needed him so much. I wrapped my arms around him but there was no response. This man was going to sleep next to me, but separately, without any love or warmth: in fact the opposite. Complete hostility.

Was this because of Eloise? Or was it because I was such a mess, a basket case with whom he could no longer cope?

The next day I went for a walk. Not over the cliff but up the lane and round to the church. I had got up early and felt dreadfully upset. Chris hated me. He couldn't wait to be rid of me. I loved him so much, but we had been driven so far apart. And this was all about Eloise. I knew I was risking my happiness, my husband and family because of my obsession with a ghost. I needed to lay her to rest.

So I went to look at Ellie's grave again. To see if it could give me any clues, any insight into her death, and figure out why she was haunting me, driving me mad. I stood and looked at the beautiful blossoming mound, the lovely floral site of her burial, and thought about her death, her complete removal from our lives, from her children's lives, and burst into tears. I couldn't make any sense of it.

'What do you want from me, Ellie? I know about Arthur now, I know about your will. What else is there for me to do?'

I walked into the empty church, sat down and tried to pray.

I prayed for my friend's soul. I asked for her to be granted peace and rest. I asked for help to heal my mind, and for the happiness of my family. I asked for Chris's love.

But mostly I just cried.

I felt a hand on my shoulder and I jumped. A tall man in a black cassock stood beside me.

Father Pete, the vicar who had presided over the renewal of our wedding vows all those years ago. He'd moved away to another parish since then and I hadn't seen him in ages, but I was glad to see him now.

'Cathy? What's wrong, my dear? There's no trouble at home, I hope?'

If only he knew. I shook my head, wiped my eyes, and asked him why he was here.

'Sarah went into hospital yesterday to have a delicate female operation. Well, I can tell you, she's having a hysterectomy and will be away for three months. I'm taking over till she gets back. But listen, Cathy. There's obviously something very wrong to make you so distressed. Do you want to talk about it?'

To my surprise, I found I did. He was always such a kind man, Father Pete. Wise, too. And maybe, because souls were his business, he could help me with Eloise.

Five minutes later we were in the Rectory. He sat me down and made some tea. Then he sat opposite me and waited.

'You know . . . you know Eloise has died?' I blurted.

He nodded sadly. 'Yes, I heard. That's her grave in the churchyard, isn't it? The one with no headstone?'

'Yes. That's why I'm here.'

'You were always very close, you two. I'm not surprised you're so upset.'

'It's not that. Well, it is; of course I'm upset. But . . . it's four months since she died, and you know that we all knew there was no hope for her. She's in no pain now – at least no physical pain.'

Father Pete raised his eyebrows.

I was quiet for a minute. I looked up at him, saw only the wise countenance of a gentle man.

'Father. Do you believe in unquiet spirits?'

He looked at me carefully.

'Will you tell me all about it?' he asked.

'I will, but first I want you to answer my question.'

He sighed. 'Yes, I do. It's part of my vocation to bury the dead, and commend their souls to God. But there are times when I've wondered.' He paused. 'You're talking about Eloise's spirit?'

'Yes.'

'And that's why you are so upset?'

I nodded. ' She . . . she . . . ' I didn't know how to say this without seeming incredibly foolish or deluded. 'She comes to me, sometimes in dreams, sometimes in broad daylight. She is desperately unhappy and afraid.'

'Why?'

'I don't know, but it's something to do with her children. She says she wants me to protect them.'

'From what?'

'I don't know that either. She wants me to do something. She haunts me almost every night.'

Father Pete watched me quietly. 'Have you told Chris about this?'

I nodded miserably. My tears returned.

'He doesn't believe me. He thinks I'm having another breakdown.'

Pete knew about my problems because we'd kept in occasional touch. At once I regretted talking to him. Of course he would agree with Chris. He may have been a priest, used to talking about souls, mysteries, good and evil, but he was also an intelligent, educated man, and he surely knew a woman with mental health problems when he saw one.

Father Pete was quiet for a moment. Then he said, 'Would it help you to know I believe you?'

I looked up sharply, alert to any attempt to humour me. But his face remained calm.

'You believe me? But why? I mean it all sounds so . . . completely mad.'

He shook his head. 'Cathy, I'm not at all surprised you're here today. I've been worrying ever since I got here because something isn't right. I worked in this church for many years, and the atmosphere has changed. I felt it as soon as I came back. That graveyard has always been so peaceful. It isn't now.'

'Have you . . . have you seen anything?'

'You mean have I seen Eloise?'

I nodded.

'No, no I haven't. But I've felt something.'

'What?'

'A restlessness; a disturbance in the air. And in the church, too. A sort of insistent murmur, a nudging, as if someone is trying to tell me something.'

I was flooded with relief. At last, somebody believed me. Not just Juliana, and poor old Winnie, but someone completely outside the situation.

'So, do you believe a person can die, but die knowing something terrible is about to happen? Something only she can put right, can prevent? And even though they're dead, communicate to another living person that they need help?'

'I believe that certain individuals are receptive to disturbed souls. But I also wonder if your friend's spirit has hijacked you. I wonder if, through no fault of your own, Eloise has possessed you?'

I was astonished. What mumbo jumbo was this?

'Father Pete, forgive me, but that sounds like nonsense. I don't believe in possession. That sounds so medieval. Eloise needs me to help her. That's all I know. I don't want to, God knows, but she's made it clear I have no choice.'

'I think you do,' the priest replied.

'What are you saying?'

'Look, Cathy, I think I can help you.'

'How?'

'I can perform a service which will release you from Eloise's demands. Let you be free of her.'

I managed a shaky laugh.

'You sound like you're talking about exorcism. How ridiculous is that?'

'We don't call it that in the Church of England. But we do have a Deliverance Ministry. There is a cleric in every diocese who can cast out evil spirits.'

I was stunned.

'Are you telling me that here in Cornwall it's you?'

He gave me a small smile. 'Well, at least in the Bishopric of Truro. I've done it before, you know. It's more common than you'd think. And it's very effective. It will give you peace of mind, Cathy. And it will help Eloise to find her rightful place, to rest.'

My whole body trembled. I'd been through so much with Eloise's visitations, Juliana's grief, Ted's anger, and Chris's blank hostility. Was it possible that this priest's offer could allow me to escape? That he could banish Eloise and her impossible demands on me? That I could resume my life again, with my family, that I would at last seem to Chris, to everyone, sane again? Normal and happy?

Then reality returned.

'Look, Father Pete, forgive me, but this is madness. I am not possessed by Eloise. Even if there is such a thing, all the horror movies say it's the Devil that possesses people. Eloise is not the Devil. And anyway, although I go to church and I believe in God, I think all the stuff about evil and demons and going to hell is rubbish, frankly. It defies belief. I'm just an ordinary woman, an ordinary mother who is going through a difficult time because . . . ' I gulped. I couldn't finish the sentence. What was I trying to say? I'm an ordinary mother who is being haunted by an avenging ghost?

Father Pete looked at me levelly.

'How do you know that, Cathy? Don't you think it could be Satan who is allowing her to torment you in this way? Evil has many forms. Eloise may not be the friend you know and love. As she manifests herself to you, she could be something else entirely. An entity which is using your anxiety and grief over Eloise's death to make you – well . . . '

Mad. That's what he didn't say but meant.

'But Ellie and I were friends. We were so close. Why would she do this to me?'

'Because it isn't her, Cathy. It's an imposter. Taking advantage of you. Satan is an opportunist, my dear. He takes what he can get. And he senses vulnerability. He knows he can claim you.'

Claim me for what, I thought. Insanity?

And I was going mad, wasn't I? Chris knew that. And it was Eloise who was sending me out of my mind. Perhaps she was possessing me. And it was evil of her to torture me like this, to destroy my marriage, my beloved family.

Maybe the priest could deliver me from evil. And from Eloise.

Chapter Seventeen

'Are you out of your mind?' shouted Chris when I got home and told him. 'What on earth do you think you're playing at, inviting that bloody idiot to perform an exorcism here at our home?'

I tried to stay calm. 'He's not an idiot, Chris. He's Father Pete, the man who renewed our wedding vows and you really like and respect him.'

'Yes, well – that was before I knew he believed in Devil worship and all the rest of that crap. It's utterly ridiculous, Cathy. I won't allow him into the house.'

There was a slight, shuffling noise around the side of the cottage, near the wood store.

I looked up, alarmed. I had thought the kids were down at the beach, but suddenly Sam opened the kitchen door and walked into the room.

I felt embarrassed. How much had he heard?

Quite a lot, as it happened. He stood awkwardly in front of us, then squared his shoulders and looked steadily at Chris.

'Dad. I don't think you should be talking to Mum like this.'

I could tell Chris was furious. I moved in quickly.

'It's OK, Sam. Dad and I were just having a . . . disagreement. We'll work it out. It's just a marriage thing.'

I smiled at Sam, but he wasn't buying it.

'No, Mum. I heard Dad say he wouldn't allow Father Pete into our house. But Father Pete baptised us all in Talland Church years ago. He's great. Tom, Eve and me really like him. I thought you did too, Dad,' he said. And stared accusingly at his father.

Chris was brusque. 'Sam, you don't know what you're talking about. This has nothing to do with you. It's entirely between me and your mother.'

Sam turned to me. 'Is that true, Mum? Is it nothing to do with me? Or do you need some help?'

Chris snorted with anger. 'Sam, will you get out of here,

please? You have no idea what you're interfering in. Your mother is very unstable. Don't humour her. Leave us alone to deal with this latest crisis in her deluded mind.'

And, furiously, he added, 'Do you know she thinks she's being haunted by Eloise's ghost? And that now she wants the priest to perform an exorcism here, in this house? Your mother increasingly belongs in the asylum. We'll leave tomorrow, and get her some treatment to restore her sanity. If it's not too late.'

I didn't know what to say. I felt vanquished; utterly humiliated that Chris would talk to my son about me like that. As if I were truly mad, some kind of reject who ought to be put away.

Then Sam came in like an avenging tiger. He stood up to his dad, and rearing up to his six foot four inches, he easily matched Chris.

'Do not talk to Mum like this. We know she's not well, we've known it for ages. But she's been brilliant, the way she's been so determined to get better. And she has. This Eloise thing, I'm not saying I understand it, but Mum's not a fool. And you shouldn't treat her as one. Whatever's going on here, you should treat Mum with respect.'

Wow! I had a champion. I was deeply grateful, but full of a mother's guilt.

'Sam, darling. This is just to do with your dad and me. I

don't want you to get involved. Seriously, I think you have to leave us alone. Perhaps take my car out to meet Tom and Evie?'

'I will, but only if Dad tells me he won't bully you again.'

Sam moved towards me, took me in his arms.

'Mum. I've seen you so sad, so unhappy, and I've always wanted to hold you and make you better. This Eloise business. I think I can help. And if Dad says he won't stay here when Father Pete comes to the house, then I will, Mum. I promise I'll be here.'

Chris, furious, stormed out onto the patio. Sam, his back rigid, followed him.

I could hear their voices clearly, see the way they faced each other off.

'Why are you humouring your mother like this?' Chris demanded angrily. 'You must know she's ill?'

'Dad, you've been treating her as if she's mad for years. She's not, you *know* that. She's hugely sensitive, and feels things most of us don't, but that doesn't mean she's lost her marbles.'

'Oh, really? So what school of psychiatry do you belong to, then? A sort of New Age discipline, which allows women who believe they're being haunted to think they are behaving completely normally?'

'Dad, I just think you're being too hard on Mum. She may

have a different view on life than you, but that doesn't mean she's lost her mind.'

I could practically hear Chris grinding his teeth. 'OK, Sam. You think your mother's just being "sensitive." Fine. *You* handle it from now. I'm going back to London, to treat patients who respect what I say.'

Sam sneered. 'Is that what it's all about, Dad? Your own self-esteem? How your patients adore you? Is that what makes you believe in yourself?'

Chris elbowed Sam aside, and rushed back inside the cottage. He ignored me and ran upstairs. Minutes later he was back down with his bag packed. He stood in the kitchen and glared at me.

'I'm going, Cathy. I simply can't put up with this any more. I'll be at home in London. You really need to think what you're doing here. Our marriage is hanging by a thread. If you want to save it, you'll have to change. I'm serious. You need to think. I can't live like this any more.'

And with that, the love of my life walked out of the door. All of my future happiness went with him.

I couldn't bear it. I swallowed my pride and fled after him. He was already in the car.

'Don't leave, Chris. I need you,' I begged, pathetically.

'No,' he said wearily. 'It's too much. You've gone too far. This exorcism is the height of insanity. My Catherine, my old Catherine, would know that. I really can't say anything more to you.'

He drove off. Because I couldn't say any more to him either, not now. Eloise was poisoning my life, and I had to get rid of her.

That night I slept badly. But although there was no Chris with me in my bed, at least there was no Eloise to torment me in my dreams.

Why? Where had she gone?

I woke in the early hours, furious that she had destroyed my marriage. But my rage against Chris was just as great. What kind of husband was this, to abandon his wife when she so desperately needed help?

I allowed myself to get more and more angry. How dare he bugger off to London, leaving me with the children? Where was his sense of responsibility?

Tom and Evie had come back from the beach after their father left. In a phone call, Chris told them he had an emergency with a patient and they accepted it. They were used to their father disappearing at short notice. They assumed he'd soon be back.

When I woke up, the younger children were still in bed, but Sam was up. In the kitchen he put his arms around me.

'Mum? It's OK. I'll help with this stuff about you and Eloise.' He couldn't bring himself to say the word 'exorcism'.

'Sam, you shouldn't have to do this. I'm so sorry. I'd like you, Tom and Evie to go back home today, and leave me here to deal with all this . . . mess. Get it sorted once and for all.'

'Mum, I think you need me. Since Dad feels he can't be here, I will be. But I do agree with you about Tom and Evie. They need to go home.'

I felt ill with sorrow. Why was I, a mature woman, a mother, relying on my son to help me through the worst crisis of my life?

It was clearly wrong. I had to get them all away, back home to London.

And should I go home too? Leave all this haunting in Cornwall? Because it was true that she had never troubled me in London. Her spirit, her story, our link was here. I didn't know why, or how, but it clearly was.

So, I could go back to London with the children. Try and work things out with Chris. And maybe, maybe, Eloise's ghost would leave me alone. Maybe her angst would stay buried in Cornwall. And maybe I would never have to hear from her again.

I needed to think. But I was totally dumbfounded. I had no idea what to do without Chris. How wrong was it to rely on Sam? Because I was clear that if I went ahead with the exorcism, without Chris, then the man, the prop I would be relying on was my eldest son. Was this right? No, obviously not.

And yet, what was the alternative? I had to get rid of Eloise. I had no choice. And Chris clearly thought I was mad to try.

I decided to send Tom and Evie back to London on the train next day. Selfishly, I would keep Sam with me, while Father Pete banished Eloise's ghost.

But of course, I had reckoned without Juliana.

Chapter Eighteen

She rang first thing, asking us all round to lunch with her and Arthur.

Evie was ecstatic. As she gathered what was on offer from listening to my side of the telephone conversation, she began a little jig.

'Oh please, Mum, please, Mum, please say yes,' she mouthed.

And of course I did.

Sam drove the Beetle and we arrived at Roseland soon after midday.

Juliana and Arthur awaited us in the hall. She rushed forward to sweep her arms around me, then charmingly greeted the children. Arthur stood shyly behind her, grinning awkwardly as his great-grandmother introduced him to my three progeny.

'Arthur, you've met Cathy, and these are her three children, Sam, Tom and Evie. I thought it might be nice for you to have some people of your own age to talk to while you're here. Arthur is a relation of mine from Australia. He's come over for a while to find out about his roots.'

Juliana was being tactful, sparing my three children from a long-winded explanation of the past. We would tell them soon enough, I thought, and although it was so complicated, I knew my kids. They were intelligent and kind. Eloise's traumatic early motherhood would intrigue them, but they wouldn't judge her.

I looked carefully at Arthur. Yes, I could see Eloise in his eyes. But she had been beautiful, and so was he. It was easy to gauge genetic gorgeousness when both she and he were so heartbreakingly lovely.

Lunch went well. Arthur talked about Byron Bay, where he lived in Australia. The kids were fascinated. Evie was shy, of course, but the boys all seemed to get on well enough. As always the dining room looked exquisite, the table and the mantelpiece festooned with vases of roses.

And the food was delicious. Asparagus with hollandaise sauce, followed by Dover Sole with spinach and new potatoes. And afterwards, strawberries and cream. All beautifully prepared by Juliana's loyal Fowey girls in the kitchen, and elegantly, if slightly shufflingly, served by Annie and Eric.

After coffee, Juliana and I went out into the garden. The children were already immersed in a game of football on the lawn.

Juliana asked me how I was, and where Chris had so suddenly disappeared to. I really didn't want to tell her; the way he left, what he'd said, seemed so final there was no way back. Instead, I talked about meeting Father Pete in Talland Church.

'How is he?' she asked. 'Is he still the same lovely man he always was? He was so understanding, so caring and intelligent. I'd love to see him again. Should I ask him round to dinner?'

I gulped. I had to tell her about Father Pete's proposal to exorcise Eloise.

With huge trepidation, I did. And as I tried to explain why the priest and I felt we had to try this extraordinary experiment, she stared at me in horror.

'What are you saying, Cathy? You want to get rid of my daughter?'

'No, of course not. I loved her, you know that. And I miss her terribly.'

'Then why do you want to use this total nonsense to ...
what? I don't even know how to say it. To banish her, as if
she is evil?'

I wanted to weep. 'No, I *know* she's not evil. But she's
haunting me, Juliana. She's devastating my life. It's because of
her that Chris has left me.'

'Left you? You didn't tell me. He's left you? Why? And
how is it because of Eloise? My daughter is dead, for God's
sake. Surely you can't blame your marriage problems on her?'

'He's left me because he thinks I'm losing my mind. And
the reason for that is ... Eloise is haunting me. Juliana, I'm
in torment. I don't know what's going on. I only know that
since she died, Ellie has been trying to get me to do something. I've no idea what, but she has taken over my life. She's
left no room for Chris or anything else. And now he thinks
I'm mad, with reason, given my clinical history. So that's it.
I have to find a way to restore my own sanity. And if Father
Pete says he can help, then that's good enough for me.'

Juliana stood up, agitated but magisterially cool.

'You must do what you need to. I'm very upset, of course
I am. I know I'm being stupid, but I really thought you had
a link to Eloise. I mean a *real* one, not like the fanciful rubbish inside my head. But as you say, it's your life, and I am
very fond of Chris. I hate to think that my daughter is causing your marriage such problems. Although,' and she looked

at me, 'I'm not sure that it's really Ellie who's standing between you. You have had so many mental problems, Cathy. Maybe everything has become too much for you. Have you thought that maybe Chris is right, that you need more treatment?'

I looked at her, disbelief and despair coursing through my mind.

'I can't believe you're saying this, Juliana. I thought you were my friend, my ally. And anyway, you've felt Eloise too, haven't you? What about *Wuthering Heights*? You told me she left it by your bed, and then I read it and heard her too. You said you felt she was trying to reach you, to tell you something.'

'Yes, I did feel that. I trusted you to understand my emotions, to see that I was grieving for my daughter.'

'But I did understand you, Juliana. I shared your disquiet about her death. And now you're trying to tell me that I'm mad, because I can see Eloise and she needs me? Jesus, what kind of mother are you?'

She gulped, but then regained a steely composure.

'I'll tell you what kind of mother I am. One who has been through a grief you cannot begin to imagine. Oh yes, it's terrific that you can see my daughter. It made me so happy when you told me that, but what's the point if you're just imagining it all? If you are seriously mentally unstable, which is obviously what Chris believes? And I've always had the utmost respect for him. He's a very eminent psychiatrist, and he knows what he's talking about.'

Juliana stood up and swept inside her house. I was shocked. I felt my precarious grasp on reality had loosened yet again. Juliana was a touchstone for me, someone to hold onto in the middle of the night when Eloise was beckoning me towards God knows what. Juliana believed in me, didn't she? Clearly, no longer.

Did I have any friends left?

Sam ran up to me. 'You OK, Mum?' he asked. When he saw I was anything but, he took me to our little car, and ushered me inside.

'I'll get Evie and Tom, and say goodbye to Juliana.' He pecked me on the cheek and went off to round up his siblings.

What an astonishingly kind child he was. I was blessed to have him.

When we got back to Talland there was an austere message on the answerphone from Chris. He told me that he expected 'the children' to be home tomorrow. There was no way he would countenance their presence at the 'outrageous ritual' I was planning.

I was completely isolated. I had no one on my side. I saw my future as a divorced woman, mentally fragile, abandoned by my family, and also by Eloise's. Ted was a vengeful, hateful man. Juliana was furious with me because I had held out hope of an explanation of her daughter's unexpectedly sudden and premature death, a hopeless expectation which I could not possibly deliver.

I was truly alone. And yet? I had my children. And maybe that was the only way forward. Not just my children, but also Eloise's. Wasn't that what this was all about?

I felt a tiny inkling of optimism. I knelt in front of our log fire, lit because the evening had turned unseasonally cool, closed my eyes and begged her. 'Ellie. Just tell me what I need to do.'

And as I looked into the dancing, happy flames, a deep black chasm, full of emptiness and despair, opened up between the logs. And I heard a voice, so faraway, so sad, so full of tears.

'Cathy, oh Cathy. Not much time now. So much you need to know, and I have no strength to tell you. I must save my babies.'

I leaned forward, struck with an idea.

'Tomorrow then, Ellie. We'll meet tomorrow, you, me and Father Pete.'

A long sigh, and she was gone.

Fortunately, the kids hadn't heard their father's icy message about an 'outrageous ritual'. As soon as we got home they went off with their friends next door, two lovely boys totally immersed in Cornwall and its diversions, to go on a fishing boat from Looe. There were mackerel to catch, and who knew what else? Sam went too, and I was glad. He had borne too much responsibility. Whatever I was going through, however it affected Chris and our marriage, I had an absolute duty to keep the children apart from all this. Was I in the grip of some mad hysteria? No! I had to hang on to the thought that Eloise really needed me. This wasn't some romantic Cornish myth; this was real, a challenge she had set me to save her children. I could taste the danger now. It was close and pressing. Of course, if I had truly lost my sanity for the rest of my life I was doomed. Jesus, what kind of future beckoned? I would have to go into some kind of nursing home, plied with drugs, unable to talk to my babies or my husband. Because, no matter how I hated him for trying to drug me, and for leaving me when I needed his support more than at any other time in my life, I still loved him. That would always be the truth.

Later, when they got back from their fishing trip, I told Tom and Evie that their father wanted them back in London the next day. Tom didn't mind – he had friends to see there – but Eve was mutinous.

'Why?' she demanded.

I was diplomatic. 'I think Dad wants to make sure that I

have as little as possible to do – he feels I need more rest and recovery time.'

'But why can't I stay and help you do that?' There was a silence. Then Tom cheerfully piped up, 'You know why, little sister. It's because Dad doesn't trust Mum to be tough enough not to do things for us.' He beamed at me. I smiled back. Better he should think that than the truth – that mum was about to mount a ghost-busting ritual; either that, or lose her mind.

After a supper of the mackerel they'd caught that day, gutted and grilled by Sam, they watched a film, and I stole away to the phone.

Father Pete picked up immediately. I explained that the children were going back home next day, and that if possible it would be best if we performed the – er – service tomorrow night.

I had assumed we would do it by Eloise's grave, or inside the church, but he said no. It would be too public, he explained. His Bishop would never allow that. The Church of England was on sticky ground when it came to exorcism. They did offer 'Deliverance' services but they didn't like to advertise the fact, in case people thought the church was – Father Pete paused.

'A bit bonkers?' I offered.

He laughed uncomfortably. 'Well, you know, we have to be careful that the general public don't see us as being too superstitious.'

I could see his point, but I also thought it ridiculous. I mean, it was Father Pete who had suggested the exorcism to me. Why be embarrassed if he and his church thought it was the right thing to do?

But I was in no position to argue. I was desperate to get the thing done.

Pete cleared his throat. 'Also, Cathy, I think it's safer if we do it in your own home.'

'Safer?' I asked. 'What do you mean?'

'Well, only that these rituals can sometimes be a little unpredictable.'

'How do you mean, unpredictable?'

'It's just that some people can react . . . not badly, exactly, but some individuals find the experience quite extreme. I'm not saying that will happen to you, but it's best if you feel safe in your own home, surrounded by familiar things.'

I was quiet. A warning voice sounded in my head. 'He thinks this could be dangerous, Cathy. He thinks you may freak out.'

It was Eloise. I was sure of it.

I pushed the thought away. I had committed myself to this. There was no other way out of the impossible grip Eloise had on my mind.

Father Pete said he would come to the cottage tomorrow evening, and that I was not to worry. It was all pretty straightforward. I thought that was an odd thing to say, given the circumstances.

Then I told him about Juliana, and how upset she had been when I told her what I was planning.

'I'll call her straight away,' said Pete. 'I'm sure I can reassure her that what we're doing will not harm Eloise. It will help her to find peace.' And with that, the priest rang off.

Ten minutes later, Juliana called. Her voice was cold.

'I can't believe you're going ahead with this tomfoolery. I've told Father Pete exactly what I think of it – and of him. But anyway, if you are going to do something so . . . so horrible, which may affect my darling daughter, then I insist on being there. Pete says he understands, and is happy for me to attend what he says will be a service which will "liberate Eloise's soul".' Her tone was acid. 'I can't believe I ever took that man seriously. Nor that I ever believed you were Ellie's friend. But I'll be there.' And she was gone.

This was not welcome news, though I could see that Juliana was perfectly entitled to be there. For a moment, I longed for Chris to be here, to put his arms around me. I longed for comfort and affection. But I was all alone in a sea of hostility.

*

221

I had a very bad night. Eloise didn't come through to me, but I had horrible dreams; my mother, telling me how wicked I was to even think about bringing Eloise back from the dead. I tried to tell her I wasn't, that I was trying to give us both peace from what was obviously torment for her and terror for me, but she wouldn't hear of it.

'You're a wicked, selfish girl, Catherine. Always were. And always a bit soft in the head, coming up with stupid ideas like this. Look at all those ridiculous dreams you had when your father died. You know, the whole family's always thought your ideas about ghosts and suchlike showed you weren't quite right. I don't know why Christopher married you. He deserves better than you. You'll come to a bad end, you know. I've always said that.'

I woke up, tears streaming down my cheeks. I felt completely friendless. Everything was my own fault. My mother was right. She had always told me I was strange. 'You pick the worst thoughts out of your head, pin them to the wall and watch them wriggle, like worms,' she told me one day in the kitchen of our family home in Manchester. She had been proud I'd turned out to be clever and gone to university – after all, it reflected well on her – but we had never really got on. The love she had for me was conditional. I had to do well, to work hard, to earn her approval. If I didn't, she withheld it. As a result, I had been very soft with my own children. I told them I loved them totally, for ever, and always would no matter what they did. Chris was the disciplinarian in our family. He sometimes told me off for being too lax, but he also knew why. He knew my mother. Sometimes, when we talked about her after her death, he would cuddle me and laugh. 'Christ almighty, no wonder you're a loony.' And he'd kiss me, and make me feel good about myself.

Thinking about Chris made me cry even more. Should I phone him? I longed to hear his voice, but not the cold one he'd used to me of late. If I told him I would come home today, get the train to Paddington with the kids, would he be sweet to me again? Could we get over all this, would he love me again?

But I knew absolutely what his conditions would be. No more nonsense about Eloise. And that could only mean no more Cornwall. Because here I couldn't escape her. And that would mean selling the cottage I had loved for so many years. It would mean my Cornwall, my clear green mornings, my beautiful blue crashing surf, would be denied me for ever.

A small price to pay to save my marriage? Perhaps. But I would always resent him for it. Talland Bay had become everything to me. A small piece of paradise, where, until Eloise's unwelcome visits, I was happier than anywhere else.

I felt a surge of defiance, even confidence. I could have both, I thought. I could have Chris and keep Cornwall, if only I could be released from Ellie's spirit. And that was what Father Pete had promised me. I just needed courage, just for one more day. And then everything would be okay, back to normal. I was sure of it.

Chapter Nineteen

Next morning I kissed Tom and Evie goodbye. Sam was driving them to Liskeard Station, and then, he promised, taking me out to lunch. Evie was furious. 'Why do you two get to go out to lunch, when Tom and I have to go home?' she hissed.

Of course, I knew why she was so cross. It was because she was leaving Arthur here, the boy she was sure was going to be the love of her life.

I hugged her, told her that a few days rest would really help me and that she could come back next weekend, and whispered, so her brothers wouldn't hear it, that Arthur was staying with Juliana for quite a long time. So she would definitely see him again.

Mollified, she kissed me and climbed into the car with Tom and Sam. Lots of extravagant waves later, they were gone.

I didn't know what to do with myself. I felt like the young student in the film *An American Werewolf in London*, as he, not knowing he has been bitten by a werewolf and is about to turn into one himself, pads restlessly around Jenny Agutter's flat as the new moon heralds his transformation. I hoped I wasn't going to turn into anything other than a woman relieved of the burden of a ghost, but I felt strange, nervous and apprehensive. Something very peculiar indeed was going to happen tonight. That much was obvious. Even if the whole proceedings turned out to be nothing more than a risible failure, I had committed myself to a course of action that was alien, not only to my beliefs, but to all twenty-first century philosophy as I understood it. And as Chris understood it. And Juliana.

What in God's name was I doing?

Sam came back, and we went next door to the hotel for lunch. Needless to say he wasn't 'taking' me out. Mum, as always, paid the bill. But I was grateful to him for staying with me, for his gentleness, and refusal to acknowledge that something terrifying was going to happen tonight.

After lunch, he went back to the cottage while I walked down to the beach and, after wandering around the rocks, sat down at the pretty little café for a cup of tea. Staring out at our beautiful cove, I found myself relaxing. The sea was calm, the sun was bright, and as so often in our small, magical environment, nature's warm benevolence was almost tangible. It was impossible to imagine a threat here on our beach, to think that evil had any place in our peaceful hamlet.

'Yoo-hoo, Cathy!' came a voice from the cliff path. I looked up. It was Winnie and her husband Wilf, accompanied by their ancient Labrador, Jasper. I stood up and waved, and they headed towards my picnic table. I asked Neil to bring us more tea, and they sat down with the satisfied glow of an elderly couple who had gone for a brisk walk and felt the benefit.

I hadn't seen Winnie since the Sunday when she had told me that she'd seen Eloise in the churchyard. That had been hugely disquieting. But today, of all days, when I was due to face up to my dead friend in a macabre ritual aimed at removing her from my life, I felt the hairs rise on the back of my neck.

Winnie brought Eloise up straight away. 'I was really hoping I'd bump into you again soon, dear,' she said as she fussed with Jasper's lead. 'Because Wilf and I saw Eloise again this morning, didn't we, Wilf?'

Wilf, always a man of few words, nodded.

'And the funny thing is,' continued his wife, 'we saw her at the exact same spot as last time. In the churchyard. But this time,' and she glared at me pointedly, 'Wilf was with me and he saw her too, didn't you, Wilf?'

He nodded again.

I remembered how cross she had been with me when I told her she could not possibly have seen Eloise. She thought I was implying she had memory problems, and elderly folk hate that. With good reason, I thought. Chris had told me my mind was unreliable when I talked about seeing Ellie's ghost. It's horrible to be so completely dismissed as mad, or in Winnie's case, senile. I felt apologetic, but still could not think what to say.

'It's funny, though,' the old lady went on. 'I tried to speak to her just like last time, but she didn't seem to know we were there. And then she just walked away, but I didn't see where she went. One minute she was there and the next she'd disappeared. It seemed a bit rude, and I never thought Eloise was rude. She was so well brought up, and she's always had such lovely manners. Always happy to stop for a chat if we bumped into each other at the shops in Polperro. Anyway, I was a bit miffed, wasn't I, Wilf?'

A wary expression crossed Wilf's face. He nodded again.

'So I thought I'd try to find her and give her a piece of my mind. She couldn't have got far, not with the graveyard being so hilly and steep. I thought maybe she'd gone into the church, so I marched in after her. She wasn't in there, but that bossy old so-and-so from the ice-cream shop in Looe was. What's her name, Wilf?'

Wilf, still wary, now looked hunted as well.

'Clara Boot,' he said glumly.

'Boot by name and Boot by nature, if you ask me,' his wife huffed. 'Anyway, she was doing the flowers, although what right she thinks she's got to do that I've no idea. She doesn't even live in the parish. So I asked her if she'd seen Eloise, because she'd just been in the graveyard, and then disappeared without saying hello. I told Clara Boot that it seemed to me that manners in this part of Cornwall seem to be on the wane. Too many incomers, if you ask me, and I wanted to have a word about it.'

She paused dramatically, then leaned towards me and lowered her voice.

'And do you know what that old Boot said then? I've never heard anything so wicked in my life. She said "But Mrs Wharton, whatever do you mean? You can't have seen Eloise Trelawney. The poor girl's dead, didn't you know?" Well, I was so shocked I had to sit down. Clara Boot asked if I was all right. Of course I was, but what was she playing at, telling me evil nonsense like that? I needed to get some fresh air, so

I went outside, and she followed me. "Look over there, Mrs Wharton," she said, pointing towards the spot where we'd seen Eloise. "That's the poor girl's grave there. She was only buried in January, so there's no headstone yet. You have to let the earth settle first." Well, I knew that of course. Did she take me for a fool? "She died of cancer, you know," the silly woman said. 'Such a tragedy, her so young and those gorgeous little girls of hers left motherless. Her husband was beside himself with grief." Well, I'd had enough. Why was she telling me such nasty lies? I've lived here all my life. Does she think I wouldn't know if a local girl had died? And then she said, "But of course, you've been poorly, Mrs Wharton. You were in the hospital, and since you came out you haven't been out and about much. That's probably why you didn't know she'd died." Well, how dare she patronise me like that? I've got lots of friends round here. Of course I'd have known if something like that had happened and I told her so. Then she said, with that false look of sympathy she has, "Oh well, dear. It's because you were so poorly. They probably didn't want to worry you." Well, I turned round to her and told her what I thought of her. I told her she should be ashamed of peddling such, vicious, nasty lies. And right there on holy ground. It was blasphemy, I said. Didn't I, Wilf?'

'Yes, dear,' said a wretched-looking Wilf.

Winnie was silent for a minute. Then she looked at me

with tears in her eyes. 'We saw her, you see. Both of us. She can't be dead, can she? Of course not.'

I didn't know what to say. She was pleading with me to tell her everything was right with her world, that Ellie was still alive, but I couldn't do it. I couldn't further upset or shock her either, by telling her Mrs Boot was right. She looked as if another revelation might kill her. I knew it was cowardly of me, but I would ask Father Pete to drop in on her and tell her. Somehow, he would make it all right. So I just smiled, took her hand and squeezed it reassuringly.

'Everything's fine, Winnie. Everything's fine. Go home and put your feet up. You've had a busy day. Hey, we'll have that sherry soon, OK?'

I looked at Wilf. He stared at me meaningfully, just for a moment. Wilf knew what was going on, I thought. He knew the truth, but he wanted to protect his wife. They both got up from the picnic table. Poor Winnie hadn't touched her tea. Shakily, she reached for her husband's arm. I kissed her cheek.

'Look after her, Wilf.'

He nodded, and as they walked away with a docile Jasper on his lead, he turned his head around and mouthed, 'Thank you.'

After they'd gone, I looked up from the beach to the church, perched so peacefully on the cliff, protecting our little hamlet, serenely gazing out to sea. It looked so comforting, so strong, as if nothing could disturb its centuries-old role of keeping watch over us, keeping us safe. I walked up the hill and through the lychgate. And there, to my right, was Eloise's grave. Quiet now. Still covered with fresh flowers. Who put them there, I wondered? I couldn't imagine Ted tending her burial site, choosing the beautiful white and pink roses she loved so much. Not with such anger in his heart. It must have been Juliana. And suddenly I was seized with guilt. I should have offered to look after Ellie's grave. I only lived up the lane, far closer than Juliana, who at seventy-five must find it tiring to come here from Roseland so often. But then, she probably found comfort in looking after her daughter, even in death.

I sighed, stared at the grave, willing Eloise to appear to me as she had to Winnie Wharton. But the air was still, the graveyard deserted and full of tranquillity, the smell of the roses irresistible to the senses. In spite of myself, I felt calm.

Chapter Twenty

It was seven o'clock. Sam and I were in the sitting room at the cottage, trying to pretend nothing strange was going to happen. He had lit the fire and I'd put the lamps on, even though it was still light outside. Warmth and brightness seemed essential. We were about to do something alien, something which we associated with cold, dark terror. Somehow I was determined that what was to happen in my house would follow my rules. It would not be frightening; it would be a celebration of Eloise's freedom, and my release from fear.

Father Pete arrived at the kitchen door. Gaily, in a suburban haze of good manners, I offered him a drink. To my relief he accepted a whisky. Actually, looking at him, he seemed glad of a shot of alcohol. He was pale, awkward, and ill at ease, just what you want when you have in your home a priest in charge of an obscure religious ceremony involving a ghost and Satan. If *he* didn't feel confident it would work, then God help Sam and me.

Actually, it was Sam I was most worried about that night. He was acting like the young host of a parental party, anxious to be helpful, heartbreakingly jolly.

After twenty minutes of small talk, I'd had enough.

'I really think we should get this underway. Can you talk me through what's going to happen, and what I need to do?'

'We should wait for Juliana, Cathy. She wanted to be here. And I think it would be better if we switched the lights off.'

Why? I wondered. Because the occult was necessarily dark? But why was I allowing the occult to invade my gorgeous, homely little Cornish nest?

All the calmness I'd felt down at the beach today, and the peace that had shimmered through me at Ellie's graveside, began to recede. I couldn't wait any longer for Juliana. This was about Eloise and me. Not about her mother.

At my signal, Sam switched the lamps off, although the log fire still continued to burn, incongruously cheerful in the sudden gloom.

Father Pete had brought along a black holdall. From it, he took a purple stole, candles and a flask of oil. I felt suddenly sick. What in God's name had I let myself in for?

I took a gulp of wine. The priest was talking to himself, mumbling over his holy accoutrements. He started lighting the candles, placing them around the room, paying particular attention to the mantelpiece and hearth. Nervously, I asked him why.

'The hearth is the home of family life, Cathy. If we cleanse that, we cleanse you and you and your loved ones of evil.'

Hysteria bubbled up in my chest. This was ridiculous. There was no way I could take part in this absurd ritual. I glanced at Sam. He was obviously trying to suppress laughter.

OK, that's it, I thought. I moved towards Father Pete, about to tell him that the whole thing had been a stupid mistake, and to apologise for taking up his time.

And then there was a stupendous crash. The kitchen door flew open and immediately slammed shut. Terrified I clung on to Sam. There, in my kitchen, in front of the hob, stood Juliana.

And next to her, malevolent and thunder-browed, stood Ted.

His eyes glittering with hatred, he stared at me. 'What the hell is going on here?' he said. I looked at Juliana.

'Why is *he* here, Juliana?' I asked.

'I thought he had a right to know that you were planning something obscene, to desecrate the memory of his dead wife. That you were suggesting she's possessing you, that she's evil, that you need to be purged of her presence. That's pretty horrific, you know, Cathy. And Ted agrees with me.'

I laughed, remembering how Ted had insulted his 'dead wife' when I met him on the cliff path. I was angry now.

'Juliana, he *hated* Eloise, hated her for not leaving him all her money. He told me so. And he threatened me.'

Juliana was implacable. 'I think what you're doing is disgusting, Cathy. And I knew you wouldn't listen to me. So I asked Ted to come with me.'

'Oh, I get it. You think he'll scare me off, intimidate me. Well, you're wrong there. This is between Eloise and me. Nothing to do with him.'

A light breeze had been ruffling the branches of the weeping willow outside. As I said those words the wind rose, and the tree's cascading branches began to thrash, as if in agitation. My mood had completely changed from indecision and unease. Ted's presence had focused my anger. I was determined now to go ahead with Father Pete's procedure. I was sick of threats, fear and broken nights. I turned to the priest.

'Go on, Pete. Let's get on with it.'

Ted stepped towards me, his face ugly with fury. In a second, Sam stood between us. He was taller than Ted, which gave him an advantage, but he was also much slighter. Ted was stocky, his muscles honed from all that surfing.

'I don't think you should threaten my mother,' Sam said quietly.

Ted stared at him for a moment. 'And I don't think she should be desecrating the memory of my wife,' he replied.

'Whatever you think my mother is doing, she is perfectly entitled to ask a priest to help her in the privacy of her own home. You don't belong here. Now go, or I'll call the police.'

'Let him stay,' said Father Pete unexpectedly. 'He will see that we mean no harm.' He turned to Ted. 'I understand your concern, Ted. But all I am doing is offering a prayer for the repose of Eloise's soul. Surely you can't object to that? And you, Juliana. Of course I know how deep your grief is. But stay and join us in our prayers, in this house which your daughter knew and loved, and with the dear friend who loved her, and wishes her nothing but peace.'

There was silence. Juliana had tears in her eyes. She walked across the room and hugged me. Now I was in tears myself. Ted stayed where he was. He looked sullen, but the ferocious anger had subsided.

The light outside was waning. Father Pete began to pray. We bowed our heads.

He prayed for God to deliver Eloise to eternal rest. Then he lit the candles around the hearth and mantelpiece. He wrapped his purple stole around his neck and beckoned me to join him by the fire. Obediently, I stood next to him, and he folded the other end of the stole around my shoulders.

The others, grouped in shadow behind us, were tense and mute.

I felt momentarily horribly self-conscious, and then, more and more I was drawn into the priest's insistent will.

'God, please bless Your servant, Catherine. Please deliver her from torment, and let her mind be at rest. By Your grace, bring her peace.'

He opened the flask of holy oil, and murmured a blessing over it. Then he dipped his fingers into the liquid, and turned to me.

'Catherine, I bless you in the name of the Lord.' And he traced a cross on my forehead.

He held a small ceremonial crucifix before the candle in the centre of the mantelpiece, bowed his head and again began to pray. I listened to his words with reverence and dread.

'Lord, please let Your servant Eloise rest in peace. Take

her to Your side, and release her from the unholy world she inhabits now.'

I heard a murmur of protest behind me. Juliana didn't like that, but the priest's voice grew stronger as he continued his prayer.

'We beg Thee, Lord, in Your infinite wisdom, to allow Your servant Eloise to leave her beloved friend Catherine to go about her business unmolested by evil spirits. We beg Thee to banish those demons which seek to destroy Catherine's peace of mind, and that of her family. Above all, to banish the demon masquerading as her friend Eloise, which is causing her so much heartache. For by Your Grace, we know such visitations are a manifestation of Satan, and must be vanquished.'

His voice grew louder, powerfully confident.

'In Thy name, Lord, I demand this evil spirit, this entity which calls itself Eloise, be banished from this house, and from Talland Bay, and cease to trouble Thy servant Catherine. For this creature is not Eloise at all, but a toy of Satan. In the name of the Father, the Spirit, and the Holy Ghost, let it be gone, to join its devilish master. Thanks be to God. Amen.'

There was total silence. I was aware of nothing but the light of the candles flickering in the surrounding gloom. I felt a little sick. I swayed and thought I might faint. I turned to look at the others. Sam, awestruck by the unexpected power of Father Pete's words. Ted, stunned and disbelieving. And Juliana, white-faced and terrified.

And suddenly all hell broke loose. The wind that thrashed the weeping willow in the garden began to roar. Branches crashed and fell from trees on the roof and all round the house. The noise was deafening.

Even the sea joined in. Our gentle cove became a raging monster. With disbelief I saw waves hurl themselves against the windows of our cottage, which was tucked away in a little hollow half a mile from the beach. It was as if the ocean itself had risen to avenge Eloise's ghost, and marched up the lane to drown us in its protest.

I thought I heard Juliana scream. I did too. But worse was to come.

As the sea crashed and roared against the house, I heard a voice shriek over the stupendous noise. It pierced my ears and my heart. It was Eloise.

'Cathy, no! How can you do this? How can you banish me like this? It's not what you think. I'm not evil. *He* is. I thought you knew, I thought you understood. If you leave me now, my children will die. Please, Cathy, please. I beg you to help me.'

Finally, I fainted.

*

When I came round, a trio of worried faces hovered over me; Sam, Juliana and Father Pete. I struggled to sit up, and they helped me to the sofa, onto which I collapsed. My legs were shaking and my mind was jittery with shock.

Sam brought me water, but Father Pete thought I needed something stronger and gave me a glass of whisky. I gulped it down, and my queasy stomach settled a little. I looked at Juliana.

'Did you hear her?' I asked. She looked mystified.

'No, dear. Hear who?'

I was angry now. All three of them looked concerned, but they clearly hadn't a clue what I was talking about. Hear who? Who did they think I meant? Why were we all here?

'Eloise, of course. You didn't hear her voice?'

They shook their heads, then looked at each other. I knew that look. It meant they thought I had lost it again.

'She spoke to me. Screamed at me in fact. She said I'd got it all wrong. She said she wasn't evil. She said *he* was.' I looked frantically around the room. 'Where is he?' I shouted.

'Ted?' said Father Pete.

'Yes. Ted. He's the problem. Always has been.'

Juliana looked anxious. 'He just left. He was ... well, he was angry. He just said he'd had enough of this ... ' Ever genteel, Juliana looked anxiously at Sam and Father Pete, but then she decided to go for it. 'He said he'd had enough of this "fucking bollocks", and was off.'

'But how could he leave? What about the sea?'

'The sea, Mum? What do you mean?' Sam's handsome face was puzzled and worried.

'It's all around the house. Right up to the roof. Can't you see it?' And even I knew I sounded hysterical. Because, when I looked at the windows, there was nothing to see but the black Cornish night.

'But didn't you hear it? The waves. They were crashing against the windows. It was terrible. I thought we were all going to drown.'

There was an uncomfortable silence. Then Father Pete spoke quietly.

'I blame myself for this. It was a wretched idea to put you through such a difficult experience, when you were so upset and fragile.'

Here we go again, I thought. The old mental illness stuff. But I wasn't having any of it. I blazed at them.

'Look, I know what I saw. And what I heard.' I glared at Eloise's mother. 'And you above everyone should listen to me, Juliana. Your daughter has just told me Ted is evil. And she said that unless I help her, your grandchildren are in terrible danger.'

She flinched. 'Cathy, please, this has to end. You're scaring me.' She turned to Sam. 'I think you had better telephone your father. She needs help. I also think Chris needs to get her out of Cornwall. She should be in a caring environment near your home in London. And then maybe she'll leave me alone to mourn my daughter in peace.'

'Juliana, I beg you. You know yourself something was wrong about Ellie's death. You told me you didn't believe she could die so suddenly when earlier she had seemed perfectly well. I'm on your side; I'm on *Ellie's* side. She's scared for her children. You must believe me.'

Juliana's face was a mask. She looked as if she was struggling to stay calm.

'Yes, you're right about what I thought about her death. But that was months ago, and I've thought about it since. I believe Eloise would have wanted me to help take care of her daughters, and to do that I have to co-operate with Ted. Making a monster out of him isn't going to help anyone, least of all Rose and Violet. And Cathy, you've changed. You seem to be almost unhinged. I just can't stand to see you like this. You're obsessed with Eloise – with this, this – ghost you say you keep seeing. She's not a ghost. She was my beloved daughter. My wonderful memories of her are all I have left. And you're poisoning them, Cathy. You're poisoning my thoughts. I won't have any more of this nonsense.'

She swept out. Father Pete looked apologetic, gave me an encouraging pat on the shoulder, and went to the door with Sam. I could hear their worried voices murmuring on the patio.

So there I was. Alone again.

Chapter Twenty-One

I went to bed straight away. Downstairs, I knew Sam would be calling Chris. Of course he would. Despite his heroic efforts to support me, he was only a boy, worried sick about his mentally ill mum.

I took one of the sleeping pills Chris had left in the bathroom cabinet and I fell asleep in minutes, dreading that I would meet Eloise.

I didn't. But I did meet a man. Someone I felt I knew, even though I'd never seen him before.

This man was on horseback, and he was riding on

Bodmin Moor. He was about my age, tall and blond. He couldn't see me, but in my dream I followed him, down the ghostly lanes, through the night where swirling scarves of mist were draped around gaunt tree branches twisted by the wind.

He was riding purposefully, as if he had a specific destination in mind. When he finally pulled in his reins and dismounted, I knew at once where we were.

The Stone Quoit of Trevetheyan. The five and a half thousand year old burial chamber of Cornish Kings and Princes, the ancient haunted monument to which Jack had brought a frightened thirteen-year-old Eloise, all those years ago.

When I woke, I knew exactly who the man in my dream was. And Eloise had surely sent him to me, as a message, a sign, a map. I had to find Jack. He must be the key to my quest to save Ellie's children.

But I had no idea where to start. Was he still in Australia? Arthur could tell me for sure. And of course Juliana, who had written to Jack after Eloise died. Although I didn't relish talking to Juliana again after last night, I owed it to Ellie to face this unpleasant prospect.

Suddenly I realised that my feelings towards my friend had turned full circle. Until last night I had begun to hate her for causing me such anguish, for destroying my relationship with Chris. That was why I had wanted the priest to exorcise her. But after she came through to me at the end of Father Pete's prayers, I no longer doubted her. I believed her. She needed me. If I didn't help, her children would die. I knew that absolutely; it was a moment of total clarity and conviction.

I felt different, energised. It was as if the swirling mist in my dream had been blown away, removed from inside my head. For the first time in weeks, I thought I was seeing straight. Ellie's ghost was real. She existed in a terrified limbo, tortured by her fears for her kids. It was my duty and responsibility to respond to her, and I wouldn't doubt her again.

It was with an almost joyful heart that I went downstairs, to find Sam eating Frosties in the kitchen. He looked up as I joined him at the table, obviously wary.

'Morning, Mum,' he said tentatively. 'How are you feeling?'

I smiled at him 'Better than I have for a long while, thank you, darling.'

He looked startled. 'I thought that, after last night, you'd be upset.'

'Nope, I feel fine. I'm sorry if I embarrassed you last night, darling. I suppose it was all a bit ridiculous, but believe it or not, it did me the world of good. I feel completely different this morning.'

'Brilliant. So you've decided to let the whole Eloise thing go?'

Of course I had decided to do nothing of the sort, but I wasn't going to worry my son any more.

'Yes, darling, I'm fine now. I just want to enjoy this lovely weather.'

And through the windows the sun smiled down. The grass and flowers in the garden seemed impossibly bright. I couldn't wait to get outside.

The look of relief on Sam's face would have been comical if I hadn't felt guilty at deceiving him. My determination to help Eloise was absolute, but from now on I was keeping it to myself.

'Er, Mum.' Sam looked shifty. 'The thing is, I called Dad last night.'

'Of course you did, darling. I wouldn't have expected anything else.'

'You don't mind?'

'I don't mind at all. What did you tell him?'

'Well, obviously I told him you'd fainted, and then got very ... er, upset and confused.'

'Oh yes? And what did he say?'

'Well ... ' Sam looked uncomfortable. 'He said he wants to come down and see you.'

'Oh, really? When?'

'Today.'

I kept my face calm for my son, but inside I was horrified. I knew Chris would be very angry with me, and I'd hoped for a bit more time before I saw him again. There would be a massive row, a confrontation I'd find deeply upsetting.

'OK,' I said, trying to sound cheerful. 'Did he say what time he'd arrive?'

'No. He just said he'd get away from the hospital as soon as he could.'

'Perhaps you could call him and let him know we don't need him now. Tell him I'm perfectly fine.'

Sam looked alarmed. ' I don't think he'd take any notice of me if I did. He's pretty cross. With me, I mean,' he added hastily.

'I doubt that, Sam. If he's cross with anyone, it's me.'

'He blames me for ... for encouraging you to let Father Pete do his thing here last night. Said I was completely irre-sponsible.'

I sighed. 'Look, Sam. You have been nothing other than a wonderfully supportive son. And I'm sorry I got you into hot water with your dad. It's really not your battle. If Chris is coming down here today, then I'll explain that I was mis-guided last night, but now I've come to my senses. And that you've been a huge help.' I stood up, walked around the table, and kissed the top of his head.

'There is one thing, Sam. Would you mind driving me over to Roseland today?'

'Mum, is that really a good idea? I mean, Juliana was pretty miffed with you last night.'

'I know,' I said smoothly. 'That's why I want to see her as soon as I can. To apologise for upsetting her, and to tell her this whole saga is at an end.'

'That's probably a good idea. When do you want me to take you?'

'No time like the present.'

And within minutes, we were off.

It was a beautiful day. The hedgerows were brilliant with roses and honeysuckle, and as we drove across to Roseland, the sea gave us glad golden winks from the horizon. It was business as usual for Kernow. Cornwall was in holiday mode again. Paradise had revealed its glorious green, blue and gold landscape one more wonderful time.

I was in an intensely happy mood. Even the thought of returning to a stern, accusing Chris didn't alter my suddenly sunny disposition. And even the memory of Juliana's furious face as she left the cottage last night couldn't dampen my skittish thoughts.

Because, as we bowled down to Bodinnick, crossed over to Fowey, past Daphne du Maurier's gorgeous house at the side of the Ferry boarding point, I was bursting with joy. I felt as if Cornwall had opened its heart to me again, had shown me why I belonged here and what I had to do. I was at last totally in tune with my heart; completely at one with what I now saw as the biggest task of my life: to rescue Eloise's children, and to save my friend's soul.

But when we arrived at Roseland, I quailed momentarily. The front door was firmly shut, something I had hardly ever seen before. It was as if Juliana was warning me to keep out. I wondered if I should have phoned instead. But no, she would never have talked to me on the phone; she would have rung off straight away. At least this way she would have to see me face-to-face.

Sam was more than happy to stay in the car. I think he dreaded seeing Eloise's mother again. I walked up to the gravel path, squared my shoulders, and knocked. There was a long pause. Could she be out? But I'd seen her car parked just inside the gate. More likely she'd seen our approach, and was refusing to open the door.

'Juliana? Juliana, please let me in. I want to tell you how sorry I am, how stupid I've been about Eloise. I'm devastated that I've caused you so much grief. Please let me talk to you.'

Another pause, and then the massive wooden door swung open. Juliana stood motionless on the flagged stone inside the hall. She looked thunderously angry. I walked up to her and put my arms round her. I kissed her cheek gently. For a moment she froze. Then she dissolved in my arms, and rested her head on my shoulder, crying quietly. Slowly I guided her through the hall and into the sitting room. I sat her down on the sofa, and settled next to her, stroking her lovely silver hair.

Annie was standing in the corner, her face a mixture of fury and distress. She moved towards her mistress, but Juliana motioned her away. She took a deep breath, took a tissue from a box on a side table, and blew her nose. Then she said, quite calmly, 'I'm quite all right, Annie. Please, would you make us some tea?'

Annie threw a poisonous glance at me and stalked off. Juliana looked me full in the face.

'Cathy, I should tell you that I was very angry last night. I still am. It was so shocking that someone Ellie loved so much could betray her as you did.'

'You're right, Juliana. I did betray her. I can only say I am desperately sorry. I don't know what came over me.' I was choosing my words very carefully. Although I was genuinely contrite that I had made her so upset, I needed her help to find Jack. And that meant I had to reassure her that her daughter was at peace, that I'd been wrong about her desperation. I'd have to keep the truth to myself.

Juliana looked at me. 'You know, although I wish I hadn't

been so rude to you last night, I still think you need some help. You've told me yourself how ill you've been. Surely you should let Chris look after you?'

I gritted my teeth. Time to pretend I agreed with her. 'He's coming back today, actually. I'm sure we can sort things out.'

'Good.' She looked relieved. 'The thing is, Cathy, Ellie was so fond of you. She always said she could trust you with her darkest secrets.'

Then why didn't she? I screamed silently. Why wait until you're dead, Ellie? Why put me through all this angst, when nothing I can do can possibly bring you back to life? But I held my tongue. No point in going through all that again, even with myself. *Especially* with myself.

Annie brought tea, obviously still very cross with me. Juliana smiled at her. 'It's fine, Annie. Cathy's explained everything to me.'

'And has she apologised to you, madam?' she growled.

'Yes, very much so. It was all a terrible misunderstanding, brought on by our shared grief about Eloise. And of course Cathy has been ill herself. It's all water under the bridge now. Isn't it, dear?'

I nodded. 'I hope so. Thank you for forgiving me, Juliana. I'm not sure I deserve it, but I promise you I'll make up for it.' I looked at Annie. 'And I'd like to say sorry to you too,

Annie. You've been so kind to me, and I know it hurts you when your mistress is upset.'

Annie seemed mollified. 'Well, thank you, miss. That was a handsome apology.'

'But am I forgiven?'

'Yes of course, miss. Now I'll have to get on with lunch. Excuse me, madam.'

And off she went. I was feeling bit sick. I knew I'd made a big mistake with the exorcism, that I'd betrayed Eloise by believing that she was possessing me, by trying to banish her, but that was all I regretted. There was still a huge and dangerous problem out there, a direct threat to Ellie's daughters. But I had to be nice as pie to Juliana. I needed to know how to contact Jack, Ellie's childhood sweetheart.

I turned the conversation to Arthur. I mentioned how charming he was. Juliana was gratified, and giggled. 'He is, isn't he? But I'll tell you who he's really charmed by. I do believe he's a bit sweet on your daughter.'

'I think the feeling's mutual. How long is he staying over here?'

'Quite a while, I think. He's thinking of enrolling in sixth-form college here, and maybe even going to university here. Eloise left him quite a bit of money, so he has the freedom to do what he wants.'

'So he knows she's his grandmother, then?'

'Yes, but he's finding it hard to get used to. Isabella, his mother, took it all rather badly when she found out Eloise was her birth mother. She had no idea she was adopted, and was very close to the woman who brought her up: Jack's mother, who died a year ago. So obviously the solicitor's letter telling Arthur he stood to inherit was a shock. Isabella asked her father about it, and he told her that she was adopted at birth in Cornwall, and then brought out to Australia. Obviously Isabella was very upset when her father told her about Eloise. She said she felt betrayed, that she'd been living a lie.'

'When you say Isabella asked her father about Ellie, do you mean Jack?'

'Oh, good heavens, no! She asked the man she believed to be her real father, her mother's husband, the man who brought her up.'

'So did he tell her that Jack is her father?'

'Not at first. He thought that she had had enough of a shock knowing her birth mother was a complete stranger. He couldn't bear to tell her that the big brother she'd grown up with was in fact her daddy. But then he talked to Jack, and Jack decided to tell Isabella the whole story. He thought that she'd feel better knowing that her adoptive parents were actually her grandparents, so they did share a direct bloodline. And of course Jack was her father, so she wasn't an orphan after all.'

'How did Isabella take it?'

'She was horrified at first. Imagine finding out that your big brother is in fact your father? But Jack was very gentle with her, and they'd always had a very close relationship. She hero-worshipped him, really. So she gradually accepted everything. And Jack was right. She was very relieved that the couple who brought her up were not complete strangers but her own grandparents. So she had always been surrounded by her own blood relatives.'

'Does Arthur know Jack is his grandfather?'

'No. He still thinks Jack's his beloved uncle.' Juliana sighed. ' "Oh what a tangled web we weave, when first we practice to deceive," eh? But I think it's for the best. Isabella has had a terrific shock, and at the moment she doesn't want Arthur to know the full truth. She thinks she's protecting him, a natural mother's instinct, but Jack thinks she'll come round in time.'

'What about Isabella? Has she inherited anything?'

'Oh yes, of course. Quite a lot. But at the moment she's very confused. She doesn't know if she wants the money or not.'

'But she was happy for Arthur to come all the way to Cornwall on his own?'

'No, she wasn't. But Jack told her she couldn't stand in Arthur's way, and so she reluctantly let him come. They speak a lot on the telephone.'

'Have you spoken to her?'

'No, not yet.' Juliana sighed. 'I'd love to, but she doesn't want to talk to me at the moment. Maybe sometime soon . . .'

I looked at her sad face and wondered what it must feel like to be rejected by her granddaughter, the child of her own beloved only daughter, now lying cold in her grave. But then she brightened.

'But the wonderful thing for me is that at least Arthur knows I'm his great-grandmother, and we get on really well. He even wants to finish his education here, as I said, if Isabella will let him. And Jack says he thinks she will. Arthur loves Cornwall; he says he feels he belongs here. And for me, just when I thought I had lost everything, that's marvellous.' She gave me a radiant smile.

I was so happy for her. It was the best possible news. To have young life in her house would transform her future. And she was healthy and energetic, and she had lots of help, even though some of it was a bit doddery. I felt gladder than ever that I had made things up with her. But I was curious.

'How do you know all this, Juliana, if Isabella won't speak to you and Arthur doesn't know the whole truth?'

'Oh, from Jack. We talk on the phone every week, ever since I wrote to him after Eloise . . . died.'

Tears sprang into her eyes. I felt mean for asking her so

many questions when her grief was still so raw, but I had a mission.

'Is he still in Australia?'

'Yes, that's where he lives. But actually he's coming over here.'

My ears pricked up. 'To England?'

'To Cornwall. He was upset to hear about Eloise, and now that Arthur's here I think he wants to keep an eye on him for a bit, especially as Isabella doesn't want anything to do with her Cornish heritage at the moment, and she isn't too pleased that Arthur wants to stay. I told you she said she won't stand in his way, but she's not prepared to come here herself. So Jack's coming to give Arthur some family support.' Juliana sighed. 'It's such a shame that Isabella doesn't want to know me. Can you imagine how wonderful it would be if Ellie's daughter were to stay here? But I mustn't be greedy. Arthur himself is a blessing I never dreamed I'd have. Jack arrives this week, in fact – I'll ring you when he gets here, because you really must meet him. Eloise would have wanted you to.'

I was elated. What incredible news. Jack was coming to Cornwall. The dream Eloise had sent me last night was surely a prophecy. I had to meet him, as soon as I could. He was the missing link, the key to Eloise's fears. My good mood this morning had not been misplaced.

There was one thing, though, that I had to raise with Juliana. Ted. I had to be tactful after last night. I tried to think of the best way to raise my anxieties.

'I'm thrilled for you that Arthur's going to live here. It's the best news. But you know, Juliana, you really haven't lost everything, even without Arthur. You have two beautiful granddaughters. Surely they will always be a comfort to you?'

Her face fell. 'Cathy, I know you mean well. But I told you before that Ted won't let me play much of a part in Rose and Violet's lives. He hates me. And now he knows Eloise has left him hardly anything in her will, he'll keep them away from me out of spite.'

Then why, I wanted to shout, did you bring him to my house last night? Why did you enlist him as support against me? But I knew the answer. Juliana had been terrified. She'd thought I was planning to do something dreadful to her daughter's memory. She'd needed all the friends she could get. And by my actions I had alienated her, and driven her towards the son-in-law she disliked and distrusted.

'I will, of course, try my best to keep friends with him. I have to, if I'm to have any contact with the girls at all. Eloise would have been devastated if she'd known how he would separate them from me.'

But Eloise knew, I thought, exactly what was going to

happen. She was trying to take steps to prevent him isolating the twins when she died. Prematurely. She didn't have the time she needed to sort everything out. And that was why she had come to me.

Chapter Twenty-Two

Outside Juliana's I found Sam aimlessly kicking a football about. He took me back home to Talland and I had my heart in my mouth when we went down the drive, scared that Chris might have come back. But his black Jaguar was nowhere to be seen, so I still had a bit of quiet time left.

I knew that when Chris did arrive, I would have to be on my mettle. I was absolutely sure now that Eloise's desperate demands were real, and that her urgent commands to me to help her children were genuine. I'd stopped caring if the world thought I was mad. Or even if my own hus-band did not trust a word I said. I was off on my own adventure and my determination to solve the horrible mys-tery my mind had imposed on me, months earlier after Eloise's death, and her subsequent invasion of my dreams, was absolute.

So, at last, I felt in charge of my own fate. But I had lost a lot of my naïvety. I would dissemble if I had to. I would lie to Chris. I would follow my heart, and maybe, if I saved Ellie's children, I could save myself.

Three hours after Sam and I got back from Juliana's, while Sam, thank God, was down at the beach, Chris's car pulled in by the front lawn.

I stood up, and took several deep breaths. I had to be calm, confident and welcoming. I was prepared for a major row, but I also had to try and show him that I had changed; that my feelings about Eloise were no longer apocalyptic. In other words, that I had seen the error of my ways. And I had to make him believe me.

Chris opened the door with a masculine sigh. The sound meant to imply to us feckless women, who'd been at home all day, that their man had spent many hours on the road, hunting and gathering, and now needed to be praised and cosseted for their virile efforts.

I knew that sound. I also knew that if I let myself respond to it, there would be the most almighty fight. And I really couldn't deal with that. So I smiled, moved towards him, and held my face up for a kiss.

I didn't get one. He glared down at me stonily from his great height.

'Where's Sam?' he asked, with a total disregard for me.

'At the beach,' I replied.

'I'll go and fetch him.'

'Why? He's not a child. He'll come back when he wants to.'

'I need to talk to him,' Chris said curtly.

'Don't you mean you need to talk to me?'

He just stared at me, then turned back to the kitchen door.

'Oh Chris, can't we just sit down and talk things through before Sam gets back? Please, darling. I know I've behaved very stupidly. I'm sure Sam's told you that last night was a disaster. You were right. I should never have got involved with Father Pete.'

I could see him wrestling with his pride. He was gratified that I'd told him he was right, but I could tell he didn't think my apology had gone far enough. I swallowed. Although I had fully intended to appease him, I could feel my temper stirring. I mean, he had drugged me when I was at my most vulnerable, and I didn't remember him apologizing for that.

Oh God, at this rate he'd be leaving again not five minutes after he arrived. I took a deep breath. I would have to abase myself selflessly, however furious I felt. I needed his help as well as Juliana's. If I had to humiliate myself to get it, so be it.

'Chris, love, please sit down. You must be exhausted after that drive. Let me get you a drink.'

Slowly and reluctantly, he sat down in an armchair. Presumably, since we normally sat together on the sofa, to prove that, so far, he wanted to be alone. I poured him a glass of wine. He took it in an ungracious way, and I took my usual place on the sofa.

'What did Sam tell you about last night?' I asked.

He was silent. He was going to sulk. I felt like kicking him. But I had to get him on my side. At last, he stared into the distance, avoiding my eyes, and said in a cold and distant voice, 'He told me you fainted, and then came up with a cock-and-bull story about the sea rising up over the house. Oh, and then he said you told everyone Eloise had spoken to you, telling you her kids were in danger. He also told me everyone was incredibly embarrassed at the way you behaved, even Father Pete.' Now he did look at me. 'I can't believe you put our son in that position. You made him ashamed of his own mother in public. You're a disgrace, Cathy, you really are.'

I gulped. My eyes filled, though whether they were tears of shame or anger I couldn't tell. Quietly I said, 'I'm sure Sam didn't say he was ashamed of me.'

'He bloody well was, and so am I!' Then the anger really exploded. 'I can't tell you what an embarrassment, what a burden you've become to the children and me. Your break-down was bad enough, with the kids seeing you comatose in bed all day. And I can't tell you how much my colleagues pitied me.'

Ah, yes, of course. Chris had been embarrassed by his failure to prevent his wife becoming neurotic. He thought his fellow psychiatrists, sympathetic to his face, were much more critical about him behind his back. And that, of course, affected his self-esteem, and men don't take kindly to that. Pathetic!

'And then,' he stormed on, 'just when I thought our marriage had a chance of getting back to normal again, you start seeing bloody ghosts. It beggars belief, and I've had enough. I made an appointment with a solicitor yesterday, and I'm seeing him next week.'

This was awful. Even worse than I'd expected. And I couldn't control my tears now.

'Chris, please give me another chance. I know I've been a burden to you. I know you've made sacrifices for me, your research, writing your book. But I'll make it up to you, I promise. I know I've been delusional, but last night gave me a terrible shock. It made me realise how close to madness I've become. I really want to get better, I swear. I won't talk about Eloise again. Please, please, help me.'

I was lying through my teeth, but I still felt real despair. I couldn't bear the thought of losing Chris. I remembered his softness, his affection, his sheer strength in better times, and how much I needed him.

I had thought I could manipulate our relationship by playing the contrite little woman. That I could get him back on my side by pretending that what had happened to me wasn't real. If I lied about Eloise, denied her in fact, he would come back to me and we would be as close and happy as we were before my mind started playing tricks. But still, despite my love for Chris, my enduring priority was Eloise. She needed me. She had told me I was her last hope in a desperate race to save her children. And even the threat of losing my husband could not deter me from doing what was right.

I suppose that's when it all became clear. I had known since I woke up that morning what I was going to do. I had managed to appease Juliana, and that gave me the optimistic hope that I could do the same with Chris. But as I watched him, I began to realise that wasn't to be.

It was extraordinary that a couple with so much love for

each other, such a strong family bond, could come unstuck through a supernatural experience. But what if my breakdown, my mental instability was somehow fated? What if I was always destined to reach this crisis in my life? What if my 'madness' had allowed Eloise to create a window in my brain through which she could reach my heart and urge me to avenge her death and save her children? Before the exorcism I had resented Ellie's intrusion into my life, the unhappiness she had caused me with my husband. But now I felt quite sure I was involved in something very dangerous indeed. I had spent so much time trying to ignore her; but no longer. This time I was not Chris's, but Ellie's.

Sam came back.

'Hello, Dad,' he said awkwardly. 'Did you have a good drive down?'

Chris, to his credit, tried to defuse the obvious tension in the room. In a tremendously cheerful voice he painted his journey from London in an improbably fabulous light.

'Fantastic, Sam. Did it in under four hours. Best time this year so far. Do you fancy some supper?' He turned to me, his face strained, including me in the invitation for Sam's sake.

But I demurred. I was too sick and upset to even think about food. Besides, I was sure Chris wanted to talk to Sam about me. I said I had no food in the house and suggested the two of them went out to eat, and so my husband and son drove into Polperro to find a pizza.

I'd already decided that Chris wouldn't want to sleep in our bedroom, so I made up the bed in my little writing cabin, at the top of the garden. It was really just a glorified shed, a sanctuary for me to escape to when I was writing my magazine articles, and I hadn't used it for many months now. But it had a single bed, electricity, running water, even a little bathroom. And a tiny TV.

When Chris and Sam came back from the village, I told Chris he could sleep in the cabin. Sensing the wave of fury from his dad, Sam disappeared to his bedroom downstairs.

'I will not sleep in your fucking cabin, Cathy,' Chris said savagely. 'What do you think I am? A disgraced husband to be banished from our bed? *You* can sleep in the bloody cabin. I'm going to sleep in my own bed. And the only reason I'm staying is because I'm so knackered after driving down from London. I've cancelled patients for the rest of the week, and Tom and Evie are getting the train down on Friday. So, I'm taking possession of my own home, Cath. The cottage *I* paid for, do you remember? While you were fiddling around with your farty little articles that paid zilch? Oh, and I paid for the London house too. So I really don't think you have any right to tell me where to sleep. In fact, I'd say you need a solicitor, pronto.'

And with that, he stormed off to bed.

Chapter Twenty-Three

I lay awake in the narrow bed of my little writing house. There was a full moon, and I left the curtains open to watch it. The soft silver light was so beautiful, illuminating my little desk by the window, reminding me, but gently, of the dreams I had had of writing novels, and the hours I'd spent with Eloise talking about Daphne du Maurier. The wind was up again, but it didn't sound threatening like last night. It sang a lullaby to which I gradually succumbed.

'Aah, you remember those times, don't you, Cathy? When we would sit here, just the two of us, drinking wine, talking about our favourite books, and how we both longed to write a novel? Well, you will, Cath. When all of this is over, you will.'

I smiled in my sleep. Lovely, soft Eloise. How could I ever have thought her threatening?

'And you're on my side now, Cathy. You have lost your fear. And that gives me strength. When you meet Jack, everything will become clear. And after you have helped me, I can rest. And you can rest as well. Don't worry about Chris. He loves you, truly loves you. You are so blessed. Everything will be fine, my dear, dear friend. We will both be happy. Believe me, Cath.'

I woke up, still in a dreamy frame of mind. I couldn't face Chris just yet, so I decided to have breakfast at the beach café and wandered down the lane to the sea. Although it was early, there were already families on the sands. I sat at one of the wooden tables outside, and ordered tea and a bacon sandwich. I watched the little ones with amused affection, lost in hazy memories of early motherhood, wishing they were my babies splashing around in the tranquil surf, and that Chris and I had no more complicated a relationship than that of loving parents, trying to do our best for our gorgeous children.

A shadow came between the sun and me. I looked up; a tall, thin figure dressed in black was already seating himself at my table. Father Pete. I felt enormously embarrassed.

He smiled at me. 'Hello, Cathy. How are you?'

I laughed bitterly. 'Oh, you know, Father. Mad.'

Now he frowned. 'Don't say that. It's not true. You shouldn't keep putting yourself down.'

I sighed. 'Well, if I'm not mad, what on earth explains my behaviour the night before last? Hysteria?'

'You were obviously overwrought, but the mistake was mine for misjudging the situation.'

'Meaning that you hadn't realised quite how batty I was when you suggested the exorcism?'

'No, I don't mean that at all. What I think is that I was too quick to dismiss your initial concerns about Eloise. I'm a priest, Cathy, and sometimes we get things wrong. I've held services of Deliverance before, and they can be astonishingly effective. But that's because the person I'm trying to help genuinely believes they are possessed by evil. And you don't. Your motive in trying to help Eloise is totally Christian. You want to intervene in a situation which, however unlikely, you yourself, not just your friend, believe poses a genuine threat to her children. Now, because Eloise has passed on, nobody believes you. Especially given your recent medical history. But I see a deep sensitivity in you. A rare intuition. And I don't think you're mad at all. But because you feel things so much more deeply than most of us, sometimes it's more than your mind can take.'

He took my hand and looked into my eyes. 'I think you are someone very special. Someone with a unique degree of empathy, which sometimes makes you suffer. And you need support, not judgement; certainly not condemnation.'

'Thanks, Pete. But, you know, welcome as your support is, and I mean no disrespect, the fact that my husband is so completely pissed off with me that he's talking about getting a divorce means that my life, because of all this, is ruined. But that's why I agreed to the exorcism. I thought it would get rid of the haunting and let me find happiness with Chris again.'

'Would you like me to talk to him?'

Good heavens no, I thought. If the priest talked to Chris I knew there would be carnage.

'Pete, you are very kind. But I'm afraid it's gone beyond that. Chris thinks I'm potty, and a disgrace to him and our children. With the best will in the world, you aren't going to persuade him I'm sane by telling him I have Christian values.'

He smiled ruefully. 'No, of course I see that. Well, I won't approach Chris. But I want you to know that I'm on your side. I made a mistake the other night, and you may need my help. Please call me if you need me.'

He got up and walked back up the hill to the church. I did feel grateful, although I was sceptical that anything Pete could do would help me in Eloise's vast enterprise. Because

I now had a glimpse of the scale of it. And it was daunting beyond belief.

Now I had to decide what to do next. I longed to see Chris, my old Chris, the Chris who would cuddle me, take me to bed, reassure me that I was great, that I was pretty and desirable. I hadn't felt either for ages. When you're depressed, the first thing you lose is self-esteem. Anyway, it was obvious I wasn't going to get any comfort from Chris, so I decided to call a cab to take me out to Bodmin Moor.

As soon as I got back to the cottage, I realised how futile this was. Where would I go on the moor? Ask the driver to take me on a tourist excursion? Ridiculous. I opened the kitchen door, dreading seeing Chris. He was there, lounging on our little yellow sofa, reading the papers. I cringed, expecting the inevitable verbal assault. But to my amazement, he looked up from the *Telegraph* and smiled. For the first time in what felt like weeks, my husband smiled at me.

'Hello,' he said, almost shyly. 'Would you like to go out to lunch?'

'Why?' I asked, stupidly.

'Because it's nearly lunchtime, and you must be hungry. You didn't eat last night.'

'I had a bacon sandwich at the beach earlier.'

'Even so. Let's go out. Just the two of us. We need to talk.'

'That's not what you said last night.'

'I know, but I was tired and angry. I bitterly regret what I said.'

No apology, though, I thought bitterly. Then I caught myself. He was in a conciliatory mood. Don't poison it, you stupid woman, I told myself. Take him at face value. For now.

We drove to our local pub, the Jubilee Inn in Pelynt. Thank God it was a short drive, not much more than five minutes from our cottage. Even so, it was an awkward journey, both of us anxious to avoid the subject of Eloise. Instead we talked disjointedly about the children, about Tom and how well he'd settled down at university, about the good results we expected from Evie's GCSEs. But the tension in the car was palpable, stifling, and it was a miserable drive. We were both unhappy, unsure about where we stood. Our communication was brittle, of course it was. We hardly knew each other at the moment. He was worried about his career, the book he was so behind in writing, and, above all, his marriage, probably wondering if he was now no longer in love with his wife. I knew I was still in love with my husband, but I was likely to lose him because of my devouring interest in a ghost, and I was still angry with him for drugging me, for talking about divorce.

When we got to the pub, we sat outside in the garden. Chris ordered a crab sandwich, but I went for comfort food: scampi and chips. After we ordered, the waitress brought us some wine. When she'd gone, Chris raised his glass to me.

'To us,' he said, with yet another smile.

I was astonished. Where had all this bonhomie come from? I awkwardly toasted him back, then said, 'Chris, I'm sorry, but I really don't understand why you're being so nice to me today. I mean, last night you were . . . ' I trailed off.

'Horrible?' he suggested. I just nodded.

'I know, Cathy. I'm sorry. Like I said, I was very angry, but I shouldn't have spoken to you like that. Sam really told me off over supper in Polperro. At first I was furious with him, too, but after we got back and you'd gone to sleep in the cabin, I began to think about what he said.'

I felt enormous relief sweep over me. Sam clearly hadn't told Chris he was ashamed of me, then.

Chris continued. 'When I was in bed, I started to think of everything you've been through. And how I, of all people, a practicing psychiatrist, should know about that. I deal with people like you all the time. And to them, I'm sympathetic and non-judgmental. How appalling that I should be so much less of a rock, for you, my wife, than I am for them.' He paused. 'Actually, it was Sam who said that to me. And I feel really ashamed. I'm sorry, Cath.'

I held my breath. I tried to think of something nice to say

to him, but I felt nothing but confusion – and, yes, appre-hension. I didn't know what was coming next.

'And now you've told me you no longer think Eloise is haunting you, and you realise how deluded you've been all these months, then I think, I really do think there's a good chance I can make you better. Of course it will take time, but once you're away from here and back in London we can get really stuck into some excellent therapy. Just as long as you truly know there's no such thing as ghosts. I can't be doing with that again.'

My mind was racing. Of course I'd lied to him that I was free of Eloise, but something much more threatening was contained in his words.

'Thank you for saying that, Chris. I know this has been hard for you. And you're right.' I forced myself to chuckle. 'I won't be seeing any more ghosts. But I hope you don't mean we need to go back to London straightaway?'

'Well, not immediately. Tom and Eve are coming down tomorrow, and I know they're looking forward to a long weekend. But after that, I see no reason why we shouldn't all go back together. We'll shut the cottage up for the summer, and then I think we should put it on the market.'

Sell our little house? Take me away from Talland Bay for ever? No, I would never let that happen. Chris was looking at me.

'Cathy, I know you don't want to leave Cornwall. But honestly, there's no other choice. This place is bad for you. I've always thought your fascination with mysticism made you vulnerable, and since we've been spending so much time down here, it's become an obsession. I need to get you back to the land of the living, to the practical day-to-day stuff of running a home, taking care of the kids, and getting a job again. I can't do that while you're spending so much time down here, so I'm going to have to insist we put this place, beautiful as it is, behind us.'

Here it was. The ultimatum I had known was coming. It was absurd, though. I knew I would never leave Cornwall. But I had to be cunning. I needed to buy time to talk to Jack and keep Eloise's children safe.

I pretended to be deep in thought. Then I said, 'All right, Chris. I'm sure you're right. We'll go back to London some-time next week.'

I was crossing my fingers behind my back. Childish and wrong, I know, but there was no way in the world that I was abandoning Cornwall, no way in the world I would let down Eloise.

That night we shared a bedroom again. But nothing else. Although he did put his arms around me after we'd gone to bed, I couldn't bear it. We were so far apart, it was like hug-ging a stranger. I murmured that I was too tired, the age-old excuse, and with an annoyed grunt he accepted it, turned over and went to sleep.

I tried to relax, but knew everything was coming to a head. I could feel it. I was glad my family was here, but I had less than a week to sort this out. In a few days, Eloise's battle would be fought.

Chapter Twenty-Four

On Saturday, Juliana called. 'Jack's here,' she said happily. 'He's anxious to meet Eloise's friends. So what about lunch sometime soon?'

'Here, tomorrow. Sunday lunch. You've cooked for us far too often lately.'

'Darling,' she laughed. 'You know I can't cook. It's not me that does the kitchen slavery bit.'

'I know, but please come here. I can't promise you Heston Blumenthal, but I'll do my best to produce a decent roast.'

'Is it OK if I bring Arthur as well as Jack? He's awfully keen to see Evie.'

'Juliana, if you didn't bring Arthur, Evie would hyperventilate. Suffice it to say there would be no joy at our table tomorrow.'

'Great. We'll see you at around one tomorrow.'

Chris was not best pleased about my planned Sunday lunch. He was fond enough of Juliana, but thought the presence of Arthur and Jack would be an uncomfortable reminder of Eloise. I told him that it was only polite to invite them, and besides, he knew Eve had a crush on Arthur. That didn't go down well, to say the least. Like any other father, Chris was deeply suspicious of boys who liked his sixteen-year-old daughter, and the fact that Arthur was Eloise's grandchild made him even more uncomfortable. He harrumphed a bit and I laughed at him, and for a while, everything seemed back to normal. Me teasing him, him pretending to be grumpy, the kids happy to see us happy. We had a lovely day that Saturday, actually, and I began to allow myself to hope that Chris wouldn't sell the cottage after all. We went shopping for the next day's lunch and later I watched him kicking a ball around with Tom and Sam on the front lawn, and couldn't believe he would part with this place and its wonderful memories of the children when they were babies. We'd always said we'd never sell; we wanted to watch our grandchildren grow up here, and to leave the house to our three kids when we finally passed on ourselves.

Evie and I were sitting right at the top of the garden. From here you could see the sea and the church. It was perfect, such a beautiful spot. Eve seemed to pick up on my thoughts. 'Oh, Mum. I love it here. We'll never leave it, will we?'

'Not if I've got anything to do with it,' I muttered.

She looked puzzled. 'What do you mean? Dad loves it too, doesn't he?'

I cursed myself for making her anxious. Maybe it would have been more responsible if I'd told Evie at least part of the truth. But what could I say? She knew nothing about Eloise's roaming ghost, and I wouldn't dream of involving her. It was bad enough that Sam knew about his mother's mental problems, without my baby being upset about them too.

'Yes, of course he does, darling. I just don't think he loves it quite as much as I do, that's all.'

She looked knowing.

'Men!' she said, in an attempt to sound sophisticated. 'They really don't get it most of the time, do they?'

I wanted to laugh.

'No, dear. They don't, I'm afraid. Still, they have their uses.'

She cradled her head in her hands.

'Mum?' she said softly. 'Do you think Arthur likes me?'

'I know he does, baby. Juliana says he's pretty keen.'

She blushed and giggled. 'What shall I wear tomorrow?'

'Something casual. You don't want him to think you've made too much of an effort. Just jeans, I think, and a pretty top.'

She nodded thoughtfully. 'How long do you think he'll stay in Cornwall?'

I thought carefully about what to tell her. I didn't want to raise her hopes too high. On the other hand, Evie might be a useful weapon in my campaign to convince Chris to keep the cottage. So I told her the truth.

'Actually, love, he's planning to stay for quite a while. Juliana told me he wants to go to sixth form college in Truro next term. And, if he does, he'll live with her.'

Evie hugged herself. 'That's amazing. So I can see him more or less whenever I want? Maybe even every weekend?'

Whoa, I thought. This could get out of hand quickly unless I put a brake on it.

'I don't know about that, sweetheart. There is the small matter of sixth form in London for you.' She looked crest-fallen, and I relented. 'Look, I'm sure you'll be able to keep in touch. I mean, you're mad about texting, and there's always Facebook.'

'I know, but it's not the same as hanging out with him. You'll come down with me sometimes at weekends, won't you, Mum?'

'Course I will,' I said heartily. 'Now, what shall we do about supper? Fish and chips from Looe okay?'

Evie couldn't have cared less.

'Whatever,' she said dreamily, and we walked down to join the boys.

That night, after a peaceful evening watching a DVD, Chris and I went to bed. Unlike the previous night, there was no awkwardness. We chatted happily enough about the children, amused by Evie's crush on Arthur, and read companionably, side-by-side. Eventually, we put the light out.

I couldn't help but feel tense. I tried very hard to yawn and generally indicate that I wanted to go straight to sleep. But Chris was insistent. He put the light back on and said, very softly, 'Cathy, we need to get back to normal. Let me hold you.'

'But you think I'm mad. Why would you want to make love to a woman you have so little respect for?'

'I have *every* respect for you, Cathy. You are extraordinarily clever and perceptive. It's just we've been through a hard time, and I'm well aware that some of it has been my fault. I love you, and I want us to get back to how we were.'

Somehow, we did.

I went to sleep feeling soothed and happy. And I managed to persuade myself everything was going to be fine. Just one night with my family, my children harmonious, and my husband loving me, had restored my faith in our future. Us. Just the five of us, as deeply entwined as we had always been.

Eloise's voice nudged into my sleep.

'Cathy, tomorrow you will meet Jack. This is it, Cath. He will show you what needs to be done. And he is so wonderful. He was always everything to me.'

Everything? What about her babies, Rose and Violet? Isabella and Arthur? What about Ted, for God's sake? But these were minor quibbles. Tonight, I felt soft, safe, loved. In Chris's arms, I was no longer threatened by my friend's insistent demands.

Chapter Twenty-Five

The next morning was chaos. I had to cook lunch for eight, and I was a lousy cook now. But I'd been really good in the old days and I was determined that the meal I produced today would at least be memorable. I suppose I had a lot to prove.

I'd been careful to get all the ingredients from Fowey, and the beef from Kittow's Butchers was always superb. But I was on edge, which made me grumpy. The boys teased me about it, which simply made me cross, but Chris, after our tender night, was helpful and attentive, and Evie was a treasure. She peeled the potatoes and parboiled them. Meanwhile I mixed the batter for the Yorkshire pudding and put it to chill in the fridge. I asked Tom and Sam to lay the table, which they did with much bickering. I felt obliged to try and copy Juliana's fabulous hospitality, so there had to be vases of beautiful flowers on every surface, three perfect courses for lunch, and port or liqueurs afterwards. But it's a bit difficult serving up a faultless, aspirational meal in an open-plan kitchen, where all the pots, pans and general detritus of cooking are on general view. Evie told me to stop fussing.

'What is it with you, Mum?' she hissed, as I was tearing my hair out about the floral arrangements. 'Juliana has known you for years. She won't give a stuff about the table decorations. She knows you haven't got servants. And for heaven's sake, Ted and Eloise lived like hippies. I can't ever remember a meal with them that wasn't like a rushed, squashed picnic.'

She was right, of course. I was being over-fastidious, not because of Juliana, but because I was nervous about meeting Jack. Eloise had given him a pretty big build-up.

Eventually the house looked presentable, even pretty. Chris had lit the fire, albeit grumpily.

'But it's far too warm for a fire today, Cathy. You must be mad.'

I chose to ignore the obvious insult. And, to be fair, he looked at me, stricken, after he said it, and obediently piled the logs onto the hearth.

And suddenly, they were here. Crowded into our sitting room, Juliana, Arthur and Jack. Chris and I busied ourselves with serving drinks. Evie busied herself with staying as close as possible to Arthur.

And then everyone sat down and gathered their thoughts. It was as if some bossy, celestial voice had shouted: 'AND RELAX.'

There was a small silence. And then I looked properly at Jack. And I knew, instantly, why Eloise had loved him. I almost fell in love with him myself, after that one long glance.

He was gorgeous. Blond and tanned as you would expect of a Cornish boy turned Aussie surf-hunk. With beautiful blue eyes and a wide, generous smile. It was obvious why Eloise had married Ted. She clearly had a type, and Ted had reawakened her passion for Jack when she met him. But as we talked, it became obvious Jack was no beach bum. He had qualified as a doctor in Byron Bay, and had specialised in treating cancer patients. How ironic, I thought. I wish he could have treated Eloise.

We sat around our big oak table, and Eve and I served up the starters, smoked salmon and prawns. Not the most adventurous beginning, but we had an excellent fishmonger in Fowey so I knew it was really good quality. Chris poured the chilled white wine.

Obviously I hadn't told the children about Jack and Arthur's relationship with Eloise. As far as my three were concerned, the two men at our table were just distant relatives of the Trelawney family. Juliana seemed on top of the world. She sparkled in a way I hadn't seen since before Ellie died.

Chris carved the beef. It looked fabulous, pink and moist. In fact, the whole course was a triumph; the Yorkshire pudding was crisp and gorgeous, the roast potatoes, parsnips and sprouts beyond my wildest dreams. Perhaps I should cook more often, I thought to myself smugly.

By now the red wine was going down a treat. I had deliberately seated Arthur next to Evie, and they were lost in a conversation that was, by turns, solemn and giggly. Chris and Jack were in earnest discussion. They were talking about the British NHS, and the way they ran things in Australia. Juliana and I just beamed at each other. What a lovely day, what a perfect occasion.

And then there was a perfunctory knock on the kitchen door. As always unlocked, it then flew open and in spilled two tiny girls, followed immediately by Ted.

Rose and Violet screamed with joy when they saw Juliana, Eve and the boys. We all leapt up immediately to welcome and cuddle them. But Ted just stood by the door, a saturnine leer on his face.

'Well, well, well,' he said sardonically. 'And there's me

thinking it's a nice Sunday afternoon, the girls are a bit lonely, I'll go and take them to visit some old friends. Only to find you all got there before me. Here you all are, having a lovely lunch, and the only person who wasn't invited was me. And the twins, of course.' He turned to his mother-in-law. 'Now, Juliana. Are you going to introduce me? That young man sitting next to Evie is, I presume, the sainted Arthur. Who is going to get so much of my wife's money. But who is *he*?' he asked, staring at Jack. 'Could it possibly be the legendary Jack, her teenage lothario? I think I should be told, don't you?'

There was silence for a minute. Then Chris stood up.

'Ted, I think we should go outside. You really can't come in to our house and insult people like this. I won't talk to you in here; there are too many people to upset.'

'Oh, really? You think people can't bear to hear the ugly truth, eh? Well, you know, so many secrets have been kept from me that I don't have much sympathy for toeing the line with you bastards right now.'

'Ted, for heaven's sake,' said Chris. ' Don't talk like this in front of your daughters. You should save your grievances for grown-ups.'

'Right, then. I'll take you, Arthur and Jack outside right now.'

I was absolutely livid. This was my lunch party he was spoiling.

'Ted, you're being ridiculous. Now sit down and have a glass of wine. Please, this just a family lunch. I'm sorry I didn't invite you but you'll remember that the last time I saw you we didn't part on good terms. To say the least.'

'Oh sure, I remember that. You were screaming about the sea rising up to drown us all, and shouting about Eloise. Really sane, I thought. What a wonderful wife you have, Chris. Mad as a hatter, but still quite pretty. Lucky old you.'

Eve and Tom were staring at me open-mouthed. Eve spoke first.

'What does he mean, Mum? What's this about the sea trying to drown us?'

'Nothing, darling. Look, Ted's obviously intent on spoiling lunch so would you three mind taking the girls downstairs to watch CBeebies? And Arthur too, of course.'

Arthur grinned, apparently unfazed by the angry stranger in our midst.

'D'you think I'll enjoy CBeebies, Evie?'

She turned to him in relief.

'Idiot,' she said happily. 'Well, maybe you will, because it's for very small brains.'

Laughing, they scooped up the little ones and made for the stairs. Tom and Sam followed, although Sam seemed reluctant to leave. He gave Ted a hard glance. As they disappeared down the stairs, I caught a strange, hungry look on

Jack's face. Probably the twins reminded him of Eloise, I thought. They did look astonishingly like her.

Again I asked Ted to sit down. Juliana backed me up and poured him some wine. Chris looked belligerent, Jack politely curious. Ted did sit down, albeit with bad grace. He stared at Jack.

'So,' he said. 'You're Jack, eh? My wife's first love.'

Juliana leaned forward.

'Ted, please be careful what you say. Arthur has no idea that Jack is his grandfather.'

'I know. It's good old Uncle Jack to him, isn't it? Don't worry; I won't spoil the comfortable illusion by telling him the sordid truth. Which is that you got my wife pregnant when she was just thirteen. Although, God knows, I could have done with a bit more honesty from her. Until a short time ago I had no idea Eloise was a promiscuous adolescent. Nor did I have a clue that she had a grandson to whom she was planning to leave a quarter of her fortune, let alone, of course, a magnanimous bequest to her bastard daughter. Yes, she was very loyal to her progeny. Pity her benevolent instincts didn't extend to her poor bloody husband.'

Jack stayed silent. He just stared at Ted, who was almost out of control.

Juliana was no longer conciliatory. She was bristling with anger.

'How dare you talk about my daughter like that! Eloise was a naïve young girl – she was never promiscuous. She and Jack made a mistake one night, that's all; and although Jack's parents adopted her baby daughter and brought her up in Australia, Ellie never got over it. She thought about Isabella every day. And when she heard she had become a grandmother, all her instincts made her want to accept responsibility. Of course she wanted to see that Arthur was provided for.'

'Oh yes, good old responsible Eloise,' Ted spat. 'Such a kind-hearted woman. It's a pity she didn't show the same sense of responsibility to me, though, the father of her daughters. I mean, what am I, just a bloody sperm-donor?'

It was my turn now.

'Ted, I said to you before, that day on the cliff path, that you are consumed with self-pity. What sort of man rants at his dead wife because she hasn't left him all her money? You've got the house, and a decent income to live on while the girls grow up. And you're a successful artist. Don't you think all this fury is beneath you? Where's your dignity? And where's your grief for Eloise? Your pity for the brave way she fought that horrible disease? And for the dreadful way she died?'

There was silence. Ted looked – well, I wish I could say he looked chastened, but he didn't. Instead, he looked shifty. But he didn't talk any more.

Chris cleared his throat and spoke quite gently.

'Cathy's right, Ted. You know that really. Everything you're saying, it's down to grief. And you won't ever move on unless you come to terms with all that's happened. And that includes the money. You don't need Eloise's inheritance. You're a talented artist. You can make your own fortune, and take comfort in the fact that your girls are well provided for. A lot of men would find that a huge relief.'

Ted stood up abruptly and strode out of the house, banging the door behind him. We looked at each other.

'Don't worry,' said Jack. 'He'll be back. He's left his car behind.'

'And his daughters,' I said.

Juliana looked delighted.

'Yes, that's marvellous. He hardly ever lets me see them, just when it's convenient for him. Cathy, I know that was all a bit upsetting, but do you mind if we finish our lunch? With the children back upstairs? Mustn't let all that delicious food go to waste, after all.'

Much later, Chris and I lay in bed, reviewing the day's events. Little Rose and Violet had had a lovely afternoon with Granny. Evie had had a dreamy day with Arthur. Jack seemed happy and at ease in our company. We drank a lot of wine, and nobody talked about Ted. We did talk about

Eloise, though. Jack asked lots of questions about her illness, and how she coped with it. Juliana supplied most of the answers, and, as she talked about her daughter, Jack became increasingly grave and sad. He lowered his voice so the children wouldn't hear.

'I wish I'd known,' he said. 'I would have come over to see her if I'd known. It was such a shock to get your letter after she died, Juliana.'

'Yes, I'm sorry, Jack. But she was adamant that I didn't tell you how ill she was; she was very secretive about it. She only told her closest friends. In many ways she was in denial. She hated talking about it. She thought acknowledging it in any way would jinx her.'

'I can vouch for that,' I said. 'Ellie kept going by being positive and convincing herself that she'd beat it. It's astonishing how upbeat she was, right up to the end.'

Ted didn't come back for his car or his daughters and eventually we put them to bed in the bunkroom downstairs. Juliana was apprehensive about leaving them here.

'What if he comes back drunk, Cathy? You know what he's like when he's had too much to drink now. Aggressive and hateful.'

Not much change there from when he's sober these days, I thought.

'And besides,' she continued, 'he'll want to drive the girls home. There's no way I can allow that if he's drunk. And he will be.'

I agreed with her. I suggested they all stay with us at the cottage. We had just enough room. The boys could double up, and we had a camp bed for Arthur. Evie and Juliana were happy to share. Thankfully my daughter's bedroom was large, with a huge four-poster bed that was easily big enough for both of them. As for Jack, he could sleep in my writing cabin.

Later, everyone went off to his or her appointed rooms, and Chris and I went to bed. Chris was disgusted with Ted.

'Christ, that man is a mess. He should be looking after his children above everything else at the moment. Not indulging himself by abandoning them while he buggers off to get pissed.'

'What worries me,' I said, 'is that his anger about Ellie's will has driven him almost mad. And that's awful for the twins. Look at the way he abandoned them today. I don't know if they're safe with him.'

Chris's voice was quiet.

'Cathy, I know you're worried about the girls. But I'm sorry. I do think you're starting to go over the top again.'

Of course he did. I had to be careful. At least he'd seen Ted in his most bitter mood. I had to be grateful for small steps.

Chris said goodnight, but followed that with an admonition.

'You really must understand that when you talk about Ted putting the twins in danger, you're going beyond the pale. He's not a nice man, I know that, but he's been through a hellish experience. Don't forget he looked after Eloise through five years of desperate illness. That changes you. Everything that's happened, finding out that Eloise had a daughter in her early teens, and that she also had a grandson, has been a huge shock to him. Of course he's going to feel resentful. He had no idea about his wife's past and didn't find out until it was too late.' He kissed me. 'It's all right, love. Stop worrying. Ted will turn out OK.'

No, I thought, Ted won't turn out OK. That's what Eloise has been trying to tell me, and what I've been trying to tell Chris.

Chapter Twenty-Six

We were falling asleep. Despite my misgivings about Chris's assessment of Ted, I was feeing really good. All my family was together under the same roof; not only them, but also the children and grandchild of my dearest friend. Her mother too, and Jack, whom she had loved so much, had settled down in my little cabin. I felt Eloise would have approved. I understood so much more about Ellie now I'd met him. I knew absolutely why she had loved him and I was sure that if they had met later in their lives, she would have married him. There was a tragedy there, I thought. How different, how much happier, Eloise's life could have been. But I was being romantic and fanciful. Ellie had had a good life, surely?

I slept, warm and happy, next to Chris. Tonight I felt his connection to Cornwall was as strong as mine. Which meant, surely, that he would want to keep our cottage?

In the early hours of the morning, there was a loud thumping at the kitchen door. I woke up, confused, to see that Chris was already out of bed, pulling on his dressing gown.

'That bastard! It's Ted, pissed and determined to wake the whole house up.'

He ran downstairs. I heard him unlock the door and immediately a massive row echoed up the stairs. I could hear Ted shouting drunkenly about Eloise, and accusing Chris of kidnapping his daughters. I heard Chris, trying to keep his voice reasonable, telling Ted that the girls were fast asleep, and it would be cruel to wake them up at this hour of the morning. Ted demanded that they should come with him, right now, so he could take them home to Fowey. Chris, still calm and reasonable, replied that he was far too drunk to drive, and the girls were safer here. Ted ranted that Chris couldn't sit in judgement over him, and said that if he didn't see his children right now he would call the police. Chris laughed and suggested Ted should do exactly that, and if he didn't, Chris would. Ted asked where the fuck was he supposed to sleep that night. Chris told him to sleep in his car. And that if he caused any more disturbance he would, indeed, get the cops down here and Ted would end up spending the night in a cell at Plymouth Police Station.

I heard the door slam shut, and the grinding of the key as Chris double-locked it. He came upstairs, annoyed but also amused.

'Honestly, Cath, he's behaving like such a plonker. An absolute idiot.'

He crawled into bed and fell asleep again almost at once. I was much more disturbed. Ted was dangerous, I thought. Far too volatile to be the sole carer of two vulnerable five-year-old girls. I didn't know what I could do about it, but I resolved to talk to Juliana in the morning. Maybe we could get him sectioned, and she could look after the twins. Chris would know about that, I thought drowsily, and sank back into sleep.

God knows how much later, there was a shot. It was unmistakeable, and swiftly followed by another. Chris jumped up from the bed.

'God, he's at it again,' he shouted, and hared down the stairs.

Chris had an airgun, which he grabbed from the cupboard as he left the bedroom. I saw him from the top of the stairs as he rushed into the kitchen brandishing his weapon.

Seconds later, Sam raced up the stairs from his bedroom on the bottom floor.

'Dad, what are you doing?' he yelled.

'Stay here, Sam. That idiot's got a gun and he's very drunk.'

'Dad, don't go outside, please. Ted's got a proper shotgun. If he's pissed, it could be lethal.'

As if to underline Sam's warning, there was another loud gunshot from the garden.

I could hear Ted whooping and I ran to our bedroom window. The garden lights were on, illuminating the pitch-black Cornish night, and I saw him open the back of the gun and shove in two fresh cartridges. Then he cavorted up towards the top of the garden, and my little writing shed. He almost seemed to be dancing.

But my attention was diverted by a scream from the ground floor. It was Juliana, in the nightdress I'd lent her. She rushed out onto the lawn.

'Ted, Ted, stop this nonsense. We are your family. Your girls are here. Please don't frighten them like this. I beg you. Come inside and let's talk.'

But Ted was out of his mind. As he reached the little cabin, he shouted:

'Jack! Come on out, mate. Let's talk about Eloise, the little slut. Did you enjoy her, her body, when she was just thirteen? What was she like? Was she firm and young? Did she have tits? Did she give you a blow-job?'

By now Evie, Tom and Arthur were up and in the kitchen. I flew downstairs, terrified of Ted's madness and what they would hear. I ordered them back into the living room, with a pleading glance at Sam to keep them well away from the grown-ups. He nodded at me, grimly aware that this was a major crisis, shepherded them into the sitting room and firmly closed the door. I loved him more than ever.

Outside, Chris and Juliana were still on the lawn. Neither of them showed the slightest fear.

'Ted, you are grieving and very drunk.' Chris's voice, strong and smooth, at his most professional, echoed strongly across the garden. 'Come inside. Sleep it off. We've got plenty of room.'

But Ted ignored him.

'Come on out, Jack,' he bellowed. 'I know you're in there. I was watching when Cathy's twee little garden lights showed you going in. Come out and let's settle this, once and for all.'

Suddenly the door to the cabin swung open, and Jack stepped outside. He was fully dressed, in jeans and a striped shirt.

'Go back inside, Jack,' I shouted. 'He's got a gun.'

But Jack merely stood absolutely still, and looked Ted in the eye.

'We were kids, Ted. It happened more than thirty years ago, in another life. And there's no harm done.'

Ted, now swaying from side to side, sounded hysterical.

'No harm done? No bloody harm? What about Arthur? He's done plenty of harm to me. Him and his mother got *my* share of my wife's money. And she never even met him. You've ruined my life, you selfish bastard. I don't see why I shouldn't ruin yours.'

Suddenly he stopped swaying. He raised his head and planted his feet wide apart. Then, to my horror, he lifted the gun up and took a steady aim at Jack's chest.

Incredibly, Jack gave a half-smile.

'Pull the trigger, Ted,' he said quietly. 'Unless that thing has a third barrel, you've run out of ammunition. You've already fired it twice, or are you too drunk to remember?'

I screamed.

'No, Jack! He's re-loaded it! I saw!'

The atmosphere changed instantly. It had been volatile and scary; now it was deadly.

Jack had gone white and Chris took half a pace forward towards the two men. His tone had altered entirely now, from the voice of reason to one of profound warning.

'Ted, you MUST NOT DO THIS.' It was a command, delivered in the deepest voice I had ever heard my husband use to anyone.

Ted didn't move, but I saw him lick his lips and squeeze his eyes tightly shut for an instant. The gun didn't waver an inch.

Chris spoke again, with the same slow, heavy delivery.

'Ted. I am telling you as one of your oldest friends: you do NOT want to do this terrible thing. You are not a killer. But if you pull that trigger, you will become one. You may kill Jack, but you will have destroyed your own life as well. You MUST know that. PUT THE GUN DOWN.'

The ghastly tableaux remained frozen. It seemed that we might all be standing there, motionless, until the end of time. But after what felt like an eternity, the shotgun began to tremble, very slightly. Then, all at once, Ted collapsed into a sitting position, gun across his knees, and in one fluid motion Chris was at Ted's side and lifting the weapon clear.

Jack slumped against the cabin doorway and buried his face in his hands. Juliana and I burst into tears. These had been the most terrifying minutes of our lives.

Chris opened the gun and ejected the two cartridges, throwing them as far down the lawn as he could. Then he gripped Ted by his arm and pulled him to his feet.

'Get the cabin key, would you, Jack?' he asked calmly.

Jack disappeared for a moment and returned with the key. Chris pushed Ted gently into the shed and turned him round just inside.

'Stay in there and sleep it off. See you tomorrow.'

He closed the door and locked it, before walking across the lawn to Juliana and me. Jack followed.

I took Chris in my arms.

'You saved Jack's life. If you hadn't been here ...'

'That man's out of control,' Chris said grimly. 'I'll get rid of the gun, but he's clearly gone over the edge. We'll have to do something radical.'

Sam appeared at the kitchen door.

'Mum,' he said urgently. 'Arthur heard some of what Ted said about Jack and Eloise. He's put two and two together and he's figured out that Jack must be his grandfather.'

I froze. 'Is he all right?' I asked.

'Very shocked. He keeps on asking if it's true. We don't know what to tell him. We had no idea.'

Juliana rushed inside the house, Jack immediately behind her. Chris put his arm round me and we followed them in.

Inside the living room, Arthur sat motionless on the sofa. Evie was next to him, her arms around his shoulders. She looked at me, her face anxious and stricken.

'It's all right, Evie. Come on up to our bedroom for a few minutes. Sam and Tom, you too. Leave Arthur with Jack and Juliana for a while.'

My three children rose obediently and came upstairs with Chris and me. There, apologizing for not telling them sooner, we explained the whole situation to them, about Jack and Eloise's baby, who had gone to Australia with Jack's parents because Eloise was too young to keep her, and how Isabella had only found out about her true parentage after Ellie died. I told them that nobody told Arthur that Jack was not his uncle but his grandfather because they thought he might be upset. The three of them listened gravely.

'I'm sure he'll be OK,' said Sam when I finished speaking. 'Arthur really loves Jack. He told me yesterday that he's the best uncle in the world.'

Chris smiled approvingly at his eldest son.

'You're absolutely right, Sam. That's a very mature observation, and I totally agree with you.'

Evie looked relieved. She worshipped her dad, and was full of pride that he was such a distinguished doctor. If Chris thought Arthur would be OK, that was good enough for her.

It was half-past four in the morning. All the children had gone to bed, including Arthur. He had had a long conversation with Jack and Juliana, as they told me the next day. Jack said it was difficult to explain the reasons why he had kept his true relationship to Arthur and Isabella secret, but eventually, at least, managed to persuade him it was for the best, and done with the most loving intentions. The sixteen-year-old boy and the man in his late forties finally shared a loving embrace.

Meanwhile, we had managed, with difficulty, to placate the neighbours, explaining that Ted was not only drunk but also suffering from post-traumatic stress after the death of his wife. They had known and liked Eloise, and were sympathetic to Ted, but understandably concerned for their own family's safety. Luckily Chris was a soothing and persuasive man. He reassured them that he'd locked Ted's shotgun away, and that Ted was safely in the cabin. Chris had gone back to my little shed after it was all over and made Ted take a sedative. As a psychiatrist, he told the neighbours he took personal responsibility for Ted's state of mind and would make sure he got treatment in the morning.

'Can you do that, Chris?' I asked as we sat around the table with Jack and Juliana, sipping hot tea. The children had gone back to bed, and mercifully Rose and Violet had slept through the whole thing.

'Can I do what?' he asked.

'Get treatment for Ted later today?'

'I'm not sure. The trouble is I don't know what to treat him for. I could give him anti-depressants and recommend a course of bereavement counselling, but I don't think he'd co-operate.'

'Then what can we do?' asked Juliana. 'I can't possibly let him look after the girls. He's dangerous. If he'd got them into the car last night he might have killed them.'

'Could you get him sectioned?' I asked.

He gave a short laugh. 'Not for being drunk and disorderly, no.'

Jack spoke for the first time.

'What about a legal care order? If we can prove that he's a danger to the children then can we have them removed from him?'

'I will not have my granddaughters taken into care,' said Juliana indignantly.

Jack looked at her. 'I wasn't thinking that. I thought we could put them into *your* care; they could live with you.'

'Could we do that?' I asked doubtfully.

'We could try,' said Chris. 'I've got good friends in the family courts. It's worth a shot.'

But as we tried to snatch a few hours sleep, with Jack bedded down on the sofa, I felt our prospects were very gloomy. Ted would fight us all the way. The girls were not only his daughters – they were his bread and butter. He wouldn't give up either without a fierce struggle. And, besides, surely any court would accept that he was temporarily mad with grief, and that taking his children away from him would wound him even further, possibly fatally.

I tried to sleep, but a faint, distant voice crept into my head.

'I told you, Cathy. I told you not to trust him. My children are in great danger. You've got to get them away from him. Soon.'

I knew I had to try.

Next morning we were all a bit groggy. Evie, bless her, had responded to the twins' demands for breakfast, which let us grown-ups sleep a little later. When we finally gathered in the sitting room, the big question was 'What are we going to do about Ted?'

I voiced it just as Jack came in through the kitchen door.

'Not a lot,' he said. 'He's gone.'

'What?' said Chris.

'He kicked the cabin door down. Easy enough, it's only flimsy wood – one good kick would have done it, which is why none of us heard anything. We were stupid to think a shed could act as a secure detention cell. Anyway, the door's hanging off its frame, and his car's gone.'

There was a moment of consternation, tinged with relief. None of us had been looking forward to this morning's meeting with Ted. On the other hand, where had he gone? And why hadn't he waited for his daughters to wake up?

We had to watch what we said in front of the little girls, but Violet had already gathered something was amiss.

'Where's Daddy?' she asked, looking keenly at Juliana.

'I should imagine he's gone back home, darling,' she replied.

'Without waiting for me and Rose?' she demanded.

'Well, he didn't want to wake you up. He will have gone home to see someone about his paintings, but it was too early to wake you. He'll be back to get you soon.'

Violet considered this. Then Rose said, devastatingly, 'Is Daddy cross again?'

'No, of course not, Rose. Daddy's just very busy at the moment.' That was me.

Rose thought about this carefully.

'I think he *is* cross again. Mummy said he was always cross these days.'

'I don't like Daddy when he's cross,' said Violet. 'He frightens me.'

'How does he frighten you, darling?' asked Chris.

'He shouts in a big loud voice. Like he used to shout at Mummy. She was frightened of him too. She used to say she wanted to take us away from him . . . '

'But,' Rose joined in, 'she couldn't because she was so poorly.'

'And then she died,' said Violet, matter-of-factly.

There was total silence in the room. None of us knew what to say. Then Rose piped up again.

'Grandma, can't we live with you? We'd rather live with

you than Daddy. And Mummy always said she wanted us to live with you.'

'Did she, darling?' There were tears in Juliana's eyes. 'Well, of course you can live with me. I'd love that. But I'll have to ask Daddy. Don't you think he'll be a bit upset if you don't live with him?'

They shook their heads in unison.

'Oh no,' said Violet. 'Every time he's cross he tells us he doesn't want us any more. He says we're a . . . '

'Burden,' they chorused together.

Evie stepped in.

'Hey, girls, would you like to watch cartoons?'

'Yes!' they shouted and ran out of the room.

'OK,' Chris said. 'What on earth do we do now?'

'Well,' said Juliana. 'We certainly have to do something. I'm not prepared to let those girls stay with him a day longer. I'll take them back to Roseland with me, and keep them there.'

'I'm not sure he'll let you do that, Juliana. Knowing him, he'll call the police and tell them you've kidnapped them. We've got to do this through the proper channels,' said Chris, 'so I need to talk to some of my legal friends. I'll get onto it straight away.' He left the room.

I'd noticed Jack had stayed strangely quiet during our worried conversation. I looked at him.

'What do you think, Jack?' I asked.

He replied, in his Aussie twang, 'I'm a stranger here. I'm not part of Eloise's family, much as I'd like to be. I am sort of a relation, but many times removed. I'm not sure I'm the right person to judge what's going on here, but it's obvious that Ted is unhinged. And that has to be bad for the children.' He looked at me. 'I don't want to tread on any toes here, Cathy, but I would like to talk to you sometime.'

'Why not now?'

He shook his head. 'No, not now.' He nodded towards Juliana, who was washing up breakfast things in the kitchen.

Everyone parted to do his or her own thing. I had a bath and washed my hair. Juliana got the little girls washed and dressed. Chris was glued to his laptop. The older kids played footie on the lawn. Only Jack seemed distant and preoccupied. I watched him from the bathroom as he wandered up the path and into the lane. He looked deep in thought as he turned left down towards the beach.

We all re-assembled around midday. Lunch was proposed, and we decided to go to the beach café. Yet again, it was a lovely day, and with so many children of all ages, it seemed the obvious thing to do.

Jack had not returned from his early walk, but we soon saw him, distant but distinct as he stepped over the rocks. We

waved and shouted, and he saw us and bounded enthusiasti-
cally up the beach. Chris and Sam had been right about
Arthur. Juliana said Jack had been wonderfully gentle with him
last night and assured him again and again how much he loved
him, and how proud he was to be his grandad. When Arthur
got up that morning he cheekily called Jack Gramps, but then
asked more seriously if he could still call him Jack. His 'uncle'
seemed too young to be a grandfather, he said. Jack laughed
and said he was glad to hear it, and after that there was no tension in the air at all.

It was crab sandwiches all round for the grown-ups,
sausage rolls and cornish pasties for the kids. And lots of tea
for us, and Coke for them. We obviously didn't talk about
Ted, and the little ones giggled happily over their ice creams.
I watched the sea, hypnotised into a calm trance by the soft
noise of the small waves, as I always was. I felt totally relaxed.
The searing visions of my dead best friend had left me. Now,
the responsibility for her children's safety was no longer mine
alone. Others shared the worry, and that was such a relief.

After a long, happy lunch, Chris said that he had to get
back home. He had emails and phone calls to make. Jack and
Juliana also said they needed to get back, although they would
wait for the girls before they returned to Roseland. The little
ones, however, didn't want to leave the beach, and neither did
Eve and Arthur. Sam and Tom had an appointment with a

fisherman in Looe, along with some local friends. So we all separated, and went our different ways.

Back at the cottage, I walked over to the cabin to inspect the damage Ted had done. As Jack had said, the door had been comprehensively kicked in, but it would be easily repaired. I went inside. Here, everything was a mess. The linen had been stripped from the bed, and heaped on the floor. The bookcase I had so lovingly stacked with du Maurier, Philip Pullman, Stephen King and Ann Tyler had been overturned. My ancient copies of *Jane Eyre* and *Wuthering Heights* had been ripped to shreds, as had my paperbacks of Donna Leon and J.K. Rowling. Candles had been thrown around the room; beloved ornaments, like my china rabbit bookends, had been smashed. I was incredibly upset. This wasn't the work of an opportunistic thief. The man who had done this was a friend, someone I'd known for many years, a man whom I had not believed could so suddenly become such an enemy.

As I left the cabin, too shocked yet to begin the dreary task of cleaning up, I glanced at my desk. I always kept wads of paper there, and pens. I was a bit of a Luddite, preferring to write first in longhand rather than my MacBook. The desk was strewn with sheets of paper, some screwed up and thrown on the floor, others torn angrily into pieces. There was one sheet of A4, though, that had been positioned, carefully, in the centre of the desk. Ted had clearly meant me to read it.

I did. It was horrible, explicit, deranged.

Eloise you little slut you bitch how could you do this to me all the times I helped you when you were ill and you cut me out of your will all because of what you did one night with a farmhand's son when you were only thirteen well now I've met him typical Australian beach-bum don't believe for a minute his claims to be a doctor I'm glad you're dead I wish you'd died years ago just after you fucked that kid that way you wouldn't have ruined my life I loved you once I doubt you ever loved me at the end I hated you so much I'm glad you saw that I'm glad you were scared of me and now that fucking loopy friend of yours says you're haunting her I hope so I can't stand her either with a bit of luck you'll drive her completely round the bend and put her in an Asylum

The rest was illegible. Pure hatred, fuelled by drink. I picked the paper up. I wanted to show it to Chris, wondering if it might help us to get the girls away from Ted permanently.

Chris read the note and raised his eyebrows.

'Charming,' he said.

'Could it help us to get the girls into Juliana's care?' I asked.

'I'm not sure. It's not illegal to write a poison pen letter to your dead wife but it *is* irrational so it might help. I'll keep it anyway.'

Jack came in from the garden.

'It's beautiful, this place. The view from the top garden terrace is stunning. I'm not surprised you love it so much, Cathy.'

I looked meaningfully at Chris.

'Thanks, Jack. Yes, I do love it. I want to be buried here.'

I saw Chris purse his lips, then Jack saw the note and cocked his head.

'What's that?' he asked.

'It's a love letter from our mutual friend,' said Chris. 'Here, have a look at it.'

'Oh no, surely not, Chris,' I blurted. 'It's incredibly hurtful and unpleasant.'

'Jack was nearly shot by Ted last night. I don't think a deranged letter will surprise him. The man is temporarily mad, and I'm sure Jack can take it.'

Jack gave me a sweet smile and took the note. He read it with equanimity.

'Right,' he said when he finished it. 'At least we know what we're dealing with, then.'

'Do we?' I asked. 'I think we have a huge problem. And I don't know what to do about it.'

'For the moment, Cathy, I think we should have a cup of tea.' This was Juliana, and she was right. We needed to calm down.

And then Eve and Arthur burst into the house. Alone.

'Mum, Dad, Ted came to the beach. And he took Rose and Violet with him, even though they didn't want to go. They were crying and saying they wanted to stay here with their granny and us. But he took no notice, just picked them up and forced them into the car. He wouldn't even speak to us.'

I was distressed that Evie was so upset. I told them it wasn't their fault and cursed Ted yet again for causing such emotional damage so carelessly. I gave them both a mug of hot chocolate, and they went downstairs to watch TV.

'I think we ought to call the police,' I said to Chris. 'We should tell them what happened last night.'

'I'd rather not do that, Cath. Ted's a friend and he's grieving – I'd hate to see him behind bars. Anyway, he'd probably get a conditional discharge, given his emotional state.'

I looked at Juliana, certain she'd support me. But what she said surprised me. She sounded amazingly calm.

'I agree with Chris,' she said. 'We have to be realistic about this. Ted is the girls' dad, and he has every right to pick them up from the beach and take them home. So, what we have to ask ourselves is, are our worries about him justified, or are we prejudiced against him because he has behaved so frighteningly last night? I agree he needs treatment, that's obvious. But we have an eminent psychiatrist in our midst, so I really think we should take his advice. We owe Ted a duty of care. Or at least I do. I am his mother-in-law, after all.'

Chris spoke firmly. 'Juliana, you have absolutely articulated how I feel. I'm very ambivalent about Ted. I know he's being an asshole, but I think I understand why and I'm sure this behaviour is temporary and that certainly he won't harm the twins – who have to be our greatest concern.'

I spoke, slowly and reluctantly. 'You're wrong, Chris. You're both wrong,' I said, glancing at Juliana. 'I know you don't believe me about Eloise's warnings, but everything that's happened so far has accorded absolutely with her forebodings. You probably don't want me to talk about it, but I told you she is terrified that Ted is going to hurt their children.'

I could tell Chris didn't want to listen. Then Jack pitched in.

'Could you tell me what you mean about Eloise's warnings, Cathy?'

'It's a long story, and I don't want to upset Chris or Juliana.

I can't offer a shred of what you'd call proper evidence, but I do know that my dear friend Eloise is telling me that her death was premature, and that her children are in danger.'

'From Ted?' asked Jack.

'I believe so,' I said.

Chris looked very uncomfortable. 'Cathy,' he interrupted, 'We need to talk about facts, not mumbo-jumbo.'

I was furious.

'Do you think the way Ted's been behaving, his threats, his violence, his attitude towards the twins, is normal? Can't you at least acknowledge that everything I've been saying to you so far has proved true?'

Chris flushed. 'Look, Cathy, what I'm saying is that Ted's grief, his anger, are entirely consistent with bereavement. That's rooted in psychological behaviour, and that is why Ted's behaving in the way he is. It has nothing to do with bloody ghosts.'

Juliana stopped him.

'Chris, I know your training means it's very hard for you to believe what Cathy says, but I do think you should listen to her. Intuition is a powerful thing, especially when it's linked to love and care. Cathy and Eloise were very close, and besides, she's not the only one who's had disturbing messages. So have I. My daughter has left me many troubled thoughts, mostly to do with her anxiety about her daughters. All I'm trying to say is that we're all troubled now, aren't we? And for good reason. So Cathy's dreams in fact foreshadowed what has happened. And I don't think you should dismiss her as – what? A fantasist? Just because she reaches conclusions in a different way from you?'

After an awkward silence, Jack spoke, gently and calmly.

'I think, understandably, we're wandering off the beaten track here. What we need to do now is to establish if Ted poses a danger to his daughters, and, if so, what we can do about it. I propose, if nobody minds me making a suggestion, that we phone Ted to find out where he is.'

Relieved by such a sensible suggestion, Juliana went to the phone. She stood holding it for some time; Ted was obviously not going to answer, so she left a message in a tone so conciliatory it was almost maternal.

'Ted, my dear. I'm so sorry about everything that's happened in the last couple of days. I hate to see you so unhappy. Can't we put all this behind us and think about what's best for Violet and Rose? We both have their interests at heart. And I do, so much, want you to be happy as well. We have all had such a difficult time over the last five years. We owe each other the patience to find peace and harmony. And to love each other. Please, Ted, let us make the girls' lives happy and worthwhile. Call me back when you can.'

I have to say we all felt stunned. I had no idea that Juliana was such an accomplished actress. I could certainly see where Eloise's dramatic talent had come from.

'And now,' she said, 'All we can do is wait.'

And we did. All evening. Ted didn't phone back, and our frequent calls to him on the landline went unanswered. His mobile was switched off.

Sam and Tom came home. The kids were hungry and I sent them out in my Beetle to bring back pizza from Polperro. After a subdued meal around the kitchen table, Juliana said she, Jack and Arthur really had to get back to Roseland. We kissed goodbye, aware that we had reached a time when a crisis loomed frighteningly close.

'Tell me if he calls you,' I begged Juliana. 'We need to make a decision about his state of mind. And be careful. If he's still as mad as last night, he might come to Roseland. You know he's dangerous.'

'Don't worry about Juliana,' Jack said. He smiled. 'I promise you I can handle Ted.'

We waved goodbye. In truth I was glad they'd gone. Not because I didn't like their company, but because the last two days had been such a strain and I wanted to wind down.

We all watched *Jaws* and it did the trick. It removed us from the tension we'd felt all day, and substituted a fictional suspense which was much easier to deal with. Later, all three of our children went to bed, humming the *Jaws* theme tune, teasing each other with pretend shark attacks. I felt reassured that their sleep would be haunted by nothing more sinister than the odd circling fin, and I knew that would be far preferable to the sound of Ted's shotgun in the garden.

In bed, Chris and I were both reluctant to talk about Ted and the twins. There was a sense of imminent danger that neither of us wanted to confront. But, to my dismay, just after we switched the light out Chris turned to me.

'Cathy, I think you should know that I'm still planning for us all to leave the day after tomorrow.'

'Surely not after everything that's happened with Ted? What about Rose and Violet?'

'They've got Juliana and Jack. They'll be perfectly safe.'

'How can you say that? Ted's a madman.'

'I'm sure Juliana is perfectly capable of looking after her grandchildren. I'll make enquiries about psychological treatment for Ted, of course, but I can do that from London. I told you, I'm determined to sell this place and I'm not going to let Ted's behaviour stop me. And Cathy, you agreed to come home.'

'Yes, but not now. I'd never forgive myself if anything happened to the girls and I wasn't here to protect them.'

He turned his back to me in bed.

'Cathy, I've told you. It's precisely because of this kind of obsessive thinking that I need to get you back to London. I agree Ted's volatile, but his anger's directed at Jack and Eloise, not his daughters.'

'And me. I told you he almost pushed me off the cliff.'

Chris sighed. 'So you said. All the more reason to get you back to London, then.'

I was speechless. He was almost mocking me. Even Ted's out of control attack on Jack had not convinced Chris that Ted was a threat to me as well.

I couldn't bear another row, so I kept silent. But as he slipped into an untroubled sleep, I cursed Chris. I was not going back on Wednesday. I was going nowhere until those girls were safe.

When I finally slept, my dreams were panicky. I was trying to find Eloise. In the dream I knew she was dead, but I needed to talk to her about something terrifyingly urgent. I had no idea what it was, but I felt very frightened. If I didn't see Eloise tonight, something unspeakable would happen.

Suddenly she was there. I could see her at the foot of the bed. She was holding her arms out to me, as if to hold me, and although I didn't move physically, I felt her embrace.

'You're panicking, Cathy. Calm yourself. There's much to do tomorrow. Just listen to Jack. Talk to him, and whatever he asks you to do, do it. He knows the danger. He senses it.'

And she faded.

I woke up very early, determined to talk to Jack. It was only just after six a.m., but when I called his mobile he immediately picked up, sounding alert and tense. He listened carefully to my rushed words.

'Listen to me, Jack. Eloise came to me again last night. I know I sound mad, and I know you saw in Ted's letter that I thought she was haunting me. But the truth is, she is. Has been almost since her death. Juliana can sense her spirit too, but she can't hear her. For some reason I'm the only one who can. Jack, she's been telling me for months not to trust Ted and also that the children are in grave danger. I haven't been able to work out why. Eloise can't, or won't, tell me. But last night she said you would know, in some way, what needs to be done. She says you can sense it.'

There was a pause, then Jack told me calmly that he was on his way to Talland immediately.

I left Chris sleeping. The house was silent as I dressed and made tea. Jack arrived sooner than I would have thought possible. He walked into the cottage, smiling and self-possessed, and I felt stronger for seeing him. We sat on the sofa in the snug.

'I need to talk to you, Cathy. You're right, I haven't seen Eloise and she hasn't contacted me in any way. But I have felt something is wrong, and I had a powerful urge to come to

Cornwall. I told Juliana and the folks back home that I wanted to keep an eye on Arthur. The truth is I felt compelled to get here not just for Arthur, but also for Eloise. I couldn't understand why, until I met Ted here the day before yesterday. Then everything fell into place.'

'I could tell you didn't like him. Well, no one would, the way he's been behaving.' I paused. 'Jack, were you ... are you ... still in love with Eloise?'

He smiled. 'It's not that simple. Ellie and I were together so briefly, such a long time ago. I thought about her a lot when I was growing up in Australia, but life goes on, and inevitably you forget.'

'Are you married, Jack?'

'I was, but it didn't last the distance. We're divorced now. But I like being on my own. I wouldn't want to get married again.'

'No children?' I asked.

He hesitated. 'No, apart from Isabella, and I really have come to love her as a sister, not a daughter, although I'm very protective of her. I've had a good life in Australia. I don't regret leaving Cornwall at all. I doubt I would have had the opportunities and education I've had over there if I'd stayed here – I'd have had to push very much harder to get into med school, for example, with the education I was getting at the village school.'

'So, if you've been happy out there . . . '

'I have,' he replied sharply.

'Then why do you dislike Ted so much?'

He smiled. 'You think I'm jealous of him, don't you? Because he was married to Eloise? Nothing could be further from the truth. No, I don't like Ted because I think he's capable of great cruelty. Even violence.' He hesitated. 'There's something else too. From everything Juliana's told me about when Eloise died, I just don't quite understand it. I'm an oncologist, and I've worked with hundreds of terminal patients, but their eventual, inevitable end doesn't happen in the way Eloise's did. I mean, they're not fine, energetic, mobile and chatty on the morning of their death, only to die so quickly and suddenly just a couple of hours later. It doesn't often happen like that. Usually there's an obvious period of decline. Of course, Eloise had her own doctors. I'd quite like to talk to them about it, to get their opinion. I may be quite wrong, but it just doesn't quite add up.'

Chris walked in, wearing his dressing gown. He looked surprised, and not terribly pleased, to see Jack, but greeted him pleasantly enough.

'Hello, Jack. What brings you here so early? Is something going on?'

'No, no. I couldn't sleep, and drove down here on the off chance that someone was awake. Fortunately, Cathy was up and in the kitchen. She very kindly offered to make me a cup of tea.'

Chris looked quizzically at me. 'Really? Well, that's a first. Cath rarely surfaces much before noon.'

'Chris, you know that's not true.'

He smiled. 'Well, you're not exactly an early bird. But it's good to see you, Jack. Cathy and I are leaving Cornwall with the kids tomorrow. So this is probably the last time we'll see you before you go back to Australia. When are you going back, anyway?'

Jack didn't respond to Chris's slightly hostile tone.

'I'm not quite sure yet. I want to make sure Arthur's happily settled with Juliana. It's going to be a big change for him, going to college in England, and he may change his mind, in which case I'll take him back home with me. So I'll probably still be around when you guys next come to Cornwall.'

'We won't be coming back, Jack.' Chris said with utter calm. 'I'm selling this place.'

Jack looked at me in consternation.

'But why? I thought Cathy loved it here?'

'I do,' I said quickly.

'Then why sell?'

It was Chris who answered.

'Because it's not good for Cathy's health. I would have thought you'd already gathered that. When Ted said the other day that she sees ghosts and holds séances, he was absolutely right. It's not normal, and it only happens in Cornwall. So I'm getting her out of here, back to London where she can forget all this nonsense about Eloise.'

I was mortified. Chris was doing it again, humiliating me before someone who was almost a stranger. It was as if the last couple of days, his renewed affection, had never happened. Why was he talking like this? Did he see Jack as some sort of threat?

I couldn't bear to look at either of them. Mumbling something about clearing up the mess that Ted had left, I walked up to my little writing house. The door still hung crazily from its hinges, and the chaos inside rocked me even more than the day before. Still shaking after Chris's contemptuous dismissal of me to Jack, I thought making a start on cleaning it up would keep my mind off my misery. Anyway, if Chris really was so intent on abandoning the cottage this week, and I had no reason to doubt it, I couldn't let any prospective buyer look at the mess Ted had made of my life. Because that's what it felt like. A violent intrusion into my most private space.

People are always going on about how men need a shed to retreat to. But I think the same goes for women, too. I don't think you get much privacy as a middle-aged married woman. You share your bedroom, your bathroom. You share your living space, your deepest thoughts and anxieties with your family. And that's what you want, of course, that total identification with your life as a wife and mother. That whole Mother-ship thing, the feeling of being the fount of care, love and wisdom, the only person who will defend your family to the death, is as seductive as it is exhausting. But this, my little cabin, was totally mine. I didn't really like even Chris visiting it. Just like Virginia Woolf, everyone needs a room of one's own.

I found a couple of bin liners and started to pick up the rubbish. I began with the bed, carefully remaking it so it looked like my sanctuary again. Chucking the torn books and papers into the sturdy bags was easy, but upsetting. To me, books were deeply personal. But, I thought, I would replace them, each and every one. And then I thought, what's the point? We were going to leave Cornwall tomorrow. What was I doing? Trying to tidy my life up so that newcomers wouldn't glimpse how much this place meant to me?

I bent down. I'd seen something white underneath the desk. I fished out two tiny scraps of paper. They were tickets to the Daphne du Maurier Festival in Fowey the previous year. They were for a theatrical production. I looked at them, puzzled, until I remembered that I'd found them in the pocket of Eloise's leather jacket. She had lent it to me last summer when I was shivering on her lovely sea terrace on a day that turned unexpectedly cold. As I looked at them, I recalled her happy face, her laughter as she told me the play had been terrible, the generosity with which she draped the coat over my shoulders, and I burst into tears.

That's how Jack found me, curled up on the bed, sobbing.

'Don't cry, Cathy. I'm sure Chris didn't mean to upset you like that. In fact, he apologised to me after you'd gone. Said he was just feeling tired and grumpy.'

I didn't buy that. He hadn't taken the trouble to come to the cabin to apologise to me. I shook my head.

'It's OK. I'm not crying about him. It's the whole mess – Eloise, moving away from Cornwall.'

'I think his decision to take you away from here is mostly an impetuous response to the strain you've both been under. I don't think he really means it. Once he gets back to London, I'm sure he'll reconsider. You two have spent so much time here with the kids. He won't want to spoil those memories.'

His words comforted me, even though I didn't believe them. Then Jack said, smiling, 'But I'm surprised that you're taking this lying down. You're a strong woman. Why should Chris make all the decisions? If you don't want to sell the cottage, then don't. He can't force you. I assume it's in both your names?'

'Yes, but you see, Jack, I'm not a strong woman. Not

strong at all. I'm – what's the word Chris uses? Fragile, that's it. As in mentally unstable.'

'I don't think you are,' he said gently.

'Honestly, I am. I've had a breakdown, and now, as Chris told you, I'm seeing ghosts. Well, just one ghost. Eloise. Anyway, it's all academic. If I refuse to leave, Chris will simply leave me. He's already done it once. And I couldn't bear to split the family up. It would break the children's hearts.'

A shadow fell across the doorway. It was Chris. He coughed. I wondered if he'd heard what I'd said. But, thank God, he looked crestfallen rather than cross. So maybe he had overheard me, but it didn't look as if he was going to take me to task.

'Cathy,' he said in a subdued voice. 'Sorry for speaking that way. Didn't mean it. As usual I got things wrong. Sorry.'

As always, I forgave him. He was my crosspatch, my own sulky husband. But I loved him. I knew I always would.

We went back into the house. The children were up, and we ate toast and cereal for breakfast. The atmosphere was relaxed and happy. Chris stopped talking about our departure next day, and Jack regaled the kids with stories of Oz. How they spent all day on the beach at weekends, cooking barbies and drinking beer. Tom said he wanted to move to Australia, it sounded so good. There was a lively debate about which was best – Britain or Australia. And then the phone rang. It was Father Pete. He sounded agitated.

'Cathy, I'm sorry to intrude. But I'm worried about Ted. I just bumped into him, and there's something very wrong.'

'OK, Pete. Tell me what's happened.'

He told me he'd been driving past Lantic Bay when he'd seen Ted's car in the cliff Car Park, and a minute or two later he watched as Ted and the two little girls walked across the top of the cliff. He stopped his car, opened the door and shouted hello. He said that Ted ignored him at first, but finally stopped and turned to face him. He looked sullen, Pete said, and the girls were subdued. He asked them where they were going. Ted looked at him as if he was mad.

'To the beach, of course. What else do you do with bloody kids in Cornwall?'

'But the thing is, Cathy, they had no beach stuff with them. No buckets or spades, no shrimping nets, no towels. They looked terribly forlorn, especially the girls. Anyway, they walked on, past the footpath down to Lantic Bay, and I was so sure things weren't right that I followed them. At a distance. They didn't see me. But suddenly Ted took them down the path that leads to Watchman's Cove. That's a terribly desolate, isolated beach. There are warnings about riptides along there, and tourists avoid it like the plague. It's incredibly inaccessible, even for experienced climbers, and those girls are – what? Four or five? Anyway, I stayed up on the road for a good ten minutes, and I couldn't see them at all. I thought maybe I was being silly, but you know, Cathy, I'm a priest. I'm used to talking to people, used to sensing what lies beneath their words. Ted was not himself. In fact he sounded slightly deranged, and the little girls looked so frightened.' He paused. 'When I got back to the Rectory, I couldn't get them out of my head. And Watchman's Cove – well, it can be a death trap, because the tide comes in so fast. So I looked for the Tide Times.'

I knew instantly what he meant. The small yellow booklet which was the essential little bible everyone in Cornwall kept by their door.

'The tide's coming in fast. High tide's in an hour and a half. If they're still at Watchman's Cove they'll soon be cut off.'

'But Ted knows Watchman's well. He'd know better than to take the girls down there when the tide's coming in. Maybe he didn't realise, but as soon as he got down there he'd see how dangerous it was. Perhaps they've already left to go home.'

'I'll call his mobile to check,' Pete said.

'OK,' I replied. 'But you know the signal's so erratic round here. You call his cellphone and I'll ring the landline at their house. Ring me back as soon as you've heard.'

The phone at Ted and Eloise's lovely home rang out for ages. Nothing.

Chris sounded impatient. 'What's going on?'

'Father Pete saw Ted and the girls heading down to Watchman's Cove—'

'Well, that sounds good,' said Chris. 'He's taking them out for a jaunt.'

'No, Chris. He's not. Father Pete said Ted sounded strange and they had no beach gear with them and who'd take two little girls to Watchman's Cove when the tide's coming in?'

I grabbed our own copy of the Tide Times, peering at the tables that affected our stretch of coast. I thrust it at Chris, who still seemed unconcerned.

'Cathy, you're being ridiculous. Ted's probably misread the tide times. When he finds that it's coming in, he'll just take the girls back home to Fowey.'

Just then our landline rang. It was Father Pete.

'I can't get through to Ted, Cathy. Of course the signal's terrible, but I really think I should go to his house in Fowey. Just in case he's realised how bad the tide is, and taken the girls back home.'

'OK, Pete. Keep in touch.'

I was thinking hard. Why take the girls to Watchman's Cove? It was hideously difficult to get down to, and even worse climbing the steep, rugged path to get back up to the road. And there were always flags warning about how fast the tide came in; it was definitely not a tourist destination. And not a place for small children either. Tiny and rocky, its only distinction was the odd little cave in the cliff wall. It had two chambers, one on top of the other. Chris used to say it resembled an unshelled peanut, inclining to the right at 45 degrees. Teenagers sometimes hung out in it as a dare, scrambling out at the last minute as the sea began to seep into the lower chamber. They loved the risk, because, if you left it too late, you wouldn't get out at all. The cave, both chambers of it, was completely flooded at high tide. Hence the sign warning against entering the deceptively friendly little cavern unless the tide was out. At any other time, the place was a death trap.

'What can we do?' I asked Chris, trying to keep my voice calm.

'What do you want me to do?' asked Chris in a sulky tone. 'Make a fool of myself by calling the Coastguard out on a wild goose chase? When Ted may be already on his way home?'

'He's not, Chris. He's not. I just know.'

Chris erupted.

'Oh, here we go again. Is Eloise talking to you now? I keep telling you I've had enough and I mean it. You're being ridiculous. You've got this mad melodrama lodged inside your head and you're never going to let it go. Well, sod you, Cathy, I'm going for a walk.'

He stalked out of the door. Leaving me again, I thought bitterly. Just when I needed him most.

Jack was still there, watchful and calm.

'I believe we need to go to Watchman's Cove.'

I looked at him gratefully.

'Thanks, Jack. I do too. Let's go.'

We left my kids behind. They protested, but I didn't want them anywhere near another disastrous encounter with Ted. Oh my God, I thought, surely he wouldn't really harm those poor little girls?

On the way to Lantic Bay, I started to panic. We pulled into the car park at the top of the hill, and got out. Jack touched my arm and pointed.

'Look,' he said. It was Ted's car, almost hidden behind a strip of gorse. So they were still here. But where?

We took the footpath leading to Lantic Bay, then turned onto the steep and precarious track which led down to Watchman's Cove. It was hard going, and to make it worse, we were trying to hurry. When we reached a stile about halfway down, I stopped to catch my breath. From here we could see the rocky little beach. We could also see something else. The tide was perilously high.

I was horrified. If Ted and the girls were indeed down there, they were in great danger. What was going on? Ted had lived in Cornwall long enough to know about these sneaky little hidey-holes. Fun for boy scouts, maybe, properly supervised. But for two little girls and a flaky father? Ted knew what he was doing. And it seemed to me to be recklessly terrifying.

Jack shook his head as he watched the encroaching tide.

'That guy is sick,' he said under his breath.

'But why, why would Ted want to harm his own children?' I asked him.

'Because, Cathy, they're not his. Actually, I think they're mine.'

Chapter Twenty-Seven

As I stared at Jack, incredulous, my mobile rang. It was
Father Pete. The reception was faint and intermittent. I
struggled to hear what he was saying.

'They're not at the house,' I heard him say scratchily.

'I know. His car's parked up at Lantic Bay.'

'Have you seen them yet?'

'No, I can't see them, but Pete, the tide's nearly in.'

'I'm calling the coastguard. Stay safe, don't go on the
beach – I'll be with you as soon as I can.'

'What in God's name is happening?'

He hesitated. 'I don't want to panic you, but Ted left his front door wide open, and I found a suicide note on the kitchen table.'

I thought my heart had stopped.

'Look, I'm on my way. I'm calling the coastguard right now and I'll try and pick Chris up on the way.' He rang off.

So, this was it. This was what Eloise had tried so hard to warn me about. She had charged me to protect her children. And I had failed her. I buried my head in my hands.

'Forgive me, Ellie. Please forgive me.'

I was shaking. Jack took me in his arms.

'Cathy,' he said urgently, 'what is it?'

'Ted left a suicide note. Father Pete's just found it at his house.'

'Christ Almighty,' he said. 'Come on, we've got to get down there.'

I nodded and we stumbled down the path. Never had the steep descent felt so perilous. I tripped on stones and roots many times, twisting my ankle and falling to the ground. Jack helped me up and almost carried me down to the cove. The pain was excruciating, but was as nothing to the terror in my head. Then, finally, we could go no further. We stood on a rock, at the foot of the path, and watched the sea as it crept inexorably up the tiny beach.

I couldn't see Ted or the girls, but the ocean was getting close to the cliff wall.

'What was Father Pete saying about a cave?' Jack asked.

'It's small,' I said. 'Going back into the cliff. It has two chambers, one at sea level, then an opening above that. But it's very treacherous. Both caves are flooded at high tide.'

'Where is it?'

'Right in the middle of the cove.'

Without a word, Jack jumped down and kicked off his shoes then plunged into the sea.

'No, Jack!' I shouted after him. 'It's too dangerous!'

He didn't reply.

I sank down onto the rock, took deep breaths. It was breezy down here. The waves weren't huge, but vigorous, tipped with tumbling white foam. The smell of the sea was intoxicating. The whole cove felt bathed in a clean, brisk saltiness, offering a tantalizing promise of health and well-being.

Except death lurked in its depths.

Jack returned, soaking and desperate.

'They're in the cave,' he gasped. 'The lower one's already underwater, but I swam up and all three of them are perched on a ledge in the upper cave. I shouted at them. Ted just looks wild-eyed. He's got a bottle of Scotch, half empty. He's obviously drunk.'

'What about the girls? How are they?'

'Terrified. Sobbing their little hearts out. I'm going to kill the bastard.'

'Jack? Can't we get them out?'

'I can't get up to their level. There are no footholes in the rock. He must have used some kind of line, a rope to get them up there. God knows how he did it.'

But I did. 'Jack, there's always a rope ladder in the cave, attached to the cliff wall. It's so people can climb up to the upper level.'

'Well, it's not there now. He must have pulled it up behind them. Christ, what a bastard he is. I'm going back in, Cathy. I'll get them out somehow.'

'It's too dangerous.'

'I'm a strong swimmer. Born in Cornwall, raised in Australia. I'm a champion surfer, Cathy. I can handle the ocean.'

'No. Jack, look.' I pointed out to sea. A bright orange dot had appeared on the horizon, rounding the headland that divided the cove from Lantic Bay. 'It's the inshore lifeboat. Father Pete said he would call them. They will rescue the girls.'

'I'm not sure they'll get here in time. I'm going back. Tell the crewmen about the cave, where I am.'

And he dived back down to the flooded beach.

*

'Cathy!' Chris's voice rang out from behind me. I turned round, and he and Father Pete were scrambling down the path. Pete's cassock was holding him up, and Chris reached my side long before the priest negotiated the rocky ground.

'Cathy, my love. I'm so, so sorry. I've been such a pig-headed fool. My darling, are you all right?'

I clung to him.

'The girls. They're in the cave with Ted. Jack saw them on the ledge in the upper chamber, but he couldn't reach them.'

'Where is Jack now?'

'He's gone back into the cave. Chris, I think it's too late. The tide's already flooded the lower chamber.'

Chris looked out to sea.

'It's all right, Cathy. The lifeboat's here.'

The wonderful sight of the orange reinforced dinghy gave me the biggest thrill of my life. I looked at the four burly crewmen on board, and prayed that they would be able to get Rose and Violet out of the cave and away from their father. I was in shock, far too numb to remember Jack's shattering assertion that Ted was not, in fact, their dad.

The crew saw us and shouted, 'What's going on here?'

Chris climbed down what was left of the rocks until he was only feet from the stationary boat.

'There's a madman in there, bent on killing himself. And he's got two little girls with him. They are only five. They've climbed up into the higher cave, but that will flood within minutes. And there's also another man who's gone into the cave to rescue them.'

'Right,' said the coxswain. 'Then we'd better get going.'

What followed next was a blur. Two of the sailors jumped into the sea and disappeared as they dived down into the cave. The others stayed on board the boat, and spooled out the line that the first men had taken with them.

I stared at the boat for what seemed hours, but in reality it was only a few minutes. Then the two men reappeared beside the dinghy, each of them struggling with an extra burden. With the help of the two sailors on board, they heaved their cargo on board. Then they bent down, hidden to us, as they tended the children they'd rescued.

One of them reared up and shouted, 'It's OK. They're both fine. Wet and frightened, but safe and well.'

I collapsed against Chris and sobbed, 'Thank God, thank God. The girls have been saved.'

But Chris looked grim. 'Where's Jack?' he shouted to the crew.

'Their father?' the oxswain yelled back. 'You were right when you called him a madman. Fought us off and tried to push the kids under the water. He wouldn't come with us. We're going to radio the coastguard and get them to send divers. It's too dangerous now for us to go back in.'

'No,' said Chris. 'Not him. The guy who went in to rescue them.'

'I don't know. We didn't see him.'

Dear God, I thought. Not Jack. Not brave Jack whom Eloise had loved so much, who had risked his life to save her children.

And then a shout from the crew.

'Throw a lifebelt down. Throw a lifebelt.'

And then, the most wonderful sight. Jack, clearly tired but still swimming, bobbed up in the water. He seized the belt they'd thrown him and was hauled up into the boat.

He choked and coughed as he was hauled up out of the sea. He was safe.

Chris yelled to the lifeboat crew. 'How fast can the diving team get here?'

'I've already radioed them. They should be here in a few minutes.'

I watched Chris's face. We both knew that would be too late.

'We've got to get these kids back to Fowey,' shouted the Cox'n. 'They need medical attention.'

And the boat powered off. 'What can we do, Chris?' I asked. 'I want to check on the girls, but we can't just abandon Ted. We should really wait for the diving team.'

'Don't worry about that, Cathy,' said Father Pete. 'I'll stay here and wait for the divers. You and Chris should go to Fowey and look after the girls. I'll call you when there's any news.'

Chris drove us back to Fowey. We were both quiet. I could tell he was full of remorse about his refusal to believe Rose and Violet were in danger. Every so often he took his left hand off the steering wheel and draped it round my shoulder, squeezing me hard.

When we finally got to the doctor's surgery in Fowey where the little girls were being treated, he stopped the car. Before I could get out he pinioned me in his arms.

'Cathy, my Cathy, can you ever forgive me? All your instincts about Ted were right. I am so, so sorry my darling. I've behaved so badly, doubting you as I did. I was rude and arrogant, convinced I knew best and what I actually think I was doing was refusing to accept that I had only seen the surface of Ted and couldn't believe he was so far from the man I'd thought he was for all those years when we were friends. It affronted the professionalism I pride myself on, so it was easier for me to be in denial. I've been so unkind to you and I love you so much – please say this hasn't destroyed our marriage.'

I lay my head on his shoulder. I even managed a smile.

'No, Chris. It hasn't destroyed our marriage. Just as long as you say we can stay in Cornwall.'

He lifted my chin.

'Darling, we'll stay in Cornwall for ever and ever.'

We smiled at each other, and he kissed me. A long, long kiss. I felt like a dry, drooping flower, parched of love and affection, at long last receiving the precious gift of rain.

An hour and a half later, we were at Juliana's. I hadn't had the chance to tell Chris that Jack said he might be the twins' father. There would be enough time later to deal with all that.

A doctor had examined both girls, and pronounced them well. Of course, he meant physically. God knows what was going through their little heads.

Juliana hid her own shock at what had happened, cuddling the little children, making them hot chocolate before she and Annie took them upstairs to bed. They were exhausted, but otherwise seemed OK. Interestingly, they never once mentioned their father. I wondered what psychological havoc Ted's attempt to murder them would wreak. I'd talk to Chris about it later.

Father Pete called and said the divers were still searching for Ted. I felt guilty that he was still out there on that bleak little beach, but he said he wanted to stay until the divers called it a day.

When the girls were in bed, we all drank brandy in

Juliana's pretty sitting room. We said very little. Jack was dog-tired and didn't want to talk. And it somehow seemed wrong to go over what had happened while Ted was still missing.

Finally, Chris and I left. There would be police and God knows what to deal with tomorrow. We should all rest, he said. And he was right. I longed to get back to my children, and to go to sleep. There was so much I didn't understand, and I was much too tired to take it all in right now.

When we got home, the children were subdued. They had seen the local news on TV. I'd already called them to say that Chris and I were all right, but there was footage of the divers still searching for Ted, and they were grimly fascinated by the horror of it all. We ate a scrappy meal, telling the kids that we were just too exhausted to talk about it tonight, but would tell them everything tomorrow. They protested, but Chris was adamant, and we both went up to bed before they did, knowing that they would stay up for hours speculating about what had sent Ted mad.

If I dreamed that night, I don't remember. Eloise was silent and the night was peaceful.

Chapter Twenty-Eight

The phone shrilled early next morning. I groaned and turned over. Chris, however, took the call. Next thing I knew, he was bending over me, fully dressed.

'The divers have found Ted's body and Juliana has asked the police if I can identify it, so I'm going to Plymouth. Afterwards they want me to go back to Ted and Eloise's house. I'll call as soon as I know anything.'

I went straight back to sleep. For the first time in months, I felt quiet and soft. I had nothing to worry about. Not now.

When I finally got up, Jack had arrived. He looked sheep-
ish but determined.

'Could we go for a walk, Cathy?' he asked. 'I've got things
I need to tell you.'

We walked with Sam, Tom and Evie down to the beach
and once they were settled at the café with Cokes and
Danish pastries, Jack and I turned back up the lane to the
church.

We sank down on the grass beside Eloise's grave. It was a
couple of hours since Chris had left for Plymouth. It was a
perfect Cornish early summer day. I felt relaxed, almost dozy.
Honeybees buzzed around the flowers on Ellie's grave. I felt
nothing but quiet peacefulness. And, of course, burning
curiosity.

'Tell me, Jack.'

He sighed. 'Six years ago I got divorced. I wasn't desolate,
exactly, but I was a bit lonely. When you're divorced, you
tend to go backwards to find out how you went wrong. I
found I was desperate to see Cornwall again and I can't really
explain it even now. I wasn't pining for England, or for
Eloise. I just knew I wanted to come home. So I flew back
to Heathrow, hired a car and drove down here.

'I didn't stay in Fowey. I didn't want to risk bumping into
anyone I knew from the old days, let alone Ellie. And God
forbid that I should see Juliana again. I thought they all hated

me. I'd got a thirteen–year–old girl pregnant, and disappeared to Australia with my parents and the baby. I was an outcast, I knew that, but still I wanted to come home to the place I loved so much; it's ridiculous, really, but despite all the idyllic surfing at Byron Bay, I couldn't forget Polzeath and Daymer Bay.

'I stayed in St Mawes, at the Tresanton Hotel. It was beautiful, fulfilled all my old dreams about Cornwall, but I couldn't resist going back to Fowey, just for one day. I mooched about the place, had a pint sitting by the harbour, thinking about old times. Then I walked over to Readymoney. And that's where I found her, on the beach. She was sunbathing on a towel. Her body was pale by Australian standards, white really, but perfect. My heart flipped over as soon as I saw her. I didn't know if I should talk to her or not. I'd made up my mind to go, but she became aware of me. She stared, and sat up. She was frowning at me; then she took off her sunglasses and said, "Jack? Can that really be you?" I could have walked away at that point, told her she'd mistaken me for someone else. But I didn't. She mesmerised me.

'Anyway, the upshot was that I went back to her house. Ted was away, painting in St Ives. We talked and talked. She was desperate for news about our daughter, Isabella. I told her about Arthur, and she was astonished to hear she had a grandson. She said Izzie must have had him really young, just like her. I said yes, she was a teenage mother, but very happily married to a lovely guy who adored her and their child. Eloise smiled. "I'm glad to hear it," she said. And then, "Lucky her." I told her about my failed marriage, she told me about Ted. I sensed, even at that point, that there were difficulties, but she didn't go into detail. Eventually, I needed to get out of the marital home. I felt almost embarrassed to be there. Obviously I didn't belong. But I couldn't resist asking to see her again, on neutral territory. She had stirred me more than I could ever have imagined.'

'And did you?' I asked.

'See her again? Yes. She agreed to come to my hotel for dinner that night. I think even then we both knew what was going to happen. Anyway, she felt safe at the Tresanton. Nobody knew her down there, and, after a couple of drinks, she completely opened up. She told me she was desperate to have a baby, and that she and Ted had been trying for a long time. They'd had various tests, and the doctors said Ellie was ovulating normally and should have no problem getting pregnant. But it wasn't happening, so at the fertility clinic they suggested Ted should have a sperm test. She told me Ted was furious when she told him, and refused point-blank at first. Thought it was a slur on his virility. But eventually, very sulkily, he agreed.'

Jack sighed, and settled back against the churchyard wall.

'The doctors said he had a very low sperm count. He wasn't completely infertile, but it was obvious it would be very difficult for them to conceive naturally. They suggested the two of them should go for an assisted pregnancy. IVF, or an even more sophisticated procedure which would mean Ted's sperm was injected directly into Ellie's egg, and then placed inside her womb. Ted went berserk, according to Eloise. He simply couldn't face the prospect that he was infertile. It went against every idea he had of himself. Brilliant artist and successful surfer-dude. He refused to believe he couldn't impregnate his wife. And, when I bumped into her, that was there they were at.'

I knew what was coming. He looked at me ruefully.

'Yes, you've got it. Eloise spent the night with me at my hotel. We made love many times. She was intoxicating. But the next morning, she said she had to get back to Fowey. Ted was due back later that same day.'

'But didn't you try to persuade her to stay with you?'

'I told her I loved her, and she said she loved me too. But my roots, back then, were in Australia. My whole career was there, not to mention Isabella and Arthur. And she said she could never leave her mother alone. So we parted. It was very hard. In fact, it was devastating.'

'So that was it? You went back to Australia? Did she write to you? Did she tell you she was pregnant?'

'No. I never heard from Eloise again. I thought of her, all the time. I even wondered if I should come back to Cornwall, to try to persuade her to be with me. But I didn't think I had the right to interfere in her life. I figured, if she wanted me, she'd get in touch.'

'So how did you find out about Rose and Violet?'

'Eloise told her mother that she'd heard from some acquaintance in Oz that Isabella had a son. She said she wanted to make some provision for them in her will. By that time, she knew she was ill. So Juliana moved heaven and earth to get in contact with me in Australia. She never told me Ellie had cancer, but she did say she'd had twin daughters.'

'And you realised they were yours?'

'Well, calculating that they'd been born nearly nine months after she and I made love, I immediately thought they might be mine. But then again, she and Ted were having fertility treatment, which might have succeeded at the same time.'

'But didn't she tell you Ted had refused treatment?'

'Yes, but I never heard from her again. As far as I was concerned, she could have got pregnant by Ted as soon as we parted. Anyway, Cathy, to be honest I tried not to think about it too much. It was too complicated, too messy, and it hurt.'

'So you still don't really know if the girls are yours? You still think there's a possibility they might be Ted's?'

Jack hesitated. 'I suppose you're right. Of course I have no absolute proof. But as soon as I saw them I felt ... ' He paused, then continued. 'I felt I recognised them somehow. I felt I knew them.'

I closed my eyes. Eloise, I thought. Please love, help me to make sense of this. Here we are, beside your grave. We've been through hell over the last couple of days. I've been through hell for months. Can't you give me some answer, a symbol at least, to show the worst is over, some explanation at least, for Christ's sake?

No answer. Eloise came when she needed me, not when I needed her.

We got up, left the grave and the churchyard, and headed down to the beach. Sam, Tom, Evie and Arthur were swimming in the sea. Jack sprinted down to the water's edge. 'When you're ready, kids, it's time for lunch. Get dry and join us at the café.'

We had lunch at the picnic tables on the beach. The four young ones seemed almost inappropriately playful, given Ted's death yesterday. But I sensed they were relieved that the crisis, which Ted had initiated, had brought so destructively into their lives, with his rage and hatred, was over. And that the little girls were safe. I don't think my children ever warmed to Ted, not really. They were hugely fond of Eloise, and her daughters, but Ted was always slightly aloof. He had thought highly of himself, his talent. He had tolerated Cornwall, because its light let him paint beautiful pictures, but really he did not have an artist's temperament. He wanted to be a celebrity, he wanted to be feted and adored. He wanted his beautiful wife to be an accessory. His rich, glamorous, gorgeous woman was there to shine a light on his success.

But Eloise was never going to be that woman. And then, she got cancer.

Which actually would have fitted into Ted's celebrity life just fine. Brilliant artist has mortally ill wife. How tragic, how romantic.

All this was going through my head during lunch, but I felt bad. Ted had behaved appallingly since Eloise's death, but he was a bereaved husband. And Eloise had betrayed him, just as he had told Chris. Except he didn't know about Jack, didn't know that his daughters may not have been his.

Or did he?

We'd finished lunch, and the kids had gone back their beach games, when Chris crunched his way down the gravel path from the lane to our table. He looked grim.

'I need to talk to you both. I haven't told you everything that happened yesterday. But I don't think we should discuss it here, on the beach, with the kids around. Can we go back to the cottage?'

This time I went down to the small squelchy sand puddles which marked the start of the ocean. I grabbed Sam's attention and told him we were going home. He splashed out of the shallow waves.

'Are you OK, Mum?'

'I'm fine, sweetie. It's just that Dad wants to tell us about the police's view about Ted's drowning, and it might be a bit upsetting for Eve and Tom. So would you keep them here for another hour or so?'

'OK. So long as you promise to tell me everything when we get back.'

'Everything, Sam. Thanks.'

As I left the paddling zone, I heard Evie yelling, 'I love you, Mum.' Her perennial sign-off.

The three of us walked up the lane and into our cottage. Chris hadn't said a word since we left the beach. I felt nervous as we entered our sitting room. I knew I was about to hear something bad. On the other hand, what could be worse than Eloise's visitations, which had almost destroyed my sanity and my marriage?

Chris sat us down, and poured drinks for all of us. Jesus, I thought, this is not good. Chris was a bit of a puritan. He certainly didn't splash the alcohol around.

'Right,' he said. 'I went over to Plymouth this morning and

identified Ted's body. Not nice. But definitely him. And then I went back to their house in Fowey, with the Superintendent. Father Pete told you Ted left a suicide note on the kitchen table. But he didn't tell you what he said. The Superintendent showed me. It was addressed to Juliana, and it was cruel. It wasn't just about killing himself, and the way he intended to do it. He wrote all the stuff we know, that Eloise had cut him out of her will, that his share of her money had been left to Arthur and Isabella. But he also wrote something else. He wrote that when Eloise told him, shortly before she died, that she'd had a baby when she was thirteen years old, he felt betrayed. Yes, I know it's ridiculous. He didn't even know her then. But it was when he heard about Isabella and also Arthur, and her decision to include them in her will, that he finally flipped.'

Chris paused. 'Cathy, I'm really sorry to tell you this. But in his suicide note, Ted said he and Eloise had a terrible row about Arthur. And he confessed that he was so angry with her that he tampered with her drugs. We all know that she was on heavy medication, pain relief for the cancer. But Ted, in his fury, made sure she took too much morphine. That's what killed her. Prematurely, although of course she was going to die anyway, sooner rather than later.'

I was staggered. I collapsed onto my little yellow sofa, the place where I'd spent so many hours daydreaming about

Eloise, our children, and our wonderful life here in Cornwall.

'No. Not that. Surely not that? Ted killed his own wife? He murdered her?'

'Yes. I'm terribly sorry, darling. I know how horrific this sounds.'

'But why? Why in God's name, when she was so close to death anyway?'

'It was about money, as everything seemed to be for Ted. He'd hoped she hadn't got round to putting Arthur and Isabella in her will, but she had.'

'So he killed her for nothing? Just to stop her leaving money to her daughter and grandson?'

'Yes. I'm afraid so.'

'Poor, poor Eloise. Oh my poor little friend. He killed her because she was trying to do the right thing by her own children and grandson, and when he found out, he was so angry about losing money that wasn't even rightfully his that he felt he was entitled to murder her. For profit. That poor girl who had spent so many years trying to face up to her own mortality, who had suffered so much, who felt such grief about leaving her little girls. And that bastard took her life out of malice, anger and avarice. What a disgusting, horrible man he was.'

'Yes. And after her death, when the solicitor told him that

not only were Arthur and Isabella going to inherit a lot of her money, but that he, Ted, was to get nothing but the house and what he called "a paltry allowance" to look after the girls, well, in his words, that's what drove him mad.'

I looked at Chris.

'Am I supposed to feel sorry for him? Because, God knows, he got what he deserved. Talk about Karma. But why did he suddenly decide, months after her death, to kill himself and take the children with him?'

'Because,' Chris said, 'he found something. Something that drove him over the edge. He discovered that he wasn't their father.'

I glanced at Jack. How could Ted know? Even Jack was not a hundred per cent sure. He looked at me and shook his head, indicating that it was as much a mystery to him as it was to us.

Chris continued. 'Cathy, I know how much you loved Eloise. But she did something to Ted that most men would feel is unforgiveable. Not only did she have an affair, but she told Ted their two little girls were his. When he found out, just a couple of days ago, that they were someone else's, he simply couldn't face bringing them up. And I'm not really surprised, given the state of mind he was already in.'

I bristled. 'Are you trying to make excuses for him? Because don't, Chris. Eloise was my best friend, and Ted was a murdering bastard. Are you really saying that Eloise deserved what he did to her? And that you're not surprised he tried to kill the girls as well as himself, because he found out she'd had an affair? I know you're a professional psychiatrist, but please don't talk to me like this.'

Chris took my hand. 'Darling, I'm not making any excuses for him. What he did to Eloise was vile. And what he tried to do to the children was unforgiveable. All I'm saying is given his state of mind, finding out they weren't his finally took what was left of his sane, rational mind away from him.'

'But how? How did he find out? Did Juliana know? Did she tell him?'

Chris shook his head.

'No. Juliana had no idea. This is going to be a terrible shock for her. The only person who knew was Eloise herself. Until Ted found something. He was in a terrible state, as we knew. Furious with her and with himself for killing her.'

'Only because he didn't get a bigger share of her money. He killed her for her fortune, only to find she hadn't left him any. He wouldn't have been furious with himself if she had. He would have been glad he'd got away with it. He was a gold-digger, pure and simple.'

'I agree with you. Remember I told you he wasn't a nice

361

man? But still, I think any man who found out that he'd been deceived about the paternity of his kids would find it hard to forgive.'

Jack looked Chris straight in the eye.

'You know, don't you? You know that Rose and Violet are mine?'

Chris looked startled.

'No. Of course I don't know that. What are you talking about? I only know that Ted found a document hidden among Eloise's things. It was a DNA analysis. She'd taken hair from the girls and, without his knowledge, from Ted, and sent them away to a lab specializing in genetic testing. What the lab found was that the chances of Ted being their father were non-existent. And the document was dated five years ago. She obviously knew the girls weren't Ted's soon after they were born, but she never told him.'

Jesus. So that was why he wanted to kill the little girls as well as himself. He couldn't cope with the idea that he had been cuckolded. That the children he had been charged with looking after, and in his mind unfairly recompensed for his care of them, were in fact the bastard daughters of another man.

I felt a flicker of pity for Ted. He had said bitterly the other day that Eloise had regarded him simply as a sperm donor. Now it was clear he wasn't even that. I remembered Eloise's desperate wail when she appeared to me in my garden. 'Oh Cathy, I've done something terrible.' She knew that after her death Ted would find the DNA report. And she knew it would rebound on her girls. That's why she told me never to trust him. And to watch over her babies. And I had, thank God. Her babies were safe.

Epilogue

It was Christmas Day and Juliana's beautiful home looked, as always, stunning. The firs in the garden were strung with lights. Inside the hall, a magnificent Christmas tree glittered gorgeously, filling the house with its glorious scent. Every ancient mantelpiece was festooned with holly and mistletoe, ivy and fairy lights. We'd just finished lunch, and, full of turkey and plum pudding, Jack, Juliana, Chris and I watched our various offspring fondly as they played Kerplunk with Rose and Violet in front of a crackling log fire. Sam and Tom had brought their girlfriends, and Evie blazed with happiness as she held Arthur's hand. It was a beautiful sight, a perfect Christmas tableau.

Not quite perfect though. I watched Juliana's face as her eyes suddenly filled with tears. I leaned across to her and took her hand.

'You must be sad, Juliana,' I said gently.

'Yes. The first Christmas without her. It's very hard. But of course I knew she probably wouldn't be here by now; this time last year I knew I was celebrating her last Christmas. I mourned for her in advance, so to speak.'

'The girls seem happy though, don't they?'

'Yes, and I thank God for that. They adore Jack, you know. He's been absolutely wonderful with them.'

'Yes. It's good to see them together. Will he stay in Cornwall, do you think?'

'I think so. He pretty much wound up his affairs in Australia when he went back in the autumn and he's up for an oncologist's post at Derriford Hospital in Plymouth. I'm sure he'll get it. I'm so pleased, so delighted that he really is the girls' father. So is he. He was thrilled after the DNA test results.'

'The girls don't know yet, do they?'

'No. We both thought that after everything that's happened, they needed some peace. No more surprises for the moment. But he intends to formally adopt them, and I'm sure he'll find the right moment to tell them he's their daddy.' She smiled at me. 'And I think I might be meeting my other grandchild soon,' she said almost coyly.

'Isabella? That's wonderful. Has she come to terms with everything now?'

'Pretty much, I think. She's written to Jack to say she'll come over in the summer. She wants to see Arthur, and meet her little sisters.'

Annie and Eric were dispensing mulled wine from an enormous silver punchbowl on the sideboard. Jack shook his head as they offered him a glass.

'No, thanks. I'm still OK to drive, but I won't be if I drink any more.'

'Why? Where are you going?' asked Chris in surprise.

'To Talland Church. I want to visit Eloise's grave. I'd like to take Rose and Violet, Juliana, if that's OK?'

Her eyes were moist again. 'I think that's a wonderful idea, Jack. May I come?'

'And us,' I said. I looked at Chris and he stood up straight away.

So six of us drove over to Talland on Christmas afternoon. Jack and his little daughters, Juliana, Chris and myself.

It was almost dusk when we got to the church, but lights glowed softly from the stained-glass windows. We gathered round Eloise's grave. Jack spoke softly to the girls.

'Put these flowers on Mummy's grave, darlings. It's her Christmas present from you.'

They solemnly placed the huge bouquet of lilies and lovely white Christmas roses at the head of Ellie's resting place. Jack opened the backpack he'd brought with him. He took out two dozen sturdy white church candles. He lit each one and then he and Chris carefully pushed them into the earth. They flickered gently, surrounding Eloise like strong small soldiers standing guard.

I bowed my head, and prayed that Eloise was at peace. I was sure she was. Since the day Ted drowned, I had heard nothing from her. And although I missed her, her silence was the best gift she could have given me.

Violet looked up at Jack. 'Do you think Mummy knows we've brought her flowers and candles?' she asked.

'I'm sure she does, darling.'

Then Rose spoke, shyly. 'Jack? Do you mind if I call you Daddy?'

'Me too,' Violet piped.

There was a small silence. Juliana held her handkerchief to her eyes.

Jack's voice was thick with emotion.

'Of course you can call me Daddy. I'd be delighted if you called me Daddy.'

He took their hands, and they walked back down the path

towards the lych-gate. Juliana followed. I glanced at Chris. I could tell he was moved.

'I love you, Cathy. I'm sorry for all the nonsense I put you through this summer. I don't know what I was thinking.'

'I love you too, Chris. Everything's all right now.'

He put his arms around me and we took a last look at my dear friend's hauntingly beautiful grave, glimmering softly in the darkness, at last a sanctuary, a place of love and peace.

And as we looked, I read again the inscription on her newly erected headstone.

Goodnight, sweet Eloise, and flights of angels sing thee to thy rest.

Acknowledgements

This book owes a huge amount to my dear friend Caron Keating. Her family and mine shared many tender and lovely moments in Cornwall, where we both had homes. Caron died tragically young from breast cancer in 2004. *Eloise* is inspired by her deep passion for motherhood, which I share. And I am grateful for her husband Russ and mother Gloria's forbearance in the writing of this story, which of course is a work of fiction, and has no bearing on reality.